...ways to get to ...e. Once..."

As Dev moved toward her, she wanted to run, to turn around and bolt into her bedroom and slam the door. But she knew she had to face him down. "I don't want to hear about 'once.' What's past is past."

"Aren't you the least bit curious?"

"About...?" Oh, she was handling this just fine!

"Whether any of the old feelings still exist. If it'll be the same...worse...better."

He was taking control away from her, and she had to get it back. "Why don't we find out?"

She put her arms around his neck—careful of the glass she was holding. And with all the insolence she could summon, she pressed her lips to his.

For an instant she *was* in control. Then he came to life, and she tasted trouble. There was no way on earth she could resist the deluge of memories or the stunning sensations that made her right hand relax....

"What the—?" He jumped away from her as if burned. "Did you do that on purpose?"

It took her a moment to realize the ice and liquid in her glass had soaked him. *Did she do it on purpose?* No way had she been thinking straight enough to plan such a revenge. Of course, there was no reason he had to *know* that....

Dear Reader,

Sometimes it seems as if I know the Lyon family of New Orleans better than I know my own. Although the Lyons are fictional, I've lived with them so long and so intimately that I find myself thinking of them as if they were real. I've even explored the Lyon family tree using genealogy software, while struggling to reconcile dates and events that stretch back to the last century.

I don't know nearly as much about my own family, but perhaps the Lyons will inspire me to remedy that situation. If I ever find the time, I'd like to join those legions who are making genealogy so popular today.

But if that does happen, I doubt I'll find the same kind of excitement at home that I found at Lyoncrest. I'm fairly certain none of my family's secrets can rival those of this fictional clan. Of course, I had a little help from Peg Sutherland and Roz Denny Fox, who have Lyon stories of their own to tell....

Once you've read *Family Secrets, Family Fortune* and *Family Reunion,* you'll know all about the Lyons, too. We only hope you like them as much as we do.

Sincerely,

Ruth Jean Dale

FAMILY
SECRETS
Ruth Jean Dale

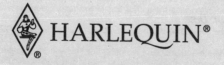

HARLEQUIN®

TORONTO • NEW YORK • LONDON
AMSTERDAM • PARIS • SYDNEY • HAMBURG
STOCKHOLM • ATHENS • TOKYO • MILAN • MADRID
PRAGUE • WARSAW • BUDAPEST • AUCKLAND

ISBN 0-373-70853-X

FAMILY SECRETS

This book could only have happened with "a little help from my friends." First and foremost, there's Peg Sutherland and Roz Denny Fox, terrific writers, all-around swell human beings and great fun to work with. And for research assistance, I'm indebted to Robyn Brownley Fennesy and Tricia Kay, who answered my distress call. On behalf of me 'n Neva Dalcour, "Thanks, y'all!"

THE LYON FAMILY

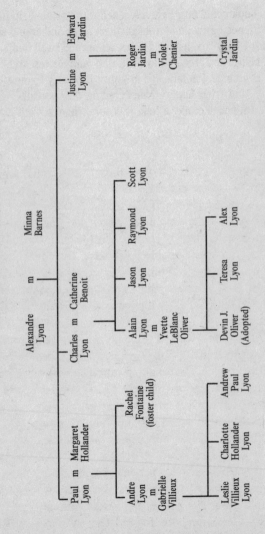

Alexandre Lyon **m** Minna Barnes

Paul Lyon **m** Margaret Hollander

Charles Lyon **m** Catherine Benoit

Justine Lyon **m** Edward Jardin

Andre Lyon **m** Gabrielle Villieux

Rachel Fontaine (foster child)

Alain Lyon **m** Yvette LeBlanc Oliver

Jason Lyon

Raymond Lyon

Scott Lyon

Roger Jardin **m** Violet Chenier

Leslie Villieux Lyon

Charlotte Hollander Lyon

Andrew Paul Lyon

Devin J. Oliver (Adopted)

Teresa Lyon

Alex Lyon

Crystal Jardin

PROLOGUE

New Orleans, Fourth of July 1999

SHARLEE INCHED HER WAY through the crowd toward the door of the rehearsal hall at WDIX-TV, trying to look inconspicuous. If she were to make a clean getaway, the time was now, while the place was still mobbed by friends, family, employees, media and Very Important People celebrating the fiftieth anniversary of the station established by her grandparents, Paul and Margaret Lyon. No one paid Sharlee the slightest heed, which was exactly the way she liked it.

She hadn't wanted to come to this overblown extravaganza in the first place but there'd been no way to avoid it without making relations with her family even more strained. Neatly lifting a glass of champagne off the tray of a passing waiter, she managed a mechanical smile for her father, briefly visible across the room. Fortunately her mother was nowhere in sight.

Why couldn't her parents understand that she, at almost twenty-five, was an independent woman who could make her way in the world without benefit of the Lyon name? She felt so strongly about this that at her job as a newspaper reporter in suburban Denver, she went by a nickname bestowed on her many years ago by a lost love—Sharlee—and her middle name, Hollander. Charlotte Lyon had been "gone" from the family nest since she left for boarding school almost nine years before.

Yet here she was, pretending for the sake of public relations that she actually belonged to this illustrious clan. Her grandfather, Paul Lyon, was an icon once known throughout the South as the Voice of Dixie; her father, André Lyon, was a devoted family man and pillar of the community who had taken WDIX-TV to new heights. Her grandmother Margaret and mother Gabrielle had both played important roles at WDIX while at the same time raising their children, loving their husbands, nurturing their community and doing it all with perfect *public* grace.

At least, Mama had done it all until the birth of her only son seven years ago. At that point, Gaby had "retired" to stay home with Andrew Paul, universally called Andy-Paul. Also living at the family manse in the Garden District were Sharlee's sister Leslie, her husband, Michael McKay, and his daughter, seven-year-old Cory. Leslie's first pregnancy had been revealed only minutes earlier, to the delight of the family.

Sharlee hated envying anyone anything, but this time she couldn't help herself. Just what she needed: an older sister who had it all, including the approval of the entire family, and an adorable little brother to carry on the Lyon name.

Her arm was inadvertently jostled, making her

champagne splash over the rim of her glass. She turned to see who the guilty party was and found herself standing behind two courtly old gentlemen deep in conversation. Her grandfather and his brother, Charles, both in their eighties. She edged closer, her curiosity roused by the almost conspiratorial tone of their voices.

"So now the history of the Lyons is an open book," Paul was saying cynically. "The truth, the whole truth…"

To which granduncle Charles replied, "I was there, brother dear. There are more secrets in this family than candles on that cake—and someday they'll all be revealed."

Sharlee frowned. What on earth were they talking about? What secrets? As far as she knew, all the other Lyons were models of decorum. Would that she could say the same about herself! But now Granduncle Charles was suggesting something altogether different, and she waited for Grandpère to refute him.

And waited.

And began to wonder. Could it be true? Secrets—perhaps Charles was talking about his own branch of the family tree.

He and his son, Alain, were not only active in Lyon Broadcasting but owned one of the most elegant French restaurants in New Orleans. She'd just eaten several cheese-and-shrimp-stuffed mushrooms from Chez Charles, reminding her of one of the few things she missed about New Orleans: the food. All of Charles's descendents had moved dutifully into

one or the other of the family businesses, and partic-
ipated in such endeavors as this grand anniversary
celebration.

Unlike Sharlee, who'd vowed early on to go her
own way and had proceeded to do so, consequences
be damned.

She had long since concluded that she was the
only person in the family with a wild streak. In her
teens she'd been the kid who got suspended from
school for practical jokes, who got into curfew trouble with the cops, who sneaked out of the house to
meet boys, who got caught drinking by the nuns. She
was also the one who was arrested in campus dem-
onstrations at college and who got into a humongous
confrontation with her mother on her twenty-first
birthday, which resulted in her decision to take a job
in Colorado, instead of moving back home after
graduation.

The result of all this rebellion was her parents'
refusal to release her trust fund on schedule. Their
lack of faith actually hurt more than being deprived
of the money—although money was nice, too, she
recalled.

This waltz down memory lane was getting her nowhere. She had a plane to catch, people to avoid.
Even so, the conversation between the two old men
had sent her reporter's instincts into high gear. Perhaps if she lingered for just a few more minutes, she
might hear a few interesting, perhaps even scandalous, tidbits about the Lyons....

But then she saw Devin Oliver heading her way,
a determined expression on his handsome face. Her

heart stood still. He looked wonderful with his curly almost-black hair and his deep almost-black eyes.

She'd managed to avoid him on this trip as she'd pretty much avoided her parents and anyone else wearing a serious expression, but her luck might be running out.

The last thing she needed was a run-in with a former lover now on her father's payroll. Turning quickly away, she ducked behind a cluster of celebrants and beat a hasty retreat, resolutely ignoring Dev's voice behind her.

"Sharlee, wait! You can't go on avoiding me forever."

CHAPTER ONE

DEV OLIVER STOOD in the open front door of the Donna Buy Ya Café on the edge of the French Market in New Orleans's Vieux Carré. It was another blistering hot August day. Across the street, a couple of little boys danced for tourist coins while the Balloon Man paused for a moment to watch and tap his toes. Farther down the block, a street musician pulled a saxophone from a ragged case, raised it to his lips and began to play.

New Orleans, Dev's home, a city like no other in the world. He smiled and was about to go back inside—a thousand chores awaited—when a flash of movement made him hesitate. He watched a long shiny limousine glide to the curb. His first thought was, *That's a No Parking zone and you're in big trouble if you stay there, mister.*

His second thought was, *I'm in no shape to be welcoming Lyons and neither is this place.*

"Shit," he said, looking down at the grubby T-shirt stuck to his torso by sweat, the dingy jeans and scruffy sneakers, all of which were the result of a morning spent trying to get the restaurant fit to open. He stepped inside. "We got company," he said to the man behind the counter.

"Anyone we know?" Felix Brown had a gentle voice but the build of a football player. He was also a hell of a cook and Dev's partner in this enterprise, assuming, of course, the Donna Buy Ya ever actually opened. For everything they fixed, something else went to hell; for every permit granted, two more hit snags. At this rate they'd be lucky to open by Mardi Gras.

Dev jerked his chin toward the white-haired grande dame alighting from the limo with the assistance of the uniformed chauffeur. "Iron Margaret herself," he said. "You ever met her, Felix?"

"Me? Get outta here. Where would I meet Miz Lyon?"

"She likes to eat. Although I don't know why she'd be visiting a shirttail relative like me." He stepped outside onto the sidewalk. "Welcome to Donna Buy Ya, Tante Margaret."

"Devin, dear." She offered her powdered and perfumed cheek for his kiss. "I've missed your smiling face around WDIX."

"Thanks." He stepped aside and held the door for her. "I don't think you've met my partner, Felix Brown. Felix, Margaret Lyon, the power behind the throne at WDIX-TV."

Felix's massive black paw enveloped hers. He stood more than a foot taller than Margaret, and she was not a petite woman.

"Glad to meet you," he said. "Hungry? It's Monday so I got the red beans and rice goin', or I could whip you up a po'boy in nothin' flat." Felix just loved feeding people; it was his raison d'être.

Margaret smiled. "Thank you, no. I'll come back and try the bill of fare when you've opened for business."

Felix looked disappointed. "Nothin' at all? How about somethin' to drink?"

"Iced tea would be pleasant."

"I gotcha covered." He gave her a thumb's-up.

She watched him trot toward the kitchen. "He seems nice," she commented. "How did you meet him, Devin?"

"We went to school together."

"Old friends tend to be the best."

Dev pulled out one of the chairs that had come with the place—either old or antique, depending on your point of view. "To what do we owe this honor?"

She sat down, her movements ladylike and precise. "The honor is mine," she countered, folding her hands neatly on the plastic tablecloth. "I'm the first member of the family to see the enterprise that's taken you away from us."

Dev felt a familiar stab of guilt. Until recently he'd worked for WDIX-TV as assistant to station manager André Lyon. It was a job he'd loved in an industry he still loved. But family politics—specifically the long-simmering feud between the two branches of the Lyon family—had finally made him too uncomfortable to remain.

He'd hesitated to leave, knowing his stepfather, Alain, would be furious. But when his mother died last January, Dev had felt free to do anything he wanted, and there wasn't a damned thing Alain or anybody else could do about it.

So he'd quit.

"WDIX will get along fine without me," he said, sitting down across from her. "It was time."

Felix plunked down two tall glasses of sparkling clear iced tea. "Do you want sugar or anythin'?"

"Sugar, please."

Felix opened one big hand and several packets tumbled onto the table. "You sure there's nothin' else I can get you?"

"Quite sure." She ripped open a packet and poured the white crystals into her glass. "Thank you so much."

"You're welcome. Now I hafta get back on that telephone. We gotta get this air conditioner workin' right. Nice meetin' you, Miz Lyon."

"Nice meeting you, Mr. Brown." Margaret poked at an ice cube in an effort to stir the sugar into the tea. When Felix was gone, she said to Dev, "That young man is your partner, you say?"

"That's right. He's got the know-how and I've got the money—or at least enough to get us started." Once escrow closed on his mother's house in the bayou, his financial situation would improve vastly.

Margaret nodded thoughtfully. "The name is quite amusing—Down at the Bayou with a local accent."

"Felix's idea. Goes with Cajun and soul food."

She picked up her tea and sipped it in silence, and it occurred to him that she seemed uncomfortable for some reason. While he searched for a way to put her at ease, she sighed and lifted her gaze to meet his.

"I'm sure you're wondering why I've intruded upon your time here today."

"I figured you'd get around to telling me sooner or later. Take your time, Tante Margaret."

Her face tensed almost imperceptibly. "That's just the problem. I'm not sure how much time I have— or more properly, how much time Paul has."

Dev straightened in his chair, all the lightness going out of his mood. "There's something wrong with Mr. Lyon?" She might be Tante Margaret, but her husband was never anything other than Mr. Lyon.

She sighed. "I'm sorry, I don't mean to alarm you. He's…as fine as can be expected. But, Devin, I need a favor, a very important favor. Since I don't wish to be in anyone's debt, I'll insist upon paying for it by backing this enterprise of yours financially."

He stiffened, all too aware of what he already owed this woman and her family. For years she and her husband had backed the *other* restaurant, the one inherited by his step-grandfather Charles sometime after the big family breakup in 1949. That other wealthier branch of the Lyon family had continued to provide infusions of cash until Alain took over from Charles in 1985, after which the restaurant apparently began turning a profit.

Charles was no businessman. Everybody in the family knew that, although nobody ever talked openly about it. They talked privately, though, and often to Dev, who'd realized long ago that he attracted confidences. As a result he often found himself burdened with secrets he preferred not to know. But Margaret Lyon was special. She'd been kind to his mother both before and after the divorce. Margaret had even dropped by the hospital during Yvette's last illness, and she'd been the only Lyon who'd attended the funeral.

Tight-jawed but trying not to reveal the pressure he felt, Dev spoke calmly. "I won't take your money, Tante Margaret. I'm already in your debt for past kindnesses. Of course, I'll do anything I can to help you."

She sighed. "I've offended you."

"Not at all. I appreciate the offer…but I just don't know what I could do for you that others couldn't do better." Suddenly he wondered what he would say if she asked him to return to WDIX. His belly clenched at that possibility.

"You're the only one who *can* do this." She drew a deep breath and spoke in a rush. "Devin, I want you to go to Colorado and convince my granddaughter to come back home before it's too late. Her grandfather's health is failing and I want…" Her eyes flashed and she changed course. "No, I *demand* that all the Lyons rally round him while there's still time."

Dev stared at her, taken aback. This was the last thing he'd expected.

She fixed him with her piercing gaze. "Please do this for me. It's very important."

For a moment he forgot to breathe. He'd had no idea the old gentleman was in anything but the best of health for someone in his eighties. At the fiftieth anniversary celebration, Paul Lyon had looked fine and appeared to be thoroughly enjoying himself. WDIX without the Voice of Dixie was unthinkable.

But so was waltzing off to Colorado on a wild-goose chase, and if there was ever a wild goose it was Charlotte Lyon—once his Sharlee but no more. She hadn't even spoken to him when she'd been home in July, which had pissed him off considerably.

"Tante Margaret, I was…close to Charlotte once, but that was a long time ago."

In fact, Dev and Sharlee had once shared a brief but fiery infatuation, when she was sixteen and he nineteen. He wasn't very proud of himself for taking her virginity, but he simply hadn't been strong enough or mature enough to turn his back on what she offered.

Her alarmed family, including Tante Margaret, had done everything humanly possible to drive the young lovers apart before they got "too involved." Only Dev's stepfather, had taken the opposite tack.

To this day Sharlee and Dev had never talked about what had happened, which left Dev's guilt intact.

"We're strangers," he said. The harshness in his voice surprised him. "What makes you think I—"

"Desperation," she cut him off. "It's for Charlotte's own good, Devin. You're my last hope. Everyone in the family has tried to reach her and failed. If you can't do this…"

Margaret's chin trembled ever so slightly. He hated to see her like this because he was genuinely devoted to her. But still…

His smile felt strained. "You asked me once before to do something I didn't want to do for Charlotte's own good,'' he reminded her.

"And to your credit, you did it.'' She didn't flinch; she'd have been a good poker player. "My motives were pure, then as now.''

"Sharlee—Charlotte's never forgiven me. She won't even talk to me.''

"How do you know what's in her heart?''

"How does any man know what's in *any* woman's heart?''

"Exactly. Devin, you must do this for me.''

"Tante Margaret—''

"*Please,* Devin.''

"I'll think about it.'' The words were dragged out of him. "But don't get your hopes up, okay? There's not much chance I can do anything even if I agree to try.''

Her silver-blue eyes were suddenly awash with tears, and she reached out to squeeze his hand in a surprisingly firm grip. "I knew you wouldn't turn me down,'' she said. "Family must always stick together. Your last name may be Oliver, but you've got the heart of a Lyon.''

Did he? Dear God! Talk about being between a rock and a hard place.

AFTER SHE'D GONE, Dev filled his partner in on what had transpired, concluding, "But there's no way I can do what she asks. Not only would Sharlee slam her door in my face, we've got too much to do around here for me to just take off like that.''

Felix grunted. Reaching into the pocket of his

jeans, he hauled out a handful of paper, which he slapped onto the counter.

Bills. Nothing but bills.

"Do what the lady wants," he advised. "Get your ass up to Colorado, or this café may *never* open."

"Sorry, Felix, but we're not taking a penny of Margaret's money." Dev gathered up the bills but resisted counting them. "I've still got some savings and a couple of stocks I can part with. If we make it until I get the money from my mother's house, we'll be okay. We're going to sink or swim on our own."

"And if we sink—" Felix laughed ruefully "—guess I can always get a job at MacDonald's, but I don't know what the hell you're gonna do."

Neither did Dev. That was what he should be thinking about instead of the way Sharlee Lyon had looked right through him last month at the party, as if she'd never seen him before.

If she'd talked to him it would have been one thing, but she hadn't and in fact never had, not in all this time. Damn, he was tempted to give it a shot just to get that monkey off his back.

SHARLEE HOLLANDER stood in front of the managing editor of the Calhoun *Courier,* trying to control her excitement.

At last! Bruce was about to give her the chance she'd longed for: a hard-news beat. No more lifestyle features, no more fashion or cooking stories, but hard news!

She'd spent three years at two newspapers trying

to get out of lifestyles, which she was, unfortunately, good at. She'd realized after the fact that she should never have taken such a post as her first job out of college, but at the time, she hadn't realized how typecast she'd be.

Bruce leaned back in his chair. "So I've decided to give you a chance, Sharlee," he said. "Heather will move up to lifestyles editor and you'll take over the city beat. You've been bugging me for this chance ever since you got here. Now go out there and cover City Hall like a blanket!"

"You won't regret it, Bruce, I swear."

"I'd better not."

She floated out of his office on a happy cloud, closing the door gently behind her. Since graduating from the University of Colorado three years before, she'd been buried in light features, but that was finally going to change.

Eric Burns, a reporter she'd dated a time or two, looked up from his computer terminal. "Congratulations. I know how much you wanted a news beat. Glad you got it." His phone rang and he picked up the handset, covering the mouthpiece with his hand.

"Thanks." She couldn't stop grinning. "I *know* I can do this."

"Good attitude," he said approvingly.

"I've got nothing if not a good attitude," she agreed, rushing across the newsroom to her desk. Damn, she loved journalism. Even when she didn't have the assignment she wanted, she loved the excitement and vitality of the newsroom. Now she was about to get her chance to show everybody that she could—

"Hey!"

Eric's shout dragged her back to the present, however reluctantly. He stood beside his desk, telephone receiver in hand. "Anyone know a Charlotte Lyon? There's some guy out front insisting she works here."

Sharlee's stomach dropped at least to her knees. No one here knew her by that name. Should she deny everything? Continue to look at her coworkers with as much innocent bewilderment as they looked at her and one another?

For a moment she really thought she could do that and then her natural curiosity surged to the fore. She just had to know who was asking for her. She rose.

Everybody in the shabby newsroom stared at her.

"I'll go see who it is," she said airily. "Then I'm going over to City Hall, just to let them know I'm on the job."

She felt the weight of their attention as she crossed the room, but she ignored it. Her thoughts were on the mysterious person who knew Charlotte Lyon.

It had to be someone from New Orleans. She hadn't told a soul there that she'd dropped the "Lyon" entirely. She refused to coast on the reputation of her family and their New Orleans media empire. She'd made that crystal clear by turning down one enticing job offer after another at WDIX-TV since graduation.

So who had tracked her down and why?

As she turned the corner, the reception area came

into view. She missed a step, stumbled, caught her balance. Devin Oliver stood by the desk, in three-quarter profile while he spoke to the receptionist in his lovely Louisiana drawl. The blonde stared at him with mouth agape and an expression of awe on her face.

Ah, but Dev looked good. Dark curly hair spilled over his forehead and those sculpted lips were curved in an enticing smile. He wore khakis and a yellow knit shirt open at the throat, biceps bulging beneath the sleeves.

She knew she hadn't made a sound and yet he turned and his gaze met hers. His eyes were as dark as his hair—almost black, fathomless, mysterious. For a second they just stood there, looking at each other over twenty feet and almost a decade.

When he smiled and started toward her, she knew she was in big trouble.

SHE WOULDN'T GET AWAY from him this time, as she had on the Fourth of July. She was going to have to talk to him whether she wanted to or not. Of course he might not like what she had to say, but that was better than the game of hide-and-seek she'd seemed intent on playing when she was in New Orleans, which was most infrequently.

That was what had finally made up Dev's mind about coming to Colorado: curiosity. He could tell she wanted to run again by the way she stepped back so quickly, by the way those beautiful hazel eyes widened, but there was no where to go with the receptionist watching so avidly.

Sharlee looked good, though, in pale linen slacks and a red silk blouse, which tightened across her breasts with the force of a quick breath. She'd matured in the years she'd been avoiding him; her blond hair was a shade darker, her breasts were fuller, her hips more enticingly rounded.

Her face had matured, as well, accenting high cheekbones and lips fuller and even more tempting...

She pulled herself together and the hazel eyes frosted over. "Why, Devin Oliver, as I live and breathe. I suppose you're going to tell me you just happened to be in the neighborhood."

He loved her exaggerated Southern charm. "No."

"Then what on earth...?"

He glanced around, noticed the receptionist still staring at them. "Is there someplace we can talk?"

"Why?" So suspicious.

"Hey, if you don't mind all your coworkers listening in—"

"This way."

She whirled around and led him down a poorly lit hallway at a rapid clip. He followed, admiring the swing of her hips, the set of her shoulders. Charlotte Lyon was a class act, all right.

They entered a small lounge complete with soda and junk-food machines, a microwave, an old refrigerator and a sign that read: It's a Newspaper's Duty to Print the Truth and Raise Hell. A middle-aged woman stood before one of the machines, obviously trying to make up her mind. Charlotte tapped her on the shoulder and smiled.

"Amy, dear, I've got to do an interview in here."

"But I don't know what I want." The woman screwed up her face at the enormity of her decision.

"The pretzels." Charlotte took the coins from the woman's hand, plunked them into the slot, then punched the appropriate button. "Health food. No fat." She placed the small bag into the woman's hands. "Enjoy."

"Oh, Sharlee, you always know!" Chuckling, the woman carried her pretzels out of the room.

Charlotte's shoulders slumped. "Have a seat." She indicated one of the mismatched chairs. "And tell me what you're doing here."

"Okay, Charlotte, but—"

"And please don't call me Charlotte!" She grimaced. "I'm Sharlee, now—Sharlee Hollander."

Her words hit him hard because he was the one who'd given her that nickname, the only one who had ever consistently called her that. "You really are pissed off at your family," he said.

She stiffened her spine and those beautiful breasts rose again. "I have no intention of discussing my family with you, Devin."

"Sorry. They're my family, too—more or less." He glanced around. "Mind if I have a Coke?"

"Be my guest."

"You want one?"

She shook her head. "I just want to know why you're here."

"Your grandmother sent me."

That stopped her cold. She sat down hard, as if her knees had buckled. "Grandmère?" she repeated faintly.

"That's right." He dropped coins into the machine and carried the can of soda to the table.

"Why?" She looked completely confused.

"I'm supposed to talk you into moving back home."

"To Lyoncrest?" The very idea seemed to appall her.

He nodded. "Your grandmother wants everyone close because…well, because she's worried about your grandfather."

"No, she isn't." Her expression hardened. "Okay, he's had a couple of heart attacks, but that was years ago. She just wants me under her thumb again—under everybody's thumb. Well, it ain't gonna happen."

He'd rarely encountered such certainty. "Even if I say please?" he wheedled, wanting to make her smile.

His ploy almost worked. Her eyes widened and a little of her tension seemed to diffuse. "You can say please and stand on your head," she said tartly. "My answer is still an unequivocal, unqualified, unambiguous *no*. I must say, I'm surprised you'd let Grand-mère talk you into this."

"I like your grandmother," he said.

"I like her, too—in fact, I love her. But neither she nor anyone else is going to run my life ever again."

That got his back up a little. "She's not running *my* life, if that's what you're implying. I just happen to think family is the most important thing we've got going for us. Maybe if you just go home for a visit—''

''New Orleans isn't my home anymore,'' she interrupted. ''It hasn't been for a long time.''

''Okay, if that's how you feel.'' He stood up. ''I've done my duty, you said no, and as far as I'm concerned, that's that. So how about joining a stranger in town for dinner, as long as I'm here?''

Before she could respond, a rumpled twenty-something guy stepped into the room. He eyed Dev curiously. ''Sharlee, Bruce wants to brief you for a planning-commission advance.''

''Now?''

''I'm afraid so.''

''Okay, thanks, Eric.'' She stood. ''I'll just be a minute, Dev.''

''Take your time.''

She left the room and he sat back down, automatically opening the can of soda and raising it to his lips. Sharlee Hollander, or whatever she chose to call herself, was really holding back. He, Dev Oliver, would sure like to know what was going on in her head.

BY THE TIME she rejoined him, Sharlee had it together again. He'd blindsided her; she hadn't been able to believe he could act as if nothing had ever happened between them, even after all this time.

Not that it mattered. She no longer knew Dev Oliver. When she had, he'd been a college student full of the same kind of ambition that drove her. He could have changed of course, but she figured he had to be alert just to survive at WDIX.

She hadn't wanted to know him, not after the way he'd treated her. Over the years she couldn't help wondering if he'd ever really been interested in her at all or if he just wanted the Lyon heiress. Certainly he'd backed off the minute he realized he'd miscalculated.

To this day she puzzled over which it was. Why he'd felt it necessary to send her a note that would rankle until the day she died. She'd memorized the hateful words and could still recite them, ending with: "We're young. Someday we'll both look back on this and laugh."

He should live so long!

But did she want to have dinner with him?

A quick mental calculation told her that she had approximately seven dollars to last the six days until payday, without breaking into an already meager savings account.

On her salary, a free meal was not to be scorned. So she swept into the employee lounge and stopped short at the sight of Dev on one of the vinyl sofas talking to a photographer. He looked up and smiled.

His smile had always devastated her with its honest pleasure. Or at least, it had when she was young and foolish.

The photographer also saw her and stood. "Nice guy," he said to Sharlee. "Take him on the tour, why don't you? Everyone'll enjoy meeting him." He nodded at Dev. "If you're around long enough, I'd be glad to take you out on one of my assignments. I think you'd find it real interesting.''

''I'm sure I would.'' Dev sounded completely sincere.

When the photographer had gone, Dev patted the sofa beside him. She responded by taking a quick step back.

''Now where were we when we were so rudely interrupted?'' she inquired, as if she really didn't remember.

''I'd just invited you to join me for dinner—an expensive and delicious one, I might add.''

''That's right. And I was just asking myself why I should. I mean, if you're just going to nag me on Grandmère's behalf, I'd be better off alone with a cheese sandwich.''

He grinned and shrugged. ''If you're trying to get me to promise not to talk about home and hearth as the price of your companionship, I'm afraid I can't oblige.'' His expression softened. ''We share a history, Sharlee, no matter how either of us feels about that now. We grew up together, loved the same people, struggled with the same problems. I don't think I could spend an evening with you and not fall back on that.''

He was right of course. She couldn't, either. So many questions she wanted to ask him, so many things she didn't know. Perhaps over dinner she'd find an opening.

Or perhaps not. In any event, she'd get a good meal out of it—and he wouldn't be able to return to New Orleans thinking he had intimidated her.

"I suppose it would be all right," she said, the words coming slow. "Where do you want to go?"

"You pick. You know the territory. I don't."

She thought about the opportunity. "There's a great place up in the mountains. It's a bit of a drive but worth it."

"I've got nothing but time."

He rose and, before she could react, took her hands in his. She pulled back with all her strength but short of yelling for help, she was his prisoner.

"Thanks," he said, looking into her eyes. "You'll have to tell me where to go, though."

Oh, if only!

CHAPTER TWO

SINCE HER OLD CLUNKER of a car was on its last legs, Sharlee had no choice but to let Dev pick her up that evening. She'd planned on meeting him at the front door of her building, but he was twenty minutes early and she got caught without her shoes by his knock on her door.

Without alternatives, she let him in—not that there was anything wrong with her apartment. It was clean and neat as a pin.

Which was a situation relatively easy to maintain since she had almost no furniture. Why bother? Nothing in her life seemed very permanent.

So all she had in her living room was a portable television, a love seat she'd bought used from a friend, a laptop computer—her pride and joy—on a folding card table with a folding metal chair, and dozens of books and magazines piled on nearly every surface and in stacks on the floor.

The kitchen was in better shape but only because the apartment came with stove and refrigerator. Her bedroom—which *he* was never going to see—had one twin-sized bed and a rickety bureau, bought at a garage sale, which had more than enough room for her small wardrobe.

"Make yourself comfortable while I grab my shoes," she said, more an indictment of his unseemly early arrival than a genuine invitation. God, no one was uncool enough to be early.

"Sorry to be so early," he said without a trace of remorse. He looked around. The expression on his face could only be labeled astonishment. He'd obviously expected more.

While he checked out her humble abode, she checked out *him*. She'd tried to forget how good-looking he was. Slim-hipped and broad-shouldered, he looked great in a lightweight summer suit and a blue shirt with striped tie. In fact, he looked sensational, although now that she thought about it, she realized there was something different about him. It took her a moment to figure out what it was.

Then she had it: his hair was much longer than she'd ever seen him wear it, actually curling below his ears. Somebody must be relaxing the rules at WDIX, she thought with amusement.

Brushing her blue skirt across her thighs, she stepped into low-heeled go-with-everything pumps. She'd refused to get really dressed up for him, since she had nothing to prove. Why should she care what he thought of her, her wardrobe or her lifestyle?

"I'm ready," she said. Straightening, she found him looking at her with a puzzled frown on his face.

"Where's your furniture?" he asked.

"I'm into minimalism," she countered.

"Boy, have you changed."

She resisted the urge to smile. "I planned this, you

know." She gestured at her sparse surroundings. "It's all the rage."

"In Colorado, maybe." He turned toward the door. "Are you ready to go?"

"Yes. I warned you it's quite a way, didn't I?"

"*Chère,* if you don't mind, I don't mind."

All the way up the mountain, she tried to forget he was already calling her *chère,* just like he used to.

SHARLEE KNEW GOOD FOOD—how to eat and appreciate it, not how to cook it.

Growing up in a family that employed a full-time cook and included a classy restaurant among its endeavors, she'd learned early to appreciate quality.

Unfortunately she could no longer afford a heck of a lot of quality. She'd dined only once before at The Fort and that had been a good year ago, again on somebody else's ticket.

There wasn't a chance she'd miss this opportunity. Without a qualm, she instructed Dev to aim the rental car west into the mountains.

The Fort lay just off the interstate near Morrison, perched on a red-rock hillside. Sharlee knew all the details from her previous journey here: how the structure had been patterned after Bent's Fort, an 1830s' fur-trading post in southeastern Colorado, how it had been constructed of 80,000 mud-and-straw adobe blocks. Since its opening in 1963, kings and presidents had dined here—and an occasional impoverished reporter.

The 27-star flag flying over the entrance was the

American flag used before Texas was annexed to the union in 1845. The round tower to the left of the entryway was used for wine storage and tastings— she knew because she'd asked.

All this and more she related enthusiastically to her companion, finishing with, "I just *love* this place! Talk about history!"

"Do you come here often?" Dev inquired as they entered the courtyard.

"I wish." She cocked her head to better hear the eerie sounds floating through the still evening air. "That's Indian flute music," she said. "Isn't it beautiful?"

"Yeah," he replied. "It is, but don't change the subject. If you're so crazy about this place, why don't you come here more often?"

Might as well tell him the truth, she decided. "Because I can't afford it on my salary. Tonight's different—Grandmère's paying." She gave him a quick questioning look. "She is, isn't she?"

"Would it make a difference?"

She considered. "Why should it?" she decided. "You're a rising young television executive. You can afford it." She led the way toward the door cattycorner to where they'd entered the courtyard.

"Actually—" he took her elbow to slow her headlong rush "—that's not quite accurate, but I'll explain later."

She darted a startled glance over her shoulder, wondering what there was to tell. Further speculation was lost as they entered another century where they were greeted by staff in costumes of the fur-trading period—calico shirts, boots and pants. Escorted through a maze of rooms, they were finally seated on the patio out back.

The last rays of the sun lowering over the mountains gave a soft warm glow to their surroundings, and the air smelled fresh and fragrant. Admiring the fountain carved of pink Mexican limestone, Sharlee couldn't keep from smiling.

She'd always been interested in history; it had been her college minor. She liked this place so much that her defenses slipped as her pleasure mounted.

She pointed to the south. "There's Pikes Peak," she said. "We'll see the lights of Denver to the east as soon as it gets a little darker."

He nodded, indicating the cannon just beyond the patio. "I guess you can't have a fort without a cannon. D'you suppose that thing really works?"

"No, sir." The busboy, dressed like a nineteenth-century fur trader responded as he filled their water glasses. "That's Bertha, our six-pounder. Last time she was fired, modern powder blew out her innards."

"That's a shame." Dev sounded amused. "What'll we do in case of attack?"

The kid grinned. "We still have Sweetlips. She's a twelve-pounder and that baby can still speak up. She's fired once in a while on special occasions."

The busboy finished his work and moved on. Dev looked around appreciatively and she was gratified to note his interest.

"I'm glad you picked this place," he said. "It's great looking but..." He raised his brows. "How's the food?"

"Wonderful." She dipped her head so she could peer at him obliquely. "Don't think I'm not aware of the chance I'm taking, bringing you here. I just wanted to show you that we have nice places in Colorado, too."

"Come on, Sharlee, you've never been afraid to take chances."

That threw her. "I…" A menu was slipped onto her plate by the waiter. Dev's intense gaze met hers and she fought the shiver that started in the vicinity of her backbone.

She *had* changed. This was the only chance she intended to take with him—ever, ever, ever!

THEY DRANK CONCOCTIONS touted as authentic to the fur-trading period 150 years ago; they ate *sallat,* an old-fashioned name for salad. The pièce de résistance was buffalo tenderloin, leaner and sweeter than beef, they agreed, although they could also have opted for elk or musk ox or even ostrich. The entrée was accompanied by potatoes dressed with onion, corn, red and green peppers and beans, which their server identified as Anasazi cliff-dweller beans, harvested from plants grown from nine-hundred-year-old beans found by archaeologists in Colorado.

And they talked—cautiously at times, easily at others, but never about anything that mattered: the weather, the mile-high altitude, the lack of humidity, his flight into Denver International. Finally, when the conversation wound down and she couldn't eat another bite, she looked at him through the shadows and said; "Earlier you were about to tell me something about the life of a rising young executive?"

"I guess I was." He cocked his head and an intriguing little dimple appeared at one corner of his mouth. "Fact is, I'm not."

"Not what?"

"A rising young executive."

Her lips parted in surprise. "Papa didn't fire you!"

"He wouldn't, so I quit."

"Because…?" She gestured, palm up, for him to explain.

"I wanted to try something else." All of a sudden he looked uneasy. "I'm opening a restaurant in the Quarter with a friend."

"Oh, come on, Dev. You expect me to believe that?" It made no sense. "If you wanted to go into the restaurant business, you could have worked at Chez Charles."

"That's just it, I couldn't." His gaze caught and held hers. "It was my first thought—family loyalty and the whole thing. Lyons stick together no matter what." He grimaced. "Fortunately Alain wouldn't allow it."

Confused by the feeling she was missing something, she frowned. "Alain? I don't think I've ever heard you call your stepfather that before. You always called him Dad."

"Yeah, but now that I'm all grown up I call him Alain." He said it flippantly, adding, "I quit my job at WDIX and Alain wouldn't hire me at Chez Charles, so there you have it. I've gone my own way and I've got to say I like it."

"This is weird." She shook her head. "Everybody in the family works at one or the other of the Lyon enterprises—except me of course. Even Leslie got suckered in to help with the fiftieth anniversary thing."

"Now there's two of us," he said shortly. "Let's change the subject. How come you're living on just what you make as a reporter? I find it hard to believe you can't afford to furnish your apartment or eat where you choose. The Sharlee I knew wouldn't take that for five minutes."

The comment hurt, even though once it would probably have been true.

Okay, would most assuredly have been true. "I don't care if you believe it or not," she said, "but it's true. I want to make it on my own."

"Yeah?" His handsome face creased in a frown. "Even so, why would you go so far as to deny your Lyon connections? You are what you were born into. We all are."

"Because...because..." She wanted to tell him about the trust fund she'd been denied on her twenty-first birthday and how diminished she'd felt. But when push came to shove, she just didn't trust him enough.

So she lifted her chin and met his curious gaze defiantly. "I was sick and tired of having so many bosses," she said. "Everybody thought they knew better than I did what to do with my life. I felt smothered. Besides—" she grimaced "—I always get so defensive when I'm around my family. All that perfection just naturally wears down an ordinary person.''

"Perfection?'' His brows rose. "Your family is far from per—''

He caught himself but not in time. What had he been about to say?

"If they aren't perfect, they've done a great job of keeping their vices secret,'' she said. She waited for him to respond; when he didn't, she pursed her lips in disapproval. "Okay, what is it you're not telling me? What do you know about my family that I don't?''

"Nothing.'' He laid his napkin beside his plate. "Well, maybe one thing. Sharlee, your grandfather's health isn't as good as you think it is.''

Her stomach clenched at the possibility he might be telling the truth, then reason asserted itself. "Grandmère just told you that to talk you into coming all this way,'' she said. "I saw Grandpère in July and he looked great.''

"I hope you're right.'' Dev looked genuinely concerned. "In case you're not, your grandmother wants him surrounded by all his loved ones, and that includes you. Is it too much to ask?''

"As a matter of fact, it is. Give it up, Dev. I won't be manipulated like this.'' But she felt a twinge when she said it. What if she was wrong?

"Dammit, Sharlee!'' For the first time his poise slipped. "Whatever your complaints and grudges against your family, you owe them some consideration. They're not a hundred percent wrong, you know. Life isn't all black and white.''

"It is to me," she shot back. "If they'd treat me like an adult, maybe. But that hasn't happened so I'm *not* going back." She stood up. "I don't want to argue with you. I'm ready to leave if you are."

For a minute she thought he was going to argue. Then he, too, rose. "Whatever you say," he agreed in a tight voice that wasn't an agreement at all.

ALL THAT PERFECTION *just naturally wears down an ordinary person.*

He thought about her words on the drive down the mountain; he might as well brood because she wasn't talking. Eventually it occurred to him that she was right about one thing: the family *had* kept her in the dark about their oh-so-very-human failings.

But she'd been their baby for a long time, right up until Andy-Paul's birth. Did the middle child feel as if her place had been usurped by her parents' midlife baby? She'd been spoiled before Andy-Paul; was she simply jealous now?

Somehow he didn't think so. There *were* many Lyon-family secrets, things known by some, but not talked about. Had Sharlee's family deliberately excluded her from that knowledge?

"We're there."

She spoke, as if she couldn't wait to get away from him. He pulled to the curb but reached across to stop her from jumping out. She turned a rebellious face toward him.

"May I come in for a drink?"

He was sure she'd refuse him. He saw "no!" in her face, saw her lips moving to form the word.

And heard her say carelessly, "Sure, why not? Even us poor folk can afford to keep a bottle of cheap vodka around."

He could hardly believe it when she led him inside the building.

DURING THE DRIVE HOME, questions had trembled on the tip of her tongue, but she'd bitten them back. She wouldn't give him the satisfaction of hearing her plead for explanations.

Besides, there probably weren't any. He couldn't possibly know more about her side of the family than she did, even though she'd been gone for such a long time.

She knew all the important stuff: how her great-grandfathers, Alexandre Lyon and Wendell Hollander, had started the radio station together; how Alexandre's two sons, Paul and Charles, had been drawn into the business while their sister, Justine, was left out entirely; how Paul Lyon had married Margaret Hollander and carried on the family dynasty.

Sharlee's grandparents had seen the opportunities and launched the television station in 1949 while Charles took over the radio side. Twenty-five years later, Sharlee's mother, Gabrielle, had met the heir, André, and fallen in love.

It had all been sweetness and light and smooth sailing, as far as anyone had ever indicated to Sharlee, everyone doing their duty while leading exemplary lives of public and private service. It raised her blood pressure just thinking about it. Hadn't anyone ever wanted to kick up their heels?

Or maybe it was sitting next to the man who'd done her wrong that was raising her blood pressure. Because *something* was sure making her palms damp and her chest tight.

So when Dev asked if he could come in for a drink, she was all set to turn him down cold when she realized that would be a cowardly response. She was his equal now, a grown woman, instead of a starry-eyed kid. She didn't have to run and hide from Dev; she could meet him and beat him at his own game.

Whatever the hell that was.

Once inside her apartment, she mixed a couple of vodka-and-tonics, then pointed him to the love seat, misnamed piece of furniture that it was. She herself perched on the folding chair.

He'd taken off his jacket and unbuttoned his sleeves. Now he raised his glass and said, "Cheers. To an evening I'll never forget."

She arched a brow and lifted her own drink. "Cheers. To an evening I never thought would happen."

They drank. She could feel her tension rising. She wouldn't have thought that she'd ever have another civil conversation with him, let alone share a dinner and allow him into her apartment. What he'd done to her had been utterly unforgivable. Even if she was the forgiving type, he'd be beyond absolution.

She'd really like to give him a taste of his own medicine, though. She started to speak, started to ask him straight out, *Dev, why did you do it? Why did you turn your back on me when—*

"I've got to give it one more try." His words cut right through her thoughts. Setting his glass on the floor by his feet, he unbuttoned his shirt collar and tugged off his tie. "Isn't there anything I can say to convince you your grandmother isn't playing games, isn't trying to trick you, *is* worried sick about your grandfather?"

"No."

"How about my chances to convince you your parents love you and want you back in the fold?"

"No." There went the old blood pressure again.

"That your sister would like to share her happiness with you, and your brother would simply like to get to know his big sister?"

"No!" She gulped down a big mouthful of her drink.

"Dammit!" He picked up his own glass but simply held it before him between both hands, a picture of frustration. "What is it about Colorado you're so crazy for? Wanna explain that?"

"It *isn't* New Orleans." She glared at him. "Besides, I went to school in Colorado. I feel comfortable here."

"So? I went to Harvard, but I couldn't wait to get back home."

"I also have a job, in case you hadn't noticed."

"Is it a great job?"

"How do you define 'great'? I'm a journalist, which is what I've always wanted."

"WDIX hires journalists."

"WDIX hires pretty faces." She'd long since convinced herself that the pencil press was vastly superior to electronic talking heads.

For a moment he just looked at her, his disappointment clear. Then he said, "Sharlee Lyon—"

"Hollander."

"Whatever—you're a snob. In fact, you're a *reverse* snob, which is even worse."

She couldn't believe he'd be so unfair. "I'm probably the only member of my family who *isn't* a snob."

His mouth tightened. "You really *don't* know your own people, do you?" Draining his glass, he set it on the floor again and rose. "At least think about your grandmother's request."

"It wasn't a request. It was an order."

"I don't care what you call it. I want you to *think* about it."

"Not a chance."

"Charlotte…!" He clenched his hands into fists, controlling himself with visible effort. "No one has ever been able to rile me the way you do," he said as if it pained him to admit it. "I don't know how you do it."

"If I do," she said, feeling a flash of vindictive pleasure, "it certainly isn't because I try."

"No?" He took a step toward her. "There are a lot of different ways to get to somebody. It isn't always in anger. Once…"

Her mouth felt dry and she took another swallow of her drink. "I don't want to hear about 'once,'" she said. "What's past is past."

"Think so? I wonder." He moved toward her, his dark eyes glittering with determination.

Sharlee wanted to run. She wanted to turn around and bolt into her bedroom and slam the door. But that was what a child would do, and hadn't she been trying to convince him, and by proxy her parents and grandparents, that she hadn't been a child in a long time?

She raised her chin and stood her ground. "Give it up, Dev. You don't do a thing for me anymore."

"No? And all evening I've been thinking otherwise."

Her pulse leaped. "That's your problem."

"It's no problem at all."

He put his hands on her shoulders. She could pull away, shove his hands aside. She could scream at the top of her lungs if she wanted to and the weight lifter across the hall would be in here before Dev knew what hit him.

Or she could face him down. Look him in the eye and let him see that this approach wasn't going to get him anywhere. "If you think you're scaring me, you're wrong," she informed him.

"Why would I want to scare you?"

He slid one hand up the slope of her shoulder until he touched her bare skin beyond the collar of her blouse. His thumb stroked lightly on the indentation at the base of her throat and she wondered if he could feel her racing pulse.

She held steady. She didn't love him anymore. She didn't even *like* him anymore; certainly, she didn't trust him.

"You're wasting your time, Devin. I'm way beyond that, where you're concerned."

The movement of his lips mesmerized her to the point that his words only registered belatedly. "Aren't you the least bit curious?"

"About what?" Oh, she was handling this just fine!

"Whether any of the old feelings still exist. Whether there's the least little spark left."

"I'm not a bit curious about any of that." But she was! She was dying to know what it would be like to...to kiss him again, nothing more. She wouldn't think about the rest of it—if she could avoid it with his hands on her the way they were now, stroking, coaxing.

"You lie." He leaned so close it took all her willpower not to flinch. "We're not kids anymore. You wonder if it will be the same, worse or better. My money's on better."

"My money's on...indifferent." He was taking control away from her and she had to get it back. "Why don't we just find out?"

She put her arms around his neck—careful of the drink she still held in her right hand. Looking into his eyes with all the insolence she could summon, she pressed her lips to his.

And for that instant, she *was* in control. Moving her mouth against his in little nibbling kisses, she felt her confidence growing. All right; it was just all right, nothing more. She could step away anytime she wanted, confident that...

He came to life as if exiting some twilight zone,

pressing his lips against hers as if he wanted to devour her. Sparks raced along to her nerve endings and she tasted trouble.

This was the man who'd taught her to kiss—not given her the first one, but taught her how powerful a kiss could be. There was no way on earth she could resist the deluge of memories or the stunning sensations that made her right hand relax...

He jumped away from her. "What the hell?" Twisting, he pulled the shirt away from his back.

The *wet* shirt.

It took her an instant to realize the ice and liquid in her glass had soaked him. All that cold must have been quite a shock.

She stared at him, mortified, trying not to giggle.

He glared. "Did you do that on purpose?"

As if she'd been able to think straight enough to plan such a revenge. It was ludicrous. She smiled, shrugged, hoped he'd believe she'd had that much presence of mind.

Surprisingly the outrage left his face. "Very good," he said approvingly, "but that was still a rotten thing to do. You owe me, *chère.*"

The endearment was beginning to sound natural. "I don't owe you diddly," she said. Pulling herself together, she glanced pointedly toward the door. "Thanks for a lovely evening."

"You're not getting off that easy."

If he put his hands on her again she'd... God only knew what she'd do, but she wasn't eager to find out. "Devin—"

"You can make amends for that dirty trick by

thinking about what I said earlier—about your grandmother, I mean.'' He gave up on the shirt and quit trying to hold it away from his back. ''Think about this sensibly and maybe you can find it in your heart to… Sharlee, I know you love your grandparents. Don't let—I don't know what it is, stubborn pride, maybe? Some grudge I know nothing about? Whatever's made you so bitter, don't let it stand between you and doing the right thing.''

With every word he spoke, her mouth tightened until it felt like a grim hard line. ''Dammit, Dev, that's not fair.''

''All's fair in love and war,'' he said. ''Promise me you'll think about it.''

She had to get him out of here. ''Fine, I'll think about it.''

He let out a sigh. ''Thanks. That's all I ask. Call me in the morning? Here's the number of my hotel.'' He picked up his jacket and drew a business card from his pocket, dropping it on the card table.

She didn't look at it. ''All right.''

''Promise?''

''Yes! Now will you go?''

He went.

And as promised she thought…mostly about that kiss.

SHE CALLED HIM the next morning before leaving for work. He answered the phone sounding alert, even eager.

''Mornin', *chère*. Nice of you to call.''

She wasn't interested in idle chitchat. "About what you asked me to think about last night—"

"Tell me at breakfast," he cut in quickly. "I saw a great-looking place between here and your apartment. I thought maybe we could—"

"We can't!" She steadied herself. "Devin, my answer is no. N-o, no. Tell Grandmère I'm sorry, but it's just impossible."

"Now wait a minute—"

"No, *you* wait a minute. There's no need for you to stay in Colorado any longer because I'm not going to change my mind. Thanks for dinner and goodbye."

She hung up the phone without letting him respond, then stood there trembling. She'd done the right thing, the only thing she *could* do. She never wanted to see him again and now she probably wouldn't.

When she closed the door to her apartment, the telephone was ringing, but she simply didn't care.

Or maybe she was afraid to care.

CHAPTER THREE

DEV CALLED ROOM SERVICE and ordered breakfast, figuring he should fortify himself before passing on the bad news to Sharlee's grandmother. She was probably expecting just such a call. Anyone who knew how damned stubborn Sharlee was would be.

But as he showered and shaved, he found himself wondering why he was so annoyed when she'd done exactly what he'd expected her to do all along. Whatever had alienated her from her family—and he didn't believe for a minute that it was simply a pileup of minor irritations—had truly wounded her.

As he had. He'd known she wouldn't be happy when he sent her that note almost ten years ago, but what else had he been supposed to do? His back was to the wall as surely as hers was. He'd spent the next year trying to smooth things over, but she'd refused even to talk to him. Until yesterday, he'd never been close enough to try.

Apparently she no longer gave a damn. The memory of that icy cold drink down his back sent a shudder through him. He'd thought she was responding to the kiss the same way he was. For her to be able to do what she'd done...

He couldn't resist a wry smile, though. She'd gotten the upper hand, all right. To a man who enjoyed a challenge, that wasn't entirely bad.

His tray arrived and he poured himself a cup of coffee. While the bacon and eggs cooled, he carried the cup to the window and looked down on the Denver Tech Center.

Hell, he might as well get the call over with so he could pack and head for the airport. Somehow he felt he was leaving a lot of things unsettled between himself and Ms. Hollander, but it apparently couldn't be helped.

He dialed Lyoncrest and wasn't surprised when Margaret herself answered the phone.

"Devin!" she exclaimed, her tone filled with hope he was going to have to dash. "You've seen Charlotte? Say she's coming home."

"I've seen her, Tante Margaret," he said, "but I'm afraid she has no interest whatsoever in coming home. I'm sorry."

There was a long silence and then she sighed. "I shouldn't be surprised, I suppose, but I was so hoping…"

"At least she didn't have me thrown out of Colorado," he said, trying to cheer her. "We actually managed to get through dinner last night without too many tense moments."

"You had dinner together?"

He heard her hope spark again and was sorry he'd fanned it. "Yes, but that's all we had. She's happy here and just doesn't want to leave. I thought I might just as well call the airport and see what flight—"

"No, don't do that."

He frowned. "Beg pardon?"

"Please try again. Devin, you cannot take no for an answer."

"I can't very well kidnap her and throw her on the plane," he reasoned. "She's got a job, she's got an apartment, she's got a *life* here."

"She'll have a better life here," Margaret said. "As for her job—it's at some dinky little newspaper, I understand."

"That's right, the Calhoun *Courier.* She seems to love it."

"Naturally she wants you to think so." The steel returned to Margaret's tone. "But she *must* come home. If she won't quit her job, I'll do whatever is necessary to change her mind, up to and including buying that newspaper myself and firing her."

Dev sat down hard on a handy chair. "You're kidding."

"I don't kid about family, dear." She sounded completely confident again.

"You'd really do that—buy the newspaper and fire her?"

"For Paul, I would do that and more. Please go back and try again. Say anything, promise anything, and then tell me *everything.*"

Dev hung up, wondering where this was going to end—and when.

SHARLEE WAS IN NO GREAT MOOD when she got into the office, so it took her a while to catch on to the fact that something was up.

Everyone was treating her too nicely, including

Eric, who came in late and rushed over to present her with two chocolate doughnuts and a big smile.

"So how's it going?" he inquired, lingering.

"Fine," she said. She nodded at the doughnuts on a paper towel. "What's the occasion?"

"No occasion." He licked his lips. "By the way, that really surprised us yesterday."

"What did?"

"Oh—" he gazed at the ceiling "—nothing, if that's how you want to play it…Ms. Lyon."

So that was it; they'd figured it out. Everyone now knew that Sharlee Hollander was really a member of the famous Lyon family of New Orleans. As news professionals, they'd know about Paul Lyon and his slew of awards, about WDIX-TV and its anniversary, thanks to extensive coverage in news magazines and trade journals. All of a sudden, she'd gone from one-of-the-gang to one-above-the-gang.

Next they'd be asking her if she knew of any job openings at WDIX. Just one more way Dev had managed to ruin her life.

ERIC WATCHED Bruce Rivers creep out of his cubicle and look around surreptitiously.

"She gone?" Bruce asked him.

"Who?"

"Sharlee! Who'd you think I meant?"

Eric shrugged. He never had a clue what Bruce was thinking and neither did anyone else around here. "Yeah," he said, "she's gone. She's got that planning-commission meeting and—"

"Don't you think I know when Calhoun bureaucrats meet? Sheesh!'' Bruce glanced around again. With his hunched shoulders and furtive eyes, he looked as if he was casing the joint. Gesturing for Eric to follow, he wheeled around and plunged back into his messy office.

Curious, Eric followed his boss inside.

"Shut the door!" Bruce hissed.

"Okay, but we're the only ones in the newsroom." And the office walls only went up about eight feet, leaving a two-foot gap on top, and half of those walls were glass, anyway, so forget secrecy.

Eric closed the door and looked around for someplace to sit. The most likely spot was a chair covered with a four-foot stack of old newspapers. Shoving them to the floor, he sat down. "What's up?" he asked.

"Whaddaya know about Sharlee?"

Eric shrugged. "Well, I think she'll turn out to be a pretty good news reporter."

"Not that!" Bruce shoved back thinning brown hair. "I mean personally."

"Oh." Eric thought hard. "Not too much, actually."

"I thought you dated her."

"Yeah, a time or two."

"So?"

"Well...she lives in an apartment on the north side of town. Not a bad location, respectable and all, but she doesn't have much furniture. Her car's a wreck, but then you know that because she's late at least once a week because of it."

"Yeah, yeah, what else?"

Eric grimaced. ''She's got expensive taste but tries to control it.''

Bruce's eyes widened. ''She would have.'' He pursed his lips. ''You know about that guy who came by to see her yesterday, right?''

''Everybody does.''

''He asked for Charlotte Lyon.''

''I know.''

''And Sharlee answered.''

''Yeah. So?''

''So she's a Lyon!''

Eric took no offense. ''You mean one of the New Orleans Lyons?'' He jerked his head toward the newsroom. ''Yeah, we figured that out.''

''The New Orleans Lyons,'' Bruce repeated, his voice filled with awe. ''The Voice of Dixie, a Pulitzer and that TV station…'' Apparently too excited to sit still, Bruce leaped to his feet and began pacing around what small amount of open space his office offered. ''I applied for a job there once. Didn't get it.''

''Too bad,'' Eric said, barely managing not to roll his eyes.

''Why do you suppose she kept it a secret?'' Bruce looked personally affronted. ''Why would she be using another name and hiding out in Colorado? I don't get it.''

''Maybe she got into trouble and they disowned her,'' Eric suggested tongue in cheek. ''Maybe she ran away from home as a baby. Maybe she's playing reporter as a lark. Maybe she was stolen by Gypsies!'' He stood up, his interest in his erratic editor's flights of fancy waning. "If that's all, I've got comp time coming and I think I'll take off."

"Okay, whatever. You run along."

Alone in his office, Bruce continued to pace. Sharlee Hollander, née Charlotte Lyon, was a good lifestyles editor and might even turn out to be a good news reporter. But surely she was worth more to him as a Lyon than as a dime-a-dozen employee.

He picked up the telephone handset and dialed information. The only Lyon he recalled by name was Paul, known from coast to coast. He dialed the number of this living legend and asked for him. After a few moments, a charming female voice with a soft southern accent came on the line.

"I'm afraid Mr. Lyon can't come to the telephone at this time. I am Mrs. Paul Lyon. May I be of some service to you?"

THE SPECIAL SESSION of the city planning commission seemed to go on forever, but Sharlee didn't mind. The most important item on the agenda—approval of a massive subdivision that would add thousands of new residents to a city already overburdened with services—was, unfortunately, the next to last item.

By the time she pulled into the parking space at her apartment, it was almost nine o'clock. She'd left home that morning just before eight and hadn't been back since, so she was tired, as well as jubilant.

She could do this. She already had a strong lead floating around in her mind—

She froze, the key held suspended in front of the lock on her door. Had she heard a noise inside?

Straining every sense, she waited. She'd left her cell phone in the car—her office's cell phone, in fact. She'd given up her own almost a year ago in favor of the new laptop computer since she couldn't afford both. If she had that phone now, she'd call 911, and if it turned out to be a false alarm, she'd just live with it.

She heard nothing further so apparently it was nothing. Unlocking the door, she walked inside.

And stopped short.

Devin Oliver stood in the kitchen doorway, a wooden spoon in his hand and a frilly red apron—Sharlee's Christmas gift from Leslie—tied around his waist. Neither of those additions made him look anything less than devastatingly sexy.

He waved the wooden spoon and said, "I heard you coming and put in the crawfish."

Annoyed, she tossed her planning-commission packet and notebook on the card table beside the computer. "What the hell are you doing here?" she demanded. "You almost scared me out of ten years' growth."

He gave her an innocent brow-raised, wide-eyed response. "Isn't it obvious?" He flipped the ruffle on his apron.

And smiled. His smile could melt diamonds.

"Not to me, it isn't," she snapped. "I never leave my door unlocked. How did you get in here?"

"Your neighbor across the hall. The neighbor who has your spare key."

She couldn't believe he'd talked his way past Brawny Bill Bolliver. "Why would he trust you?" she demanded. "You could have been a thief or an ax murderer. You could have been a maniac, for God's sake."

He looked hurt. "I've got ID."

"So? Maniacs can have ID. Besides, you're supposed to be gone."

This simply wasn't fair, she fumed. Seeing him had frightened her at first because she hadn't realized who had invaded her space; now she was frightened because she *did* realize who it was. She'd thought him safely out of her life and wasn't prepared to deal with the shock of finding him here.

"I changed my mind," he said calmly. "Or rather, your grandmother changed it for me." He turned back toward the kitchen. "Excuse me while I check my *étouffée*."

Her knees nearly buckled. "You're making *étouffée?*" It had been years since she'd had *étouffée* or jambalaya or any of the other favorites from her youth, although she'd hoped to get to a good restaurant when she'd been in New Orleans in July. As things turned out, she hadn't had time.

He hesitated and his expression softened. "*Chère,* you look like you're about to salivate. Sure, I made *étouffée*. I had to use frozen crawfish—" he made a disparaging face "—and I had to run all over hell's half acre to find even that."

She smelled it now, a savory aroma redolent of spices. "But I can't eat now," she groaned.

"Why? Did you have time for dinner earlier?"

"No, but…it's after nine. If I eat now, I'll never get to sleep."

"Whatever you say. I've already eaten, so I'll just put the rest in the refrigerator. You can have it tomorrow."

"Don't you dare!"

He laughed. "Sit down, then, and I'll serve you."

A little shiver of awareness rippled down her spine. He'd served her before—and she'd lived to regret it.

Nevertheless, she sat down at the card table, closing her eyes to better appreciate the lovely aromas wafting from her kitchen. Better to think of food than of this man who'd reappeared to screw up her life all over again.

SHARLEE GROANED and pushed aside her empty bowl. "I can't eat another bite," she declared. "Dev, that was wonderful. I didn't realize how much I'd missed down-home cookin'."

"I figured." He stacked her empty rice bowl inside the *étouffée* bowl.

"I didn't know you were such a good cook."

"I've got lots of talents you don't know about."

That startled her out of her satisfied stupor. "Is breaking and entering among those talents?"

"Ah, Sharlee." He had the good grace to look sorry, although it might have been an act. "When your grandmother told me not to come back without you—"

"Did she really say that?"

"Absolutely. She wants you home and she's not

in any mood to take no for an answer. But when she said that, I thought, hell, why not get you in a good mood by surprising you with a nice dinner? So I shopped—which isn't easy in this town—and came on over. I had to talk my way in and then after I did, I realized I had no idea when you'd be getting home."

"You still seem to have timed things well." She looked at him with renewed suspicion.

"That's because I called your office. Some guy in the newsroom said you were at a meeting that would probably run three hours, give or take. So I did everything except the last-minute stuff and settled down to wait."

She pursed her lips. "Well, I'll admit the food was great but you're not going to soften me up with *étouffée*. You're nothing but Grandmère's errand boy and I am not going back to New Orleans with you, even if you feed me great meals every day of the week."

"Okay," he said as easily as if she'd refused another slice of bread.

She blinked. "Okay?"

"Sure, why not?" He picked up the dirty dishes. "I'm glad you're sticking to your principles."

"You are?"

"Hell, yes! As long as you refuse to listen to reason, I get a free Colorado vacation. Because Margaret Lyon has made it clear that if I don't come home with you, I'm not to come home at all—period, end of discussion."

She laughed. "That's ridiculous."

"Maybe, but who am I to argue with Iron Margaret?'' He winked and carried the dishes into the kitchen. He returned with two steaming mugs of coffee.

She shook her head regretfully. ''I can't.''

''Decaf.''

He put hers down and she saw that he'd already added milk to make a primitive version of café au lait. So he remembered what she liked. But did he remember all of it or just this?

She looked away. ''I'm too tired to argue.''

''Is that the secret, then? Wear you to a frazzle and you turn all soft and agreeable?''

She didn't like being called ''soft and agreeable'' when in this man's company; it was just another way of saying ''vulnerable,'' and she never intended to be that with him again. But she couldn't quite think of a way to reprimand him so she hedged. ''I've had a hard day, if you must know.''

''Poor Sharlee. Drink your coffee and you'll feel better.''

She took a sip, then lifted her gaze and said impulsively, ''Dev, why did you quit your job at WDIX—really?''

''I told you, I—''

''No, I don't want some vague explanation.'' She shook her head vigorously. ''I honestly want to know. I thought that's all you ever wanted to do—work in television.''

His face grew serious. ''Politics,'' he said finally.

''What did *you* have to do with politics? You weren't a newsman or anything like that.''

''Family politics,'' he elaborated.

"I'm afraid I don't understand." She stifled a yawn, although she was intensely interested. A hard day and a fabulous meal had conspired to make her drowsy.

"They all wanted a piece of me," he said finally. "I couldn't be loyal to everybody, and I couldn't bring myself to make a choice and cut off the rest. So I quit."

She regarded him with new respect. "We come from a complicated family, Dev," she said with a sigh. "I can sympathize with you, but why a restaurant, of all things?"

"A café, really. It was funny how it happened. I was looking around for a business opportunity and ran into an old school friend. He's a chef, and since I practically grew up with the restaurant business, it was a natural."

"Is this your secret ambition—to own a restaurant of your own?"

He shrugged. "To be perfectly honest, I'm still not sure what I want to be when I grow up. This is something to do until I make up my mind. I liked television, but in New Orleans…" He shook his head as if rejecting his years at WDIX.

"You could leave New Orleans," she said softly. "It's not the only city in the country."

He frowned. "It's home. Everybody I love is there."

She felt a pang at his words. Everybody *she* loved was there, too, but she'd left regardless. Maybe his ties were stronger than hers, although now that his mother was dead…

"I'm sorry about your mother," she said suddenly. "Leslie told me."

"Thank you, but don't change the subject. Is Calhoun your idea of paradise?"

"Not hardly." She laughed dubiously. "I want to work in California eventually, but so does everyone else in journalism." She felt a twinge between her shoulder blades and straightened.

"You could always just move out there and start looking." He walked to the love seat, where he scooped up several small corduroy pillows.

"What would I live on until I found something? My financial situation...is not good. I've had a lot of expenses lately." Like keeping her car running, paying off credit-card debts she'd run up years ago when she'd still had expectations of a juicy trust fund. She'd scissored all her plastic more than two years ago, but it had still taken forever to get out of debt.

"You could always live on charm." He flashed that grin again. Dropping the pillows onto an area rug on the hardwood floor, he beckoned her with a crooked finger.

She automatically leaned away. "What?"

"You're a mess. I'm gonna straighten out a few of those kinks."

"What kinks?"

"The ones in your back...your shoulders...your neck. C'mon, Sharlee, we don't have all night."

She couldn't believe he was serious. "You want me to lie down on the floor and turn you loose on my back?"

"That's right. You won't regret it, either. I dated a physiotherapist for a long time—six months, at least. You can trust me. I'm good."

She couldn't trust him, not about this or anything else. He was too slick; she'd forgotten how slick, or maybe he hadn't been quite so polished before.

She said a dignified, "No, thank you," and stood up. Then, despite all her good intentions to the contrary, that ache between her shoulder blades made her groan.

"Jeez," he said, "you are one headstrong woman."

Before she could resist, he had her by the elbows, maneuvered her into place and pressed her gently down. Confused and off guard, her panicky gaze met his.

"It's okay," he said softly. "I won't get out of line, I promise."

"I never thought you..."

He flipped her over onto her stomach and her protests died away. She lay there on the middle of her living-room floor like a sacrificial lamb, waiting for the ax.

What she got was not cold steel but the press of warm strong hands. That initial contact literally took her breath away.

"This would work better if you'd take off that blouse," he murmured. "I mean, it'll work fairly well this way but—"

"It's this way or forget it," she said. And then she did groan. "My God, that feels wonderful."

"Thanks. It'll feel even better once you start to relax."

Relax. Even those strong fingers kneading the clenched muscles of her shoulders couldn't make her relax.

"I saw Leslie the other day," he said, sliding his hands down her sides while his thumbs dug into the channels on either side of her spine. He settled himself astride her, his thighs tight to hers.

Sharlee felt as if she'd been immobilized by an electrical shock. His hands moved across her back, pressing and kneading, while his legs imprisoned her. Somehow he seemed to be relaxing her exterior while arousing her interior.

"Uhh...that's probably enough," she ventured weakly. "You don't have to keep—"

"Just a minute more." Those magic hands skimmed over her shoulder blades and slipped between her arms and her torso, pressing against the sides of her breasts before moving down to her waist. She wanted to scream at him, tell him not to try anything, tell him to keep his cotton-pickin' hands where they belonged, tell him...that what she felt wasn't really a rush of surrender and he was wasting his time if he thought so.

"Better?" He paused with his hands on either side of her waist.

"Yes." It came out a strangled groan.

"We're almost finished, then."

His hands left her body to settle on either side of her head, fingers threading through her hair. The press and pull mesmerized her as he worked across her scalp and down to her neck. She felt limp as a wet dishrag, tight as a dry sponge. She felt so many things that her mind reeled.

A quick pat on the rump yanked her back to reality and his weight lifted.

"That should help you sleep," he said in a low voice.

She wanted to yell at him, say, *You idiot, now I'll never sleep because you've got me so damned worked up.* She rolled onto her back and found him standing over her, his legs on either side of her thighs.

"Yes, thanks." She made no move to rise because to do so would lead to more physical contact, and she didn't think she could stand that. How long had it been since she'd been so aroused by a man?

A long time. *Too* long, actually.

He offered a hand. "Let me help you up."

"I can get up by myself." She scooted out from under him then, one of her knees sliding lightly against his leg. She stood up, making a big production of smoothing her clothes back into place. "Th-thanks for everything—dinner, the back rub. Now I've got to get some sleep."

"Hard day tomorrow?"

"All my days are hard." *Harder, with you in town.*

"Okay." He turned toward the door. "What shall I tell your grandmother?"

"That I love her and I'm not moving back to Lyoncrest."

"She didn't say you had to move into the family

mansion, although I know she'd like that. She just wants you in town, nearby in case anything happens to—''

''In case anyone in my family wants to tell me how to run my life. No way. Been there, done that.''

''Okay. I'll tell her.'' Giving her a two-fingered salute, he paused in the doorway. ''Sleep tight.''

''I will.''

Only she didn't.

SHE APPEARED FOR WORK the next day red-eyed and tired and feeling harassed and persecuted.

Whereupon Bruce called her into his office and fired her.

CHAPTER FOUR

"BUT...BUT..."

Sharlee stammered to a confused halt, staring at Bruce with total disbelief. This was ridiculous; he couldn't fire her! He'd just promoted her, for God's sake. Dragging in a deep breath, she tried to get past the shock.

"Look," she bargained, "I went to the planning-commission meeting last night. I got a good story."

"I'm sure you did."

"And I introduced myself around, told all the commissioners I'd be covering city stuff."

"That doesn't matter any longer," he said. "You're still fired—or maybe I should say laid off."

"I couldn't care less what you call it, Bruce. I mean... Don't you at least want me to write up the meeting?"

"I'll have someone else do that. You can pick up your final check at the front desk on your way out." He looked distinctly uncomfortable. "I'm really sorry, Sharlee, but we're...we're cutting back and you're the junior reporter in news. It's just the breaks, kid."

She had to be missing something. She racked her

brain for an explanation. There had never been any complaints about her work, so what could it be?

"Okay," she said, "I'll take my old job back as lifestyles editor."

Her editor shook his head. "Sorry, no can do. You're news now and that's where I've got to cut."

"Bruce!" She stared at him in frustration—and then the light dawned. Putting her fists on his desk, she leaned over to stare him in the eye. "Did you happen to speak to any of my relatives in the past twenty-four hours?" she demanded, her voice rising.

A wash of red swept up his neck and mottled his face. "Absolutely not."

She knew bluster when she saw it. "You're lying. How dare you do such an underhanded thing! Was it my grandmother who told you to fire me?"

"I don't know what you're talking about."

He did, the lying SOB. "What did she promise you?" Sharlee pushed. "Cash? A job at WDIX?" She straightened, some of the shock dissipating while cruel reality began to sink in. "I hope you didn't sell yourself too cheap. This kind of deal doesn't come along every day."

He looked down at the desktop and his shoulders hunched. "Sharlee—Charlotte, it's not what you think…exactly. I…that is, when you—"

"Give it up, Bruce." Wearily she straightened. "I understand exactly what happened, and you know what?" She crossed to the door and opened it wide so that all those eager listeners in the newsroom could hear without straining.

"You can't fire me. I quit!"

Walking out, she gave in to her baser instincts and slammed the door so hard it rattled. Glaring around at the stunned expressions of her former coworkers, she squared her shoulders, prepared to stare them down.

Eric broke the impasse. "Tough break, Sharlee."

Then they all swung into action: "Yeah, tough break. A shame... Unfair."

Fair rarely had anything to do with life, she'd long since discovered. Sharlee drew a deep breath and walked to her desk. "He just caught me by surprise, that's all. I was going to quit, anyway."

They didn't believe her, but they all nodded understandingly. Eric said, "If there's anything I—" he glanced around "—anything we can do..."

She couldn't force a smile. "Thanks, but I can't think of a thing. Unless you know of any job openings?" She saw their helpless expressions. "I didn't think so."

Pulling open desk drawers, she began hauling out the personal items she'd accumulated over the past eleven months, trying not to think about her situation, about the underhandedness of her grandmother, about a future that no longer looked promising.

And especially, she tried not to think about where she was going to find another job.

RUNNING ON ADRENALINE, she made it all the way to her car before it really hit her.

She'd just been fired.

She'd never been fired before and it was horrible. She felt like dirt.

What was she going to do now? With trembling hands, she thrust the key into the ignition and gave it a quick turn. The engine came to life slowly. It coughed a couple of times but, all in all, behaved remarkably well.

Driving through a sparkling clear August day, Sharlee headed for her apartment—not home. It had never felt like home and she'd never made the slightest effort to make it homey. She'd never intended to be there for the long term. She'd planned to use the *Courier* as a springboard to something better, but after this it was probably a springboard to oblivion.

She stopped for a red light, the car idling like a lawn mower. Maybe she could still find some good in this. It would at least push her into doing something. She'd make a few phone calls, check the Internet, see what was out there—

A blast from a car horn woke her up and she made a hasty left-hand turn into her street. At least she still had transportation. If she had to go out of town for job interviews—

The engine sputtered and died.

Just like that, she found herself coasting down the street in eerie silence. Guiding the vehicle to the curb, she took a deep breath intended to forestall the cloud of gloom settling around her head.

She turned the key in the ignition. The engine growled. She tried again. The growl was shorter and fainter.

The third time, nothing happened. No growl, none.

"I'm doomed!" She said it out loud, leaning forward over the steering wheel with her eyes squeezed shut.

Then she straightened, flung open the door, climbed out and hiked the five blocks to her apartment, swearing under her breath with every step.

DEV WAITED IN THE ENTRY to her apartment building. Why was she not surprised?

"You!" Marching up to him, she whapped him good on the arm with her leather shoulder bag.

"Hey!" He rubbed his arm. "What's your problem?"

"I hate you—oops, that's not a problem, actually. It's a fact."

"But—"

"Devin Oliver, I could kill you for what you've done to me this time!"

A bulky form hurtled the last ten or so steps down the stairs to the right of the entryway. "Hey, what's going on? Is this guy bothering you, Sharlee?"

Brawny Bill Bolliver to the rescue, clad in a net tank top and biker shorts, muscles bulging in every direction.

"He certainly *is* bothering me," she said angrily.

"Want me to hurt 'im?" Bill pounded one big fist into the other palm. Turning, he did a double take. "Howdy, Dev. What's up?"

"She's mad at me," Dev said. "I don't know why."

"Liar."

"I can throw him out if you want me to," Bill

said, frowning. "Sorry, Dev, but someone's got to look out for Sharlee."

"I understand perfectly."

They turned to her for agreement. She longed to smack them both. Instead, she marched to the stairs leading to her second-floor apartment. "I don't care what either one of you do. Excuse me, I'm going to go slit my wrists now. I'd appreciate it if you'd just leave me alone."

She stomped angrily up the stairs.

Bill looked at Dev. "She was joking, right?"

"Right. I'll go along to make sure, though."

SHE ALMOST SUCCEEDED in slamming the door in Dev's face, but like a door-to-door salesman, he managed to wedge a toe inside.

She pushed. "Go away!"

"Not a chance," he yelled back, "at least until you tell me what's going on."

She pushed harder. "As if you don't know!"

"I don't, I swear it. What the hell's happened?"

"I've been fired!" She stalked across the room to drop her shoulder bag on the love seat.

Dev almost fell in the door. "You're kidding," he said.

"Do I look like I'm kidding?"

"No, you look like you're ready to do major damage to someone or something. Can you calm down long enough to tell me about it?"

She spun around to confront him. "Okay, I'll pretend you're an innocent bystander." She drew a deep breath. "I went into work today and my editor—my *former* editor—fired me. He mumbled something about cutting back on the news staff, but that was a crock.''

Dev let out a low whistle. ''I don't blame you for being upset.''

''You ain't heard the half of it, buster.'' She began to pace. ''He was put up to it. He talked to someone, probably Grandmère. She bribed him, offered him something.''

''Are you sure of that?''

She stopped pacing to glare at him. ''She offered *you* something, right?''

''I never said that.''

''I know how it works, Dev. What did she do? Back your restaurant?''

His level gaze didn't falter. ''She wanted to. I turned her down.''

''Then why are you here if there's nothing in it for you?''

He hesitated just for an instant. ''I told you, I like your grandmother. She's been really good to me over the years and I...well, I owe her.''

''Yes, and that's the way she likes it. They all do.'' She pressed her palms against cheeks burning with anger and humiliation. ''Why do I get the feeling you're holding something back?''

He looked distinctly uncomfortable. ''Because I am. I also came because I was curious. When you wouldn't even speak to me last month—''

''God! If I'd known a snub would lead to *this*, I would have talked your ear off.'' She tried to swallow her rage. ''I don't know what kind of deal

Grandmère offered Bruce but he fired me, and when I started home…'' She blinked furiously to keep her tears at bay. She would not let him see her cry. ''My car broke down. I knew it was in rotten shape, but I thought it would last a few more miles.''

''You had to walk home?''

She gave him a cynical smile. ''Bus service in this town is unpredictable at best.''

''Poor Sharlee.''

He moved as if to take her into his arms and she shoved him away. Sympathy would be her undoing.

''None of that! You helped do this to me, Devin. You're as much to blame as Grandmère is, so don't try to get around me with a little phony sympathy.''

''It's not phony. On the other hand, I have to admit I can see your grandmother's fine hand at work here.''

''Aha!'' His admission was sweet.

''If she did that, it was wrong. However, there are extenuating circumstances. She's doing what she thinks is best for her husband, and you, too. Can't you cut her some slack?''

''After putting me in a spot like this? No!''

He gave her a look that might have been pity. ''All right, Sharlee. If that's the way you feel, I guess there's nothing left for me to say.''

She blinked in surprise. She'd never expected him to give up so easily. ''Well, then,'' she said uneasily, ''in that case…''

Without another word he turned toward the door.

''Where do you think you're going?'' she demanded.

"Home."

"You mean to New Orleans?"

"That's what I mean, all right." His hand closed around the doorknob.

"Devin Oliver, you come back here!"

"Excuse me?" He turned, all innocence.

So upset she could hardly speak, Sharlee glared at him. "You don't seem to understand how much trouble I'm in here."

"I think maybe I do."

"The hell you do! If you did, you couldn't be so blasé about it."

"I'm not—"

"It's my turn to talk." She advanced on him with menace. "You've barged into my life uninvited and messed it up royally. You've gotten me fired—"

"I had nothing to do with that."

"Yes, you did, at least indirectly. You've gotten me fired and now you plan to just waltz on out of here again? You're going to leave me with one paycheck, seven dollars cash, four-hundred-and-thirty-two dollars in the bank, no job, a deceased car and no prospects?" She was filled with righteous indignation.

"You do have a problem," he agreed.

"Nice deduction, Sherlock."

"Now, don't be testy." He looked at her with an expression that could only be called calculating. "I've got an idea."

"Yes, and I've heard it."

He shook his head. "Another idea."

"If it's anything like the last one—"

"Calm down, Sharlee, and give me a chance. I'm trying to help you out. I may hate myself in the morning but—"

"Sounds good so far." She planted her fists defiantly on her hips.

"If you'll go back to New Orleans with me, I'll give you a job waiting tables at the Donna Buy Ya—minimum wage and all the tips you can earn."

"The Donna…?"

"Buy Ya. Donna Buy Ya. That's my restaurant—I mean, my café. Mine and Felix's."

"And you want me to wait tables? Are you out of your mind?"

"Waitressing not good enough for a Lyon?"

"It's not that, it's…" She caught herself up short. "I'm a trained journalist, for God's sake."

"An *unemployed* trained journalist."

"Do you have to add insult to injury? I can't live on minimum wage and tips, anyway."

"You can if you live above the café with Felix and me."

Her jaw dropped and she stared at him.

"And you can eat free—my offer includes room and board," he added in a guilty rush.

"You have got to be kidding. You're offering me this sterling opportunity to live with you and some strange guy and wait tables for tips and minimum wage? What is this—an ambush?"

"Pardon?" Now it was his turn to look surprised.

"Are you setting me up to be ambushed by my family? I can't imagine any other reason you'd make me such an offer, even if I am in desperate need of a break.''

"That hurts." His woebegone expression reflected his words; he really did look hurt. "I did what your grandmother asked and you said no—several times. I probably *am* responsible for your losing your job, at least partially responsible. I'm trying to offer you an option, just something to tide you over while you figure out what you want to do next.''

"Thanks for nothing.''

He grimaced. "You think putting up with that temper of yours is my idea of a good time? You think I *want* to live with you? Jeez, I told you I'd hate myself in the morning for trying to help you out, and guess what? It didn't take that long.''

"I'll starve to death before I move in with you!''

He got calmer as she got more upset. "Sharlee,'' he said, "if you haven't got the guts to go back home, just say so.''

"My problem was never lack of guts,'' she flung at him. "Just give me one good reason I...''

She stopped, a memory flashing through the anger: Granduncle Charles saying, *There are more secrets...than candles on that cake....*

And then there was Dev.

If living with her made him uncomfortable or worse, more power to her. She owed him, both for then and for now. She'd never have another opportunity so tailor-made for revenge.

Besides that, he was the only man who had ever walked away from her. *She* was the one who could pull the plug now. What if...?

Dev looked alarmed. "What is it? Are you sick or something?"

She shook her head and said, "Okay."

"Okay what?"

"Okay, you win. I'll go back to New Orleans with you on one condition."

"And what, God help me, is that?"

He *was* sorry he'd made the offer, the louse, which made her even more eager to accept it. "You're not to tell anyone in my family that I'm there, and if they find out I'm back in town, you're not to tell them where I am."

"That's ridiculous. Two plane tickets will be on your grandmother's charge card. She'll know."

"Then charge one to her card and the other to yours. You *do* have a credit card, don't you?"

"Yes, but I didn't get it for *your* benefit. It happens to be maxed out at the moment, anyway."

"What a shame. In that case, consider it a loan. You can take it out of my lavish salary." She was feeling better about this by the minute.

He heaved a disgruntled sigh. "All right, if that's the only thing that will satisfy you."

"It isn't. Promise me you won't tell anyone in my family I'm back in town."

"Sharlee…" He frowned.

"I mean it, Dev. I don't want anyone to know. Is that clearly understood?"

His lips thinned. "Okay, you don't want your family to know. Any other demands—I mean, requests?"

"Not at the moment." The enormity of what she'd

committed herself to almost overwhelmed her. "Wh-when will we leave?"

"As soon as I can make the arrangements. I'll let you know."

After he'd gone, she stood in the middle of the room, heart pounding. She had so much to do: car to dispose of, probably for junk; furniture to sell or give away; packing. Of everything facing her, packing would be the easiest. Besides her clothing and personal items, there was really nothing she wanted to keep except the laptop.

"Waitress, huh." She said it aloud, trying it out on her tongue. Regardless of what Dev thought, she was no snob. She knew without giving it any serious thought that being a waitress would not be an easy job. But she also felt sure that *good* waitresses could make decent money—didn't she always tip twenty percent herself, more for exceptional service?

Damn, the old competitive spirit was surging to the fore. She'd be the best damn waitress in New Orleans. Hell, she'd own Dev's Donna Buy Ya before she was through with him.

And maybe, just maybe, she'd own him, too.

DEV DROVE THE RENTAL CAR back to his hotel in a state of shock. He couldn't believe what he'd just done. Taking that woman into his home and his business was probably the dumbest thing he'd ever done in his life—except fall for her in the first place.

But who'd have thought she'd accept an offer made purely out of guilt?

In his hotel room, he dialed Lyoncrest and waited

for Margaret to come on the line, which she did quickly.

"Devin, dear boy, I've been waiting for your call. What's happening there?"

"Somehow I think you already know, Margaret." No "Tante Margaret"; he was too angry with her for that.

"Ahh." She breathed the word on a soft sigh. "So my granddaughter is facing adversity. But *you* shouldn't feel guilty. Once she realizes how determined I can be—"

"I think she already does."

After a long expectant silence, she said softly, "Will you kindly explain that?"

"She knows you got her fired from her job and she's furious."

"She may suspect, but she can't know, unless…that man—what's his name? Bruce something? I'm sure he wouldn't tell her."

"He didn't have to. She's not stupid, Margaret. But that wasn't all that happened to her today. Her car broke down and now she doesn't even have the means to look for another job."

"I'm sorry she has to go through this," Margaret said with another sigh. "I'm not really hard-hearted. I simply don't have a great deal of time. Everything I've done, I've done out of love—love for her and also love for my husband. There is nothing more important to me than family."

Damn, he already knew that. "Margaret," he said, "you're a control freak."

Her indrawn breath conveyed surprise and then

she laughed. "Nobody's perfect. Now, if you would just call me Tante Margaret again…"

"Tante Margaret," he said with feeling, "you're one of a kind."

She laughed lightly. "Thank you, dear. So tell me, how much longer do you think it's going to take to convince her?"

"No longer at all."

"You're not giving up!"

"No. We struck a deal. She's going to come back with me as soon as I can make the arrangements, but she's not moving into Lyoncrest. She's going to stay above the Donna Buy Ya with me and Felix and—" he didn't look forward to telling her this about her precious granddaughter "—she's going to work in the café as a waitress."

"Oh, my God!" Margaret burst into delighted laugher. "That's wonderful!"

"Is it?"

"Of course. It will buy us time to resolve this impasse, and she'll be nearby in case…in case she's needed quickly."

"If you say so. I'm glad one of us is happy about it. Because I feel like a total—" at the last instant he changed it to something suitable for elderly ladies "—jerk!"

"I'm sorry you feel that way and I quite understand. When you see how happy everyone is to have her back—"

"Don't even think about it."

"What?"

"Broadcasting the news. She didn't want me to

tell *anyone,* even you—maybe especially not you. She doesn't even want me to charge her ticket to your card, wants me to pay for it myself.''

"Do, and I'll reimburse you immediately. But to tell no one—"

"Tante Margaret, you'll know where she is. Maybe once she's actually in New Orleans, she'll get used to the idea and decide on her own to contact you.'' Or so he devoutly hoped.

"That would be best, I suppose. Oh, Devin, you've done what no one else could. I can't thank you enough.''

Now he sighed. "Sharlee is still a long way from being reunited with her family. Unless you give her space, I'm afraid she'll take off again. If she does, you may never get her back.''

"That won't happen.''

"I sure as hell hope not, because if it does, I'm the one who'll be responsible.''

Damn. More guilt. Just what he needed. "One more thing—''

"Yes?''

"I won't be calling you about this again. I've done what you asked and that's the end of it.''

"I understand entirely. In future I'll call you. Hurry home, dear, and bring Charlotte with you.''

"Hey, wait a minute. You don't seem to—'' The line went dead and he added an unheard, "understand.''

SHARLEE AND DEV arranged to meet at Denver International Airport two days later. He'd offered to pick her up of course, but she'd refused, relying, instead, on the kindness of Brawny Bill.

Regardless of what the future held, she would not give up her independence lightly. She didn't need Dev Oliver; she didn't *want* to need him.

She wanted to own him.

Such melodrama! She bit back a giggle. Even the *thought* of revenge was sweet.

Brawny Bill grinned at her from behind the wheel of his vintage Jeep. ''Somethin' funny?''

''Yes.'' She stared ahead at the multipeaked white roof of the airport, looking like a series of nomad tents on the plains. Was she leaving for good this time? She shivered.

Bill gave her a curious glance. He'd been a good friend, even buying some of her furniture and arranging for the rest to go to a secondhand store. But then, he'd always looked out for her. Mikey, his ''partner,'' hadn't minded at all.

''That Devin's okay,'' Bill said unexpectedly. ''He'll take care of you now that I won't be around.''

She giggled again, which wasn't like her, but the significance of this undertaking made her giddy. ''I hope *I* take care of *him*,'' she corrected.

He nodded agreeably. ''That's good. I guess you guys have known each other a long time.''

''All our lives.'' A long time to know without really knowing. ''Dev's stepfather is my father's first cousin.''

''Must be a big family. That's real nice.''

She used to think so.

He maneuvered through the various curves and

turns of the airport approach, then pulled to the curb in front of the United Airlines sign. Dev was there waiting for her, his suitcase on the curb beside him.

Her heart fluttered at the sight of him and at the realization that she was about to get on a plane and fly away with him. But it was way too late for second thoughts—or third or fourth.

Bill leaned over to open her door and Dev was there to help her out, his hand warm on her arm.

"Thanks, Bill." She blew him a kiss. "I'll never forget you."

"Have a happy life, Sharlee."

"I intend to, Bill. You have a happy life, too."

Why did she suddenly feel like crying? She liked the big man a lot, but that was no reason to break down and bawl like a baby. Facing days and nights with Dev Oliver—now *there* was good reason to cry.

CHAPTER FIVE

SHARLEE WAS FINE until the fasten seatbelts light went on for the descent into New Orleans. Then she realized her savoir faire was the result of wine and not nerves of steel.

This was a mistake! Casting an anxious glance at Dev, she tried to calm herself. True, she hadn't had that many options, but surely she could have found *something* less threatening than this.

So she did what she usually did when she was intimidated or out of her depth or simply scared; she clammed up—at least until they stepped outside the air-conditioned building and into the August swelter of New Orleans.

She staggered and thought for a moment she might faint, something she'd never done before.

Dev caught her arm and looked at her with quick concern.

"Easy, *chère.* Are you sick?"

She gasped. "Let me just catch my breath." The very air felt sultry and heavy, its weight pressing her down. Already she felt enveloped by dampness. She'd felt the same way when she came back briefly last month, although to a lesser degree.

"Feeling better?"

She swallowed hard and nodded. "I'm sorry. I didn't know it would affect me like this." She shoved damp hair away from her face. "It's so humid."

He shrugged. "This is news in New Orleans? C'mon, our shuttle's loading."

"A shuttle?" She glanced around in surprise.

"Hey, your grandmother would gladly have sent the limousine."

He was laughing at her. "The shuttle's just fine," she said. Ignoring her trepidation, she picked up the two lightest suitcases while he handled the rest. The sooner she was out of this heat and humidity, the better.

But she was under no illusions that the weather was the worst of her troubles.

THE SHUTTLE LET THEM OFF in front of the French Market and they trudged the remaining distance through the narrow cobbled streets for which the French Quarter was famous. Sharlee was hardly aware of her surroundings, so consumed was she with foreboding.

"Here we are." Dev stopped. "Welcome to the Donna Buy Ya Café, your home away from home."

Sharlee blinked and turned. Sure enough, that name was emblazoned across the glass front in sweeping gilt letters. Dev opened the door and gestured her inside.

She entered cautiously, feeling completely alien to this place and to her own immediate future. She also felt horrible, both mentally and physically. She simply didn't belong here.

Still, Dev's new venture intrigued her. She stopped and stood her cases upright on their wheels. Slowly she turned in a complete circle, taking in the interior of the small restaurant.

To the left of the door was a counter with six stools; ahead and to the right of the door were tables and chairs—no booths. She could see the kitchen beyond the counter and that was that. The floor was some kind of tile, smooth and so old its color was indistinguishable. A ceiling fan turned in lazy circles overhead, which was a good thing because the air-conditioning didn't appear to be working.

The whole effect was so mismatched and funky that it made her smile. There was something cheery and inviting about the place.

"You're smiling," Dev observed. "Does that mean you like it?"

"I don't *dis*like it," she countered. "How's the food?"

At that moment a huge black man came out of the kitchen. "Food's great," he said with a big grin. "I should know. I cook it."

"Felix," Dev began, "this is—"

"Yeah, I know who this is." The man marched up to her and swooped her up into a bear hug that lifted her feet completely off the ground. "Welcome to the Donna Buy Ya, Charlotte."

"Sharlee." With her cheek mashed against his massive chest, her name came out pretty much a mumble.

"Sharlee," Dev repeated helpfully.

Felix put her back down on her feet. "Let's haul your stuff upstairs, Sharlee. You'll wanna change before you go to work."

She blinked in surprise. "Hey, slow down! I just got here."

"Maybe so, but if we're gonna open in ten days—"

"Ten days!" Dev was obviously surprised.

Felix grabbed the handles of Sharlee's suitcases. "Things have been happenin' around here. I'll tell you all about it as soon as we get this little lady settled."

There was nothing for Sharlee to do but follow the two men up the stairs hidden in a hallway at the back of the café. With each step she felt herself moving farther and farther away from life as she'd known it to this point.

Not an entirely bad thing, actually.

THE SECOND-FLOOR APARTMENT consisted of three tiny bedrooms, a living room, a kitchen and one— she could hardly believe it—bathroom. This was going to take considerable compromise on all their parts, she thought wryly.

Nor did the apartment have the charm of the café. High ceilings and peeling wallpaper dark with age made the place seem almost forbidding. But there were a couple of redeeming features, such as the long narrow garden surrounded by tall buildings but visible from the living room and kitchen.

"Is that your garden?" she asked Dev.

"We kind of share it with the nice old lady who lives in the apartment on the other side." He indicated the wrought-iron balcony across from the one they stood on. "Her name's Blanche Fortier and she does the gardening in exchange for use of it."

"She does a great job," Sharlee said, impressed by the luxuriant greenery below her.

"She had the same deal with the last owner and kept the garden up even though this place stood vacant for a couple of years," he explained.

Felix hollered from inside. "I stuck Sharlee's bags in her room. Come on down when you get settled."

"Will do." Dev cocked his head and grinned at her. "Brace yourself. I'm about to show you your new home."

She grinned back. "You saw where I was living in Colorado. I'm not all that fussy."

"Then follow me."

In the dim, narrow hall, he pointed out Felix's room to the left, then his room. He indicated the bathroom through the last door on the right and finally her room, last door on the left. He paused to let her enter first. Taking a deep breath, she did.

The small room looked like something out of a late movie. Everything in it—what few things there were—was dusty and unkempt. The old cast-iron bed had been painted white who knew how many years ago and now the paint was flaked and peeled. Even from here, she could see that the mattress sagged badly.

A dark wooden table stood beside the bed, and across the room against the wall stood a chest of drawers painted a sort of moss green. A rope hung across one corner of the room with a few wire coat hangers.

And the wallpaper—yellowed roses on a background of muddy green.

But double doors had been thrown open to a balcony hanging over the sidewalk, and she could hear people walking by and smell a multitude of tantalizing aromas. Already she was wondering about the previous occupants of this room, who they'd been and what they'd done and what their stories might be.

The place reeked of history and she *loved* history.

Overhead a ceiling fan turned in lazy circles, stirring up dust. She coughed. "I see you went out of your way to get this place ready for me," she said, but she was only teasing.

He seemed to know that. "Felix opened the door and turned on your fan. What more do you want? You come here not as a Lyon but as an employee, remember?"

"I'm not complaining. It's worth every penny I'm paying."

"And I'm sure you'll be worth every penny we're paying *you*." Giving her an amused glance, he crossed to the outer door and stepped onto the balcony. "I hope the noise won't keep you awake."

"When I'm tired, nothing keeps me awake." Leaving the suitcases for later, she joined him. She placed her hands on the wrought-iron railing and sucked in a deep breath.

"Not so bad, huh?"

"What isn't?" She gave him a cautious glance.

"Being here."

She chose to misunderstand. "Here in this apartment?"

"Here in this town. It's your town, Sharlee, your hometown. It'll all come back to you."

She shivered, because it honestly didn't feel like her town. As for it all coming back to her... "Maybe that's what I'm afraid of," she said, realizing with a start that it was true. She didn't want to become entangled again. Not with family quarrels and certainly not with *him*.

He stood so close she could feel the heat of his arm near her shoulder. In his khaki pants and baby-blue knit shirt, he looked cool and comfortable. But then, he probably didn't feel the same forcefield around her that she felt emanating from him.

"Hey, *coozin!*"

The cry came from the other side of the street below. A darkly tanned young man with black hair and ragged jeans waved and grinned.

Dev straightened. "Beau! I'll be right down."

"Cousin?" Sharlee translated the Cajun dialect.

"Close as cousins, anyway. That's Beau Achord. Wonder why he's come in from Bayou Sans Fin today. You can bet he's got a reason." Dev turned away from the railing. "Come on down when you get unpacked—and don't worry. We won't really work you too hard on your first day here."

"I don't mind," she said. "I came to work."

She looked down at Beau Achord, staring up at her with friendly interest. She waved and he waved back, then trotted across the street and out of sight beneath the balcony.

She might as well unpack and get it over with, she decided, turning back into the room. But first she had to get out of these hot jeans and into something cool.

Then she'd figure out how to deal with Dev Oliver on his own turf.

BEAU ACHORD NODDED toward the back stairway, his dark eyes sparkling with interest. "Here comes your gal," he said. "Me, I'm outta here."

"Stay and meet her," Dev invited, adding, "She's not my gal."

"Will be." Beau touched the fingers of his left hand to his forehead in a jaunty salute. *"Très vite."*

"Very soon" was way too optimistic, Dev thought, watching Sharlee walk down the last few steps. She'd changed into shorts that revealed long slim legs and a T-shirt accenting high round breasts.

She looked around with obvious disappointment. "Where's your cousin? I wanted to meet him."

"You will. He was in town to pick up supplies for his boat business. He dropped by to invite all of us to a *fais do do* on the bayou a week from Sunday."

"A dance at Bayou Sans Fin?" She gave him a strange look. "I'm not sure I really want to—"

"You've got time to think about it," he interrupted, then changed the subject. "Are you hungry?"

"Starved."

"Felix cooked up a big pot of gumbo just to keep

his hand in, as he says. He's carrying a plate to Blanche at the moment, but you can help yourself.''

"What about you? Aren't you going to eat?"

"I've got errands to run. Gotta see the man about
this air-conditioning and pick up some paint. My
car's in a garage a couple of blocks away. You know
what a bitch it is to find parking around here.''

She got that narrow knowing look on her face.
"Let me guess. It's a Mercedes convertible.''

"Somebody told you.'' He hated a smart aleck,
especially one who was right. "See you later.''

"Okay.''

She didn't sound as if she much cared whether she
did or not. He was halfway uptown before it dawned
on him why.

The first time they'd made love was at Bayou Sans
Fin, at his mother's house.

Mr. Sensitivity strikes again.

WHEN FELIX RETURNED, Sharlee was sitting on the
counter with her feet on a stool, holding a big bowl
of chicken-and-sausage gumbo and rice on her lap.
She ate enthusiastically with a big spoon, which she
now waved in his direction.

"This is the best gumbo I've ever tasted!"

"Sure enough?"

"Yes, sure enough.'' She licked her lips appreciatively.

"Thanks.'' He looked around. "Where's Dev?"

"Errands, he said.'' Which wasn't very nice, running off before she even had a chance to settle in.

"Pissed you off, eh?" His quick grin was amused.

"Of course not. Why should it?"

"You're a woman. You don't need a reason."

His observation drew a reluctant smile. "I'll accept that," she said. "Felix, do you know why Dev quit his job at WDIX?"

Felix's smile disappeared. "Really? No. I think it had something to do with his mother's death, though. He changed a lot after she died."

Sharlee's appetite faded and she set the bowl aside. "I never knew her." Actually Yvette Lyon had been pretty much persona non grata in the family after she and Alain divorced. No one ever seemed to understand how he ended up with all three children, even the one who wasn't his.

"Me, neither," Felix said. "She was sick a long time. Dev ran himself ragged toward the end. After she died, it was like...kinda like she took his final...obligation with her. He was at loose ends for a while, and then all of a sudden he quit his job and went in on this place with me." He gestured with both hands.

Obligation. The word struck a chord with her. If she felt too little obligation to family, Dev might have felt too much.

"What about you?" she asked Felix. "Are you a local? Where did you learn to cook like this?"

Over the next hour she learned that Felix was indeed local, that he'd learned to cook for a family of seven siblings after his mother died and his father left him in charge at the age of eleven, that he'd learned from his aunt and refined his talent in San Francisco.

Big hands tightening convulsively into fists, he spoke with soul-deep passion. "This place has gotta go," he said. "It's Dev's money but it's my dream. This is probably the only chance I'll ever get to do it my way. The Donna Buy Ya's gonna fly or Felix Brown will know the reason why!"

She nodded. For all their sakes, failure was not an option.

DEV RETURNED with the painting supplies to find Sharlee on her knees scrubbing the shelves behind the counter. He was so surprised he nearly dropped the paint.

She pushed her hair back with her wrist and grinned. The T-shirt, damp with sweat, clung to her breasts and he tried not to stare.

"Hi," she said, dipping her sponge into a bucket of soapy water. "That took long enough."

"I got the paint," he said stupidly, thinking that he'd never seen her look sexier than she did now, sitting back on bent legs, face aglow from exertion.

"No kiddin'." She looked pointedly at the cans hanging from the wire bails in each hand.

Flustered, he shifted his weight from one foot to the other. He'd known having her around would be difficult because he couldn't so much as look at her without thinking of what had been. But the force of what he felt now came as a complete surprise.

He wanted her. He wanted her more than he ever had before, even back in the beginning when they were new to each other and just discovering the passion between them. But he wasn't going to have her. He didn't need that kind of grief again.

"Where's Felix?" he croaked.

She gave him an odd look. "In the storeroom working on those shelves that were falling off the wall."

"Okay. Sorry I bothered you." He carried the paint away.

"No bother," she called after him. "When I get into the swing of things, not much bothers me."

That he could believe. What he couldn't believe was that Charlotte Lyon could get into the swing of scrubbing shelves.

THEY PARTED AT ELEVEN that night with Felix's admonitions ringing in their ears.

"Tomorrow we paint. Be prepared. My sister DeeDee's comin' over to help because I wanna get through the entire downstairs, no excuses."

After he'd gone off to bed, Dev and Sharlee stared at each other.

Dev spoke first. "I think he means it."

"You and me both."

"Uh…" He hesitated. "Why don't you take the bathroom first?"

"Okay."

"It'll be easier once we're used to each other. I mean, who gets first dibs and who gets…"

She nodded. Tired from all the hard work, she looked much more relaxed and comfortable than when they'd arrived. "I'll try not to take too long and abuse your good nature."

"I didn't know you acknowledged I *had* a good nature."

"Of course you do," she said lightly. "If you hadn't, you'd have run straight to my grandmother and spilled your guts. The fact that she wasn't at the airport waiting for me indicates that you must, indeed, have a decent side."

She went off down the hall and he sat there brooding. She sure wasn't going to like it when she found out he *had* spilled his guts to her grandmother. Maybe he shouldn't have, but on the other hand, he couldn't bear the thought of Margaret worrying and stewing about her granddaughter when there was no need.

Life had handed him a choice that sucked. Too damned bad.

He gave Sharlee fifteen minutes in the bathroom, figuring that was plenty of time. Barefoot, wearing only trousers, in deference to their guest—he usually wandered around in the altogether—he tossed a towel over his shoulder and headed across the hall. Just as he reached for the knob, the door flew open and she stood there.

Face bare of makeup, hair slicked back, soft pink mouth rounded into an "O" of surprise, she looked good enough to eat. She had on some kind of shimmery turquoise robe belted at the waist, which nicely outlined her breasts.

She raised her eyebrows. "Excuse me, I'll just…"

When she tried to sidle past, those breasts brushed

his bare arm. He reacted as if he'd been zapped by an electric shock, jumping back awkwardly.

Even as unnerved as he was, he saw the tiny shiver dart through her. "Good night," she murmured. Head down, she rushed across the hall and into her own room.

Almost immediately the door swung open again. "I forgot to thank you for the radio," she said breathlessly.

"That's all right. I figured you needed something to entertain you."

Damn, he'd like to entertain her. Right now, this very minute, he'd like to strip that robe off her and—

"Well, it was very thoughtful of you."

The door closed again. He stared at it for a couple of minutes, trying to calm his breathing, trying not to think of the feel of her nipples brushing his arm.

Then he went inside and took a long shower.

A long *cold* shower.

LIVING WITH DEV, Sharlee quickly discovered, was not easy.

Thank God for Felix, who came and went without rhyme or reason. He could usually be counted on to interrupt any potentially explosive moment, as he had on her first morning there.

She'd stumbled into the kitchen looking for the source of a delectable aroma, right into Dev's arms as he turned to reach for the cups. Pressed against him from chest to knee, she'd frozen, her stricken gaze flying to his face.

She'd barely even realized who it was until they

touched. Not a morning person, little registered with her until that second cup of coffee. But standing there in his arms, it registered belatedly that his chest was bare, which was quickly followed by a question she simply had to ask.

"What do you have on when you sleep?"

His eyes widened. "What do I..."

She laughed breathlessly. "The radio is not a satisfactory—"

"Mornin', kiddies." Felix grinned from the doorway. "Hate to break up this little tête à tête but I gotta get to that coffeepot."

They sprang apart guiltily, which was when she noticed Dev wore striped pajama bottoms that looked as if they'd just been unfolded.

Felix reached for a mug on the open shelf. "Get a move on. We got paintin' to do today."

Sharlee groaned. "As if any of us are going to forget."

"I dunno." He grinned over the rim of his mug. "Looked to me like you two were fixin' to forget everything."

She smiled sweetly at him. "Not a chance with you around to remind us of our duty," she said. "One cup of coffee and I'm all yours."

She didn't miss the flare in Dev's eyes when she said it. Maybe this was going to work out, she thought as she carried the coffee back to her room to dress. He seemed as aware of her as she was of him. More and more, it was beginning to look like a question of who lost control first.

It wouldn't be her! And if *he* lost control and lived

to regret it…well, revenge really could be sweet, or so she'd heard.

Rummaging through her belongings, she hauled out a pair of denim shorts and a cotton blouse she could tie across her midriff, thinking of Dev, thinking of how he'd brushed her off.

Maybe she'd get her chance to do the same to him. But before she did, she'd have to make damned sure that this time, she would not be the one left to pick up the pieces.

Why had he betrayed her that way?

She was determined she wouldn't ask. The answer might be even worse than the question.

DEEDEE WAS AS LITTLE and cute as her brother was big and scary. Only nineteen, she took night classes and worked part-time as a checker in a small neighborhood grocery. Once the Donna Buy Ya opened, she hoped to have all the work she could handle there.

With a paintbrush in her hand, she was a demon, putting them all to shame with both her speed and precision. By noon, the rest of them had nearly as much paint on themselves as on the walls, but DeeDee was as clean and neat as a pin.

Sharlee, who'd vowed she could work harder if not smarter than any of them, was last to lay down her brush in favor of one of Felix's po'boy sandwiches. "Just another minute," she kept saying, until Dev marched over, took the brush from her hand and dragged her to the table.

She wasn't afraid of work, no matter what anyone

thought. She could laugh and kid around over sandwiches and sodas, knowing that she wasn't letting down her part of the bargain. She was *not* a charity case.

BY THE END OF THE DAY, Dev thought his arm was going to fall off.

The two women, on the other hand, looked…not as fresh as when they'd started certainly, but a hell of a lot better than he felt.

He'd probably feel even better if Sharlee wasn't wearing those tight shorts and a blouse that bared a lot of skin. Her long golden legs would probably dance in his dreams tonight, as her breasts had dominated his sleep the previous night.

He sighed, or maybe it was a groan.

Sharlee paused in stripping masking tape off the wall to flash him a smile. "Poor Dev all worn out?"

Felix plopped his messy brush down on a paper plate. "Poor Felix sure is. How about you, DeeDee?"

"Hangin' in," she said cheerfully. "But I've gotta get goin'. I have a class at six." She placed her brush carefully next to her brother's. "How about you, fella? Aunt Delia said you were comin' over tonight to cook jambalaya for everybody, but if you're too tired…"

"Hell, I forgot all about that." Felix turned to Dev and Sharlee. "Sorry, kids, but you're on your own tonight."

Sharlee's heart leaped into her throat. She managed a calm nod, but what she thought was, *Not to-*

night! Although she was seriously thinking about sleeping with Dev for revenge, she was no way near a decision. Before she could do anything so drastic, she had to be sure in her own mind that she was strong enough...confident enough...immune enough to his charm that it would be she who walked away, not he.

Because if he ever did that to her again, one of them would die.

She could play a little in the meantime, though. So she smiled sweetly at Dev and said softly, ''Just you and me, kid.''

CHAPTER SIX

SHE WAS DELIBERATELY TRYING to drive him crazy—or was she?

Dev couldn't be sure. Actually, where Sharlee was concerned he couldn't be sure of much except that she would probably surprise him.

Such as the way she'd worked today: always first to start and last to quit. He was impressed in spite of himself. He'd seen how simply she'd lived in Colorado, but he'd still found it hard to believe that the heiress to a good chunk of the Lyon fortune would get down on her knees to scrub, climb on a chair to paint, plunge her hands up to the elbows in soapy dishwater to clean brushes, and do it all cheerfully.

She barely seemed like the same girl he'd fallen for way back when. That girl had been a pampered princess, while this one was mature and calm and presumably wiser. Even so, the signals she sent were so mixed he couldn't act on any of them even if he wanted to.

After Felix and DeeDee left, he and Sharlee had looked at each other and suddenly something very like desire arced between them—at least, that was what *he'd* felt.

What had she felt? Expressionless, she'd turned

away deliberately, as if dismissing whatever had just happened.

Then later that night, when they were alone in the apartment, she'd had such vulnerability on her face that he'd half risen from the couch to go to her. Her eyes had opened wide, as if she'd suddenly realized the invitation she'd extended. Jumping up, she'd fled to her room as if seeking a safe haven from feelings she didn't care to confront.

Dev went outside onto the balcony overlooking the garden and tried to calm down. She might be more mature, but she often seemed a little lost, a little lonely...

And always, she was tempting.

FOR TWO DAYS they worked side by side, cleaning and painting and rearranging. Sharlee never complained and never shirked. She got along great with Felix and DeeDee and everyone else who wandered in to see how renovations were going.

Including Blanche Fortier, their friendly neighborhood gardener, who dropped by on the second afternoon specifically to meet ''the new girl.''

''I've seen you across the way,'' the slender gray-haired woman said, shaking Sharlee's hand. ''But I've never seen you using our lovely garden.''

''I want to,'' Sharlee assured her, ''but this slave driver keeps me so busy I haven't had time.'' She gave Dev a gently accusing glance.

''Guilty,'' he agreed promptly. He'd been looking for a way to give her a little time off without seeming to favor her. ''But the worst is over. Felix said we'd been working you too hard and should give you the afternoon off to get reacquainted with your hometown.''

''You're from New Orleans?'' Blanche looked surprised. ''I'd never have guessed.''

Sharlee seemed pleased by this. ''I've been gone for a long time,'' she explained. ''Actually I'm just passing through on my way to someplace else.''

''I'm from Memphis myself,'' Blanche confided, ''but this is my adopted hometown.'' She hauled a newspaper from beneath her arm and offered it to Dev. ''I thought you might have missed this in today's paper.''

''Missed what?'' He opened the folded newspaper.

''In the second section—a story about Paul Lyon. I know you used to work for him, so I thought you might enjoy reading it.'' She held up a hand and rippled her fingers. ''Now I really must go. I hear my roses calling.''

'''Bye, Blanche.'' Dev pawed through the paper until he found the right page, then began to read. The story concerned the success of the WDIX literacy program launched in conjunction with the fiftieth-anniversary celebration last month.

The accompanying photograph showed a handsome and distinguished man who looked nowhere near his mid-eighties. Dev glanced up to find Sharlee watching guardedly.

He held out the paper. ''Wanna see it?''

She shook her head.

''Suit yourself.'' He tossed the paper into the nearest wastepaper basket. ''In that case, why don't you go ahead and take off? We can manage without you for the rest of the day.''

''I can't. It's going to rain.''

''It rains practically every afternoon during the entire month of August. You won't melt.''

''How can you be so sure? Papa used to say I was made of sugar.'' Her mouth quirked in a teasing grin. She looked delectable in her usual shorts and T-shirt, her face clean of makeup and her hair pulled back with a rubber band.

''And then you grew up.''

''Shh.'' She touched a forefinger to her lips. ''Hardly anyone seems to realize that.''

So she didn't go out that afternoon, just worked right alongside the men. Later Dev noticed that the wastebasket had been emptied. Later still, he discovered that not everything had been disposed of…

It was around midnight when he padded silently from his room to the kitchen for a glass of milk. When he passed the living room, he saw a soft light on and supposed Felix was up for some reason.

Only it wasn't Felix; it was Sharlee, curled up in the big old overstuffed chair looking at something in her lap with a world of longing on her face. The muted glow of a floor lamp cast shadows that emphasized the curve of her shoulder above the thin straps of her nightgown, the sweet line of a leg folded beneath her. Her hair tumbled around her shoulders as if she'd just risen from bed. On the table next to her chair was a half-full glass of milk and a cookie with one bite missing.

She made such a lovely picture that it took him a

moment to realize that she was gazing at the photo of her grandfather, clipped from Blanche's newspaper. She must have heard him then, for she looked up guiltily, at the same time crumpling the newsprint in her fist.

"You scared me!" She said it as if he'd done it on purpose.

"Sorry. I was on the way to the kitchen for something to drink and saw you in here. Anything wrong?"

"No, of course not. I was hungry, that's all." She leaped to her feet and the folds of the white cotton gown settled around her knees. "I thought everybody was asleep or I wouldn't have…" She indicated her attire.

"No problem." He congratulated himself on sounding cool when he didn't feel cool at all. Dressed or semi-undressed, Sharlee got to him big time. Undressed—hell, he'd probably burn to a cinder. He grinned at the image. "I'm not exactly dressed for a ball myself." In fact, he'd thrown on the only pajama bottoms he owned simply because of her presence in the apartment. "We're not very formal around here."

"I've noticed." She picked up the glass and the cookie. "I'll just drop this in the kitchen and go on to bed, then."

"I didn't mean to run you out."

"You didn't."

"Then let me take that stuff for you on my way."

He reached; she reached. Their fingers brushed and he heard her soft intake of breath.

"Thank you."

"No problem."

He watched her hurry out of the room, still clutching that bit of newsprint. He liked the new softer side of her he was seeing. *She has more feelings for her family than she's willing to admit,* he told himself. *She's been hurt and she's trying to protect herself...but she still cares.*

He downed the rest of her milk and popped the remainder of the cookie into his mouth. His lower extremities ached with tension, and the pressure in his groin had built to uncomfortable proportions.

Unfortunately there was damned little he could do about it.

THERE WAS NO POINT stalling any longer, so Sharlee took them up on their offer of a break the next morning. For some reason she'd felt obliged to bury herself in the Donna Buy Ya to avoid venturing forth in the greater world of the Vieux Carré—the French Quarter.

As she felt obliged to avoid any personal topic of conversation with Dev, even though she longed to hit him right between the eyes with questions that had plagued her for so long.

She banished those irritating thoughts. She refused to look back, and even her current situation was temporary. As soon as the café opened for business, she'd start casting about for journalistic opportunities that would take her west, the direction she'd always intended to go.

With a wave and a "See you later," she headed

through narrow streets toward the Café du Monde for a cup of dark rich coffee with chicory and a *beignet*. Around her, the part residential, part commercial French Quarter sprang to life. Shopkeepers washing down the sidewalks smiled at her as she passed antique shops, restaurants, bars and apartments.

She veered from the most direct route to walk through Jackson Square, the old town square facing the river and dominated by a statue of the general himself astride a rearing steed—a perfect perch for pigeons. In the background, the soaring spires of St. Louis Cathedral rose like sentinels against a cloudless blue sky.

She felt like a tourist.

She hadn't expected that. She might loudly argue that New Orleans was no longer home, but she had never quite believed it herself—until now. Even the special aromas didn't make her feel as if she'd come home. Passing eateries on the square, she smelled roasting coffee beans, baking bread, even the pungent odor of fish and crawfish and shrimp without the slightest feeling of déjà vu.

It was almost as if she'd never been here before.

The Café du Monde lay ahead with its green striped awnings. She crossed Decatur and went inside. Even early in the morning, the café's business was thriving. She found a round table in the corner and sat down, feeling alone and out of it.

A waiter wearing the little Café du Monde hat took her order for café au lait and a plate of three *beignets,* then ambled away. While she waited, Sharlee looked around at the other customers.

Tourists, most of them. She'd apparently brought her feelings of alienation to the right place. But where *didn't* she feel alienated?

The answer surprised and dismayed her: at the Donna Buy Ya.

She was actually enjoying her work there, which required a certain amount of muscle but little if any thought. She was tired of thinking, tired of balancing a full plate. She could only hope she'd snap out of this lethargy soon, because she had a lot of decisions to make. At the moment, though, her situation suited her surprisingly well.

Except for being around Dev so much.

And stumbling upon him—or being stumbled upon *by* him—at all hours of the day or night. Take last night, for instance. She shouldn't have been sitting there in her nightgown staring at her grandfather's picture for the hundredth time. She should have known...

Maybe she *had* known Dev would appear and see her and want her. Because whether or not she decided to sleep with him as a prelude to dumping him, she certainly didn't mind giving him at least that small taste of what he'd turned away from once.

The waitress set the coffee and *beignets* on the table without a word and wandered off again. Sharlee looked down at the small square donuts covered by mounds of powdered sugar and felt the beginnings of a sneeze.

She'd loved these sugary confections once. Disappointed, she picked one up and tried to shake away the drifts of white.

Just one more thing to get through on her way to the other side.

What the hell. She'd go for broke, take back a bag of pralines and *really* put herself to the test.

DEV WAS SURPRISED when Sharlee waltzed out first thing that morning, but not as surprised as he was when his brother, Alex, walked in.

Twenty-two and a somewhat halfhearted part-time student of communications at Loyola, Alex was also the family rabble-rouser and hedonist. In fact, now that Dev thought about it, Alex was kind of the Sharlee of his branch of the Lyon family.

"Where y'at?" Alex greeted his older half brother in typical New Orleans style. Unshaven and rumpled, he didn't look as if he'd made it home last night. "You wouldn't have an oyster po'boy back there in the kitchen for a starving man would you?"

"Nope, and Felix isn't around to fix one for you. How about a bowl of leftover *étouffée,* instead?"

"Naw, my mouth's all set for a sandwich. I'll go grab me a po'boy down the block. When you gonna open this dump, anyway?"

"August twenty-fifth, and you're *not* invited. We can't afford to run out of food."

"Ha-ha, very funny." Alex suddenly looked uneasy. "Uh…that's not really why I dropped by."

"No kiddin'." Dev kept right on polishing the chrome behind the counter.

Alex turned beseeching. "Come on, Dev, help me out here. I'm in big trouble, man."

"Who with—Alain or the law?"

"With Dad, of course." He glowered. "I wish you wouldn't call him Alain."

"That's his name."

"But you used to... Ah, hell." The kid thrust out his full lower lip and kicked at the leg of a stool. "Why'd you do it, Dev? I still don't get why you quit a cushy job at WDIX for *this*."

The *this* was uttered with complete scorn.

"I doubt you ever will, kid." *Hoped* he never would was more like it. "So what've you done this time?"

"Nothin', not a damned thing." The rebellious cast to Alex's unshaven face said otherwise. "I got busy and...and didn't go home last night, that's all. No big deal. But the last time that happened—"

"Which was when?"

"Last Wednesday. Wanna make something of it?"

Dev considered his brother, a young man with smarts and looks and family connections and absolutely no self-discipline. "You're after my help, remember? Back off."

"Yeah, right." Alex settled down. "Anyway, Dad said the next time I didn't come home he was throwin' my butt out. I don't think he really meant it, but maybe you could just...you know, tell him something."

"Such as?"

"Well, that I spent the night here and tried to

phone home but...but your phone was out or something.''

Dev laughed. "Oh, yeah, he'd believe that."

"Then think up something better," Alex flared, "because—"

The opening of the door stopped his tirade and they both glanced up to find Sharlee standing there, holding a paper bag and looking sexy as hell.

"Oops," she said. "Am I interrupting..." Her eyes widened. "Alex? Is that you?"

"My God! Charlotte?"

They met halfway and he swept her into an enormous hug. Dev, watching, didn't like the gleam in the kid's dark eyes, but figured Sharlee could handle him just fine.

Which she did by stepping back and removing his arms from around her waist.

Alex looked from her to his brother and back again. "I didn't know you were in town, Charlotte. I saw Uncle André just yesterday and he didn't say a word."

She exchanged a quick glance with Dev before answering. "He doesn't know. Nobody knows but Dev. And now you of course."

Alex frowned. "Why not? I don't get it unless you two...you are—"

"No!" they exclaimed in unison.

Sharlee added, "It's a long story. Suffice it to say, I'll let everyone know when the time is right—which at the moment, it isn't."

"I see," Alex said, although he obviously didn't. "Do me a favor and keep this quiet, okay?"

"Sure," he agreed too readily. "Whatever you say." He turned back to his brother. "About what we were discussing, Dev—"

"Forget it." Dev picked up his polishing cloth again.

"But—"

"It wouldn't do any good, Alex. Alain's still pissed off at me because I left WDIX, so do you really think he'd listen to anything I have to say?"

"You could at least try."

"You got yourself into this. I'm afraid you'll have to get yourself out."

"In that case, thanks for nothing."

Sharlee touched the kid's arm lightly. "Is there anything I can do?"

"No, but thanks for asking."

"You'll keep my secret, won't you?"

"No problem."

Dev sure as hell hoped he meant it, but the look on Alex's face wasn't too reassuring. If he told Alain, there could be hell to pay.

ALEX GRABBED an oyster po'boy on the corner, then walked to Canal Street and caught the St. Charles trolley to the Garden District. Leaning back on the hard wooden seat with a groan, he gave in to his hangover.

He'd managed to hold it together long enough to talk to his brother, for all the good it'd done. He'd been grasping at straws and he knew it, but there was always the outside chance Dad and Dev had made up their differences.

Alex hadn't really cared until it affected him, as it did now. Dev was okay, a good brother and everything, but ever since their mother had died he hadn't been the same. Alex, who hadn't even gone into the bayou to attend her funeral, felt a flash of guilt, which he quickly pushed away.

He'd hardly known her, after all. Only Dev had kept in touch after she'd deserted them.

Besides, Alex had more important things to think about. Staring out of the open car at the oak trees shading St. Charles, he considered his plight. Unless he could come up with some scheme, his father was going to kill him. Since Dev wouldn't help, what did he have, what did he know, that he could bargain with?

And then in a flash of inspiration, he had it: Charlotte Lyon was back in town and nobody on her side of the family knew. That bit of information must be worth *something*.

Of course Alex had promised not to say anything, but what difference would it make if he did? She'd never know he was the guilty party, so why shouldn't he use the information for much-needed leverage with his sure-to-be-pissed-off father?

He actually smiled. The news flash that she was back and living with Dev could mean a great deal to his deliverance.

"Sorry, Charlotte," he said softly, rising to depart the streetcar at the far end of the Garden District. "But you understand. You wouldn't want your favorite cousin to be homeless, would you?"

"WANT A PRALINE?"

Felix recoiled, then leaned forward to check out the logo on the bag. "Don't eat that stuff," he said. "You want a praline, I'll make you a praline that's fit to eat."

Sharlee laughed. Dev was out somewhere working on some permit or other. She'd just finished washing the windows and was ready for a little break. "You don't have time to do what you're doin' and you want to make me pralines? I don't think so, Felix."

He gave her a sheepish smile. "You're right. But if you hadn't been around to help out here, we'd be in a lot worse shape than we are now."

"Thanks." His compliment was a pleasant surprise. "Sure you don't want one of these?"

"Oh, all right." He reached into the bag and drew out a brown disk lumpy with pecans. He took a bite. "Sugary," he judged, then popped the rest into his mouth. "You enjoy your walk this mornin'?"

"Yes." She had…sort of. "I've been avoiding my family, but when I got back, Alex was here."

"Uh-oh," Felix said.

"What's that supposed to mean?"

"That kid gets into more trouble than anybody in the family. Bet he was after something."

She frowned. It had seemed that way, but she didn't really know, so she shrugged. "He promised not to tell anyone I was here."

"And you believed him?"

"Felix! What are you saying?"

"Just that I wouldn't trust that kid. Dev's gone out on a limb for him time and again, and it always gets sawed off under him." Felix smiled evilly. "So you about ready for another chore? Because—"

"Sorry, I've got a chore—a big one." She set the bag of pralines on the kitchen counter; she'd had enough. "I'm heading upstairs where I'm going to vacuum and dust the entire apartment."

Felix groaned. "Are we about to get that 'woman's touch' whether we want it or not? Next you'll be cookin' us supper."

She laughed at that one. "Not if you live a hundred years," she assured him. "I can't cook worth beans, but I can clean, and somebody sure needs to. I'm awake half the night sneezing my head off up there. I figure it's up to me to do something about it."

"You go, girl."

And she did.

THE FIRST THING Dev noticed wasn't how clean the apartment was—although it certainly was. No, what he noticed was how red and sore Sharlee's hands looked, clasped at her waist that way. He longed to take them in his own and kiss them and press them against—

"Well," she demanded, "aren't either of you going to say anything?"

Felix, who'd come up the stairs right behind Dev, said, "Hey, I'm speechless. You speechless, Dev? I'm sure as hell speechless."

"That's more like it." She gave them a wide happy grin. "The table's set. I sure hope you've got dinner on that tray because I'm starving."

"You bet." Felix carried the large foil-covered tray into the kitchen.

Sharlee turned expectantly to Dev. "Well? What about you?"

He looked at her in her flowery summer dress with her hair all neatly combed and open eagerness on her face. Suddenly it occurred to him that she looked like an old-fashioned housewife welcoming home her husband after a hard day at the office.

"You did good," he said, disconcerted by the image. "Look, tell Felix I remembered something I have to do. I'll eat out."

Her expression changed to disappointment.

"But—"

"I'm sorry, I've got to go."

He turned and rushed from the room, taking the stairs two at a time. He was running for his life.

Sharlee watched him run, telling herself she really didn't give a damn. Why should she when he didn't care enough about her to...

She pulled such thoughts up short. If she wasn't careful, she'd find herself caring just a little too much about his comings and goings, his approval and disapproval.

So far, so good, she told herself. After all, *she* wasn't the one who'd run.

SHE GAVE DEV the cold shoulder the next morning, and he didn't blame her. The apartment hadn't looked this good since...he had no idea, because when he and Felix had moved in, it had been a mess, which they'd managed to ignore without too much trouble. Now it didn't sparkle maybe, but it didn't look half-bad, either.

He stood the unaccustomed chill in the muggy New Orleans air until after lunch, at which point he turned to her and said, "Okay, I give up. I'm sorry. I should have been more sensitive to your feelings last night—"

"Ha!" she inserted vengefully.

"—and I'm sorry I wasn't, but I had stuff on my mind."

"What stuff?" she inquired, instantly interested.

"Nothing that concerns you."

"Great. If it's none of my business, why are you bringing it up?"

"Because I want you to know that I do appreciate your efforts and I want to make amends."

"That sounds promising." She regarded him with speculative eyes. "Okay, I accept your apology. Let's see those amends."

"Okay, here they are—me, at your service." He spread his arms wide. "We're in pretty good shape around here, so where do you want to go and what do you want to do? Jump on the trolley? Go to the aquarium or ride the riverboats? Name it and it's yours."

"Why? So you can drop me off and go on about your business?" Her tone was reproachful. "Thanks, but no thanks. If you think I'm going to let you—"

"No, Sharlee," he said, "I'm not going to drop you off, I'm going with you. So what's your pleasure?"

Her hazel eyes sparkled. "That's different, then.

Okay, I think I'd like to—'' she cocked her head
''—walk along the river, maybe do a little shopping
at JAX. Is that okay?''

Shopping wasn't his best thing, but the walk
sounded good. ''Let's do it.''

He hoped he wouldn't regret it.

ALTHOUGH SHE ENJOYED having a companion, Dev's
presence made Sharlee feel no less a tourist than she
had when she'd prowled the French Quarter alone.
Although everything she saw she'd seen before, she
felt a certain detachment that was unsettling.

She'd always liked the waterfront, especially the
Moon Walk. Named for a former mayor, it offered a
green promenade between the broad Mississippi,
nearly half a mile wide at this point, and Washington
Artillery Park. A scramble of vessels, everything
from giant container ships to tug-propelled barges,
docked along the river's edge.

Upriver she could see the Crescent City Connection, the collective name for a pair of bridges linking
New Orleans with the West Bank. Immediately to
their right lay the former Jackson Brewery, long
since taken down and put together again as a shopping center called simply JAX.

She took a deep breath, then wrinkled her nose.
''Fish,'' she said, ''or at least, fishy.''

''That never used to bother you,'' he said, looking
a little reproachful.

''It doesn't bother me,'' she protested. ''It's just
that now I notice it. Before, I never did.''

"I thought by now you'd be feeling more at home."

She thought about that. "In some ways, maybe. In others..." She shrugged. "Let's not talk about it, okay? I told you this wasn't home and it isn't. I'm just passing through." Taking his arm, she hurried him along. "Let's go to JAX and get something cold to drink," she suggested with false gaiety. "I don't have any complaints, really. I'm just grateful that—"

"*Sharlee?* My God, is that *you?*"

Sharlee stopped dead. Turning slowly, she knew exactly whom she'd see.

CHAPTER SEVEN

LESLIE RUSHED FORWARD with outstretched arms, a look of unrestrained joy on her face. She hugged her sister hard, held her away to smile happily, then hugged her again.

"What are you doing here?" she exclaimed. "When did you get back? Why didn't anybody tell me? How—"

"Hold on!" Sharlee extricated herself from her sister's embrace. She noticed that Leslie was wearing maternity clothes although she was only about three months pregnant. "Nobody knows I'm back except you and Alex, who promised he wouldn't tell a soul. And Dev, of course."

"You mean nobody else in the family knows?"

"That's right."

Her sister looked thoroughly confused. "What's going on here? Why are you hiding out in the Quarter?"

"Before you two get into all that," Dev interjected, "I'm going to bail out." He gestured toward a café across the street. "I know a guy who works in there. I'll grab a cup of coffee and let you two catch up."

"Thanks, Dev." Leslie gave him a brilliant smile. "We'll be in the food court on the top floor."

The two women watched him cross Decatur Street and disappear inside a small restaurant. Then Leslie faced her sister, expression serious. "All right, Charlotte Hollander Lyon, you've got a lot of explaining to do. A *whole* lot."

They found a quiet spot inside not far from the food concessions. While Leslie waited at the table, Sharlee fetched drinks: lemonade for her sister, iced tea for herself. When she was seated, she took a deep breath and plunged in.

"This isn't the way it looks."

"What—finding you here with Dev?"

Sharlee nodded, wondering if she'd believe it herself if she wasn't living it.

"How do you think it looks?" Leslie countered.

"Like...like Dev and I have taken up with each other again. Believe me, we haven't."

Leslie pursed her lips and poked at ice cubes with her straw. "Of course you have," she said. "I find you wandering around the Quarter with him when your own family doesn't even know you're in the state!"

"But—"

"Did you even go back to Colorado after the anniversary party or did you just stay here with him?"

"Of course I went back to Colorado. He came after me. Actually Grandmère sent him after me."

"Then *she* knows you're back?"

"No, at least I don't think so. I made Dev promise

not to tell her, or at least I think I did. Now I'm not entirely sure.''

"Then I just don't get it," Leslie announced. "Grandmère knows how…cool you've been toward the family. Why would she do this? I mean, we've all tried to reason with you." She grinned. "Even me.''

"I'm sorry, Les, I just couldn't." And *shouldn't.*

"I never took it personally, but Grandmère…" Leslie shook her head. "Every day she seems more determined to keep us all together. You probably don't know this, but she steamrolled Michael and me into moving into Lyoncrest right after we were married. As it turned out, neither of us has regretted it.''

"I'm glad of that.''

"And you—she's wanted you back since you graduated from college. But I don't understand why she'd pick this particular time to play hardball.''

"Apparently—" Sharlee stopped abruptly. Her sister was pregnant. Why give her cause to worry about the state of their grandfather's health? Sharlee shrugged and finished evasively, "You know how much she likes having her own way.''

"Who doesn't?" Leslie arched her brows. "But tell me, Charlotte, where *are* you living?''

Sharlee sighed. "With Dev—and Felix Brown, his partner at the Donna Buy Ya Café. There's a three-bedroom apartment on the second floor.''

"You're living with two men? Why on earth would you do such a thing?" Straitlaced Leslie was clearly scandalized.

"It's platonic, believe me. I'm helping them get

their café ready to open." Sharlee hated sounding so
defensive. "After that, I'll work there as a waitress—
just for a little while, until I find another newspaper
job."

"That's ridiculous. You, a waitress?"

"It's honest work."

"I know. It's just that the last I heard you were a
reporter in Colorado. A few weeks later you're a
waitress in the French Quarter." Leslie gazed in-
tently at Sharlee, then said, "I guess as long as
you're happy—"

"I'm not," Sharlee said quickly. "This is temporary. I'm looking for another reporting job and as
soon as I find one, I'm out of here."

"Without ever telling your parents or your grandparents you were here?"

"I'll probably…give them a call."

"That's absolutely terrible," Leslie said. She
poked her straw up and down in her glass. "I don't
know what's behind this vendetta you seem to be
carrying for the family, Charlotte, but it's just not
right."

"It's not a vendetta." Sharlee's stomach had
clenched into an anxious knot and her hands trembled. She didn't like having to justify her actions to
anyone.

"What is it, then? What's driven this wedge between you and the people who love you?"

Sharlee hesitated, thinking again that if Les didn'
know about the trust fund or all the attempted ma-
nipulations by now, it was probably better to leave

her in the dark. Finally she said, "We just don't get along."

"Can't you try harder?"

"No, Leslie, I can't." Sharlee spoke decisively. "I am what I am and I want to run my own life. Is that too much to ask?"

"Well, no…"

"They had my life all planned out for me. After graduation I'd move back to Lyoncrest and go to work at WDIX in the news department. Then I'd work—if you can call it that—my way up and be the youngest anchor in the business. I'd follow in Grand-père's footsteps whether I wanted to or not."

"Would that really have been so bad?"

"Would *you* have liked it? But wait, there's more. I'd also learn the business from the ground up, sit on the WDIX board, follow in *Papa's* footsteps."

"Surely you're exaggerating," Leslie said. "You just *think* that's what they wanted."

"Les, they said so."

"My God! When?"

"Remember when I came home from college for my twenty-first birthday? That's when they told me my future was set." She laughed bitterly. "All I had to do to be a rousing success was show up."

"Oh, dear, they dropped that on you at the same time they gave you your trust fund?"

"But they didn't," Sharlee blurted. "When I de-clined their kind offer, they declined to release the money. They said once I'd grown up and had a steady job with a future, and they could be sure I wouldn't do something stupid with the money…"

"Oh, Charlotte." Leslie seemed on the verge of tears. "I had no idea."

Sharlee patted her sister's hand. "It's okay. I got over it...mostly. But that's why I haven't set foot in Lyoncrest since, and I don't intend to."

"Does that mean you still don't have your trust fund?" Leslie couldn't keep the astonishment from her voice.

Sharlee shook her head. "I've hardly met their exacting standards, and you know what? I don't care."

The two sisters stared at each other. Then as one they began to laugh helplessly.

"I'm speechless," Leslie said, wiping tears from her eyes. "I didn't know any of this." She added plaintively, "I wish Michael was here. He always knows what to do."

Sharlee felt a flash of envy so strong it shocked her. "Your husband seems very nice," she said. "God knows he's good-looking."

"He is, isn't he." Leslie, self-effacing Leslie, seemed downright smug. "And you know what? He loves me! *Me!* And that's changed my entire life."

Now tears welled up in Sharlee's eyes, but she blinked them back. "It's wonderful to see you so happy. You certainly deserve it."

"So do you. But I don't think you'll ever find real happiness until you make up with the family, even if you don't like some of the things they've done."

"Maybe." Unconvinced, Sharlee pushed away her glass, empty except for a few melting cubes of ice. "Come on, you know they've always treated me lik a baby. I'm sick of being protected when I don't need protecting.''

Protected. Sharlee flashed back to the overheard conversation between two old men: *more secrets...than candles on that cake....* ''Les,'' she said impulsively, ''do you know of any skeletons in our family closet—scandalous secrets, that kind of thing?''

The question obviously took her sister completely by surprise. ''Why would you ask such a thing?''

''I thought you might have uncovered something while you were researching the official Lyon family biography for the anniversary celebration.''

''Not really.'' But Leslie suddenly looked uncomfortable. ''What good does it do to talk about these things?''

''None, if everybody's perfect.''

''Well—'' Leslie pursed her lips ''—I guess I do know one family secret, actually.''

Sharlee leaned forward eagerly. ''Whose?''

''Mine.'' She paused for a moment. ''And Mama's and Grandmère's, too.'' Another pause. ''My father—my real father—was a handsome rat who was involved in a lot of...let's call it illegal activities. He was murdered in an alley just a month or two before I was born.''

''You're kidding! I thought Mama divorced him.''

Leslie's laughter sounded pained. ''I wish. After his death, Grandmère actually went out and paid off his debts for booze, gambling and women.''

''Why would she, if Mama and Papa weren't married or involved at the time? They weren't, were they?''

Leslie shook her head. "I'm not sure Papa—André—even knew Mama then. But Mama's mother was an old friend of Grandmère's, and you know how she is about taking in strays.''

Sharlee did know. Over the years, Margaret Lyon had befriended many in need, often moving them right into Lyoncrest with the family. Margaret had never called them "strays," but everyone else did. "Why have I never heard about any of this?" she wondered aloud.

Leslie sighed. "Mama was ashamed she'd chosen so badly. She didn't want anyone to know.''

"*You* know.''

"Only because Uncle Charles and Alain hired a private detective a few years back, apparently in hopes of finding something to use against André. Mama told me because she was afraid I'd hear the story elsewhere.''

Sharlee was astounded; she'd had no idea any of this was going on. "But still, she told you and not me.''

"You weren't here," Leslie reminded her. "You were the same place you'd been since you graduated from college—somewhere in Colorado trying to pretend you didn't even know us. How could they treat you like an adult when they'd hardly seen you since you were sixteen? You didn't even come home for summer vacations except for a week or two, and that took arm-twisting.''

"Didn't any of you ever hear of the telephone?''

Sharlee defended herself, although she recognized a grain of truth in what Leslie had said.

"Would you want this kind of news told over the telephone?"

"Well, maybe not," Sharlee admitted grudgingly. She thought about what she'd just heard and a reluctant smile tugged at the corner of her mouth. "Actually this puts an entirely new light on things."

"Such as?"

"I take some comfort in discovering that Mama is human, after all."

"Oh, dear." Leslie gripped her hands together on the table. "Please don't say anything. She's thoroughly ashamed of herself for getting into such a mess in the first place." Her eyes widened and she smiled past Sharlee's shoulder. "Hi, Dev. Pull up a chair."

He did. Sharlee didn't look at him.

"How's it going?" he asked cautiously.

"Okay, I guess." Leslie didn't sound too sure. "I...just told Sharlee about my father. My real father, I mean."

Sharlee jerked around to stare at him. "You knew," she guessed.

"Yeah, I did. I saw the detective's report."

"Well, that's just great. Everyone knew but me and it's *my* mother."

"Dev's not everyone. He's family. I trust him completely."

I don't, Sharlee thought, annoyed that he apparently knew a great deal more than he'd told her. "Whatever. What else do you know that I don't?"

"Nothing. Why look for trouble? I'm happy in the here and now."

Sharlee could see that was true. But she couldn't help thinking there was more, much more, to be discovered. Leslie's official family bio had been a glowing tribute to hard work, dedication, talent and family loyalty—but she was a librarian, not a reporter. Sharlee was sure it had never occurred to her sister to dig any deeper into information and opinion offered as fact.

She said no more on the subject, but she made a promise to herself that once the café was up and running, she'd find out what else lurked in the dark depths of the family closet.

And she'd start with Uncle Charles.

THE SISTERS SAID GOODBYE in front of JAX.

"You promise you won't tell anyone you saw me?" Sharlee repeated.

"I said I wouldn't—except for Michael of course. I have to tell him."

Sharlee nodded. "I suppose so."

"When's the café opening?"

"Wednesday."

"We'll come to that."

"Please don't. Felix says it'll be a madhouse. We're not making an announcement, just inviting people we figure will be tolerant, plus whoever walks in off the street."

"Okay, but I don't want to lose touch again, Charl."

"We won't, I promise." Sharlee kissed her sister's

cheek and sent her on her way, wondering what the repercussions of today's chance meeting—if indeed it *was* by chance—would be.

FELIX AND DEV called the "staff" together the day before the café was to open for final instructions and a pep talk.

The Donna Buy Ya would throw wide its doors for the first time August twenty-fifth at five o'clock. After that, they'd open for lunch from eleven until two and reopen for dinner from five until nine every day except Sunday, when they would be closed. The split shift would allow the same workers to handle all sessions.

Felix, of course, would cook. The big man was so excited by the prospect of doing his own thing in his own kitchen that if he'd had a choice, he'd have started pulling startled passersby in off the sidewalk. He'd stocked the pantry and placed orders for fresh vegetables and seafood and was raring to go.

He'd be assisted by Dev, who would also run the business side of this enterprise—hiring and supervising staff, bookkeeping, customer complaints or other problems.

"And there better not be any of those," Felix said, looking around with an ominous countenance.

DeeDee giggled. "The customer is always right, unless he's wrong," she announced cheerfully. "Don't worry, boss, Sharlee and I've got that one covered."

Sharlee certainly hoped so. She'd had a couple of sessions with DeeDee on the proper etiquette of wait-

ing tables at a funky café, which differed consider
ably from what went on at Antoine's or Chez
Charles.

"Just use common sense," DeeDee had urged
"Don't ever let a water glass or a bread plate si
empty. Don't wait to be flagged down for drink or
ders or the check and keep smilin'." She'd patted
Sharlee's arm. "Don't worry, you're a natural."

Yeah, right.

The two waitresses would also greet customer
and handle the cash register in their spare time, as
sisted by Dev.

An eighteen-year-old called Ace, who had a wide
gap-toothed grin, would handle bussing chores. The
dishwasher was Augy Deens, a middle-aged guy who
looked like a street person to Sharlee. She'd never
heard him say a word, never seen evidence of his
work ethic, but Felix vouched for him so he was in

Not a very big staff, but Felix and Dev said they'
hire more people as the need arose.

Sharlee hoped it would arise soon. This didn'
seem like a very large group to handle such a daunt
ing endeavor.

"Now," Felix announced, "we've got a little trea
for y'all. We're gonna give you dinner, served b
our own fantastic new waitress, Sharlee, under th
supervision of our fantastic old waitress, DeeDee. S
take a seat and get ready for the best jambalaya yo
ever wrapped your mouth around."

Rubbing his hands together with gleeful anticipa
tion, Felix returned to his kitchen.

DeeDee and Sharlee looked at each other, and the younger woman burst into laughter.

"This is great!" she declared. "You go, girl."

She raised one hand and Sharlee, coming out of her shock, gave her a high five. Hell, she could do this. It was no big deal.

But then she turned to her table and saw Dev and Ace and Augy looking at her expectantly. Sucking in a deep breath, she squared her shoulders. This was not, after all, brain surgery.

Grabbing an order pad off the counter, she marched up to the table. "Welcome to the Donna Buy Ya," she said brightly. "May I take your order?"

"Where's my water?" Ace made a great show of looking around for it. "You folks got no damn busboys around here? I can't order till I get my water."

Augy waved a fork in the air. "And a clean fork. Hell, this one's got egg or somethin' on it. Who washes dishes around this dump? Fire that sucker!"

Sharlee took a quick step back. "Yes, sir. Right away, sir." She fled around the counter to fill water glasses, grab fresh silverware.

And calm down. This was only make-believe and they weren't going to cause her to lose her cool. Across the counter, the two men kept up a running commentary while Dev just watched with a half smile on his lips.

DeeDee leaned over the counter, grinning. "Don't let 'em get to you," she advised. "Because you're new, they're tryin' to give you the works."

"I can handle them," Sharlee said. "Hell, if I can

stare down a mayor or a congressman, I shouldn't have any trouble with those two."

DeeDee's dark eyes widened. "You did that?"

Oops. Mistake. "In another lifetime," Sharlee said. "In another lifetime."

Colorado did seem like a lifetime away as she carried water and silverware back to the table—and curiously enough, she was having a lot of fun with this game of pretend.

She set a glass before each man and distributed fresh silverware in a very businesslike way, she thought smugly.

Ace gave her an insolent grin and deliberately pushed his paper napkin off the table.

"Ah, darn," he said mournfully. "I dropped my napkin."

"Let me get you another one, sir." She extracted a fresh one from the napkin holder on the table. "*Now* may I have your order?" She posed with her pad and pencil. "May I recommend the jambalaya? Our chef is renowned for his jambalaya."

Augy frowned. "What's in that? I'm from Illinois and we don't eat that stuff up there."

"You'll love it. It's got crawfish and—"

"Crawfish!" Ace jumped in, mock horror on his face. "Ain't crawfish what the folks around here call mud bugs? I ain't eatin' no bugs! Bring me a thick steak and I want it well-done but fork tender."

"Gimme a boo-rita," Augy said. "One of them Mexican things with hot sauce."

Sharlee just kept on smiling. "And you, sir?" she said to Dev. "What'll it be?"

"*Chère,*" he said, "you just bring me any little
ol' thing the chef's got goin' back there."

Curiously enough, Dev's order was the only one
that flustered her. Or maybe it was because those
were the first words he'd spoken directly to her since
they'd run into Leslie.

"YOU DONE GOOD."

Augy dropped a buck on the table, gave Sharlee
an awkward hug and headed for the kitchen where
he'd help with cleanup before leaving for the night.

"Yeah, you're okay." Ace gave her a shy grin and
scooped up Augy's dollar. "I'll keep these tables
bussed. You can count on it."

"I will, Ace. I had no idea how hard a busperson
worked."

"Hell, I ain't no busperson. I'm a bus*boy.*"

"Now that I look, I can see that." She gave him
a friendly wink.

DeeDee gave her a thumb's-up, then followed the
guys into the kitchen where she would, no doubt,
make a full report to Felix. With a sigh Sharlee sank
into Ace's vacated chair.

"I'm exhausted," she said.

Dev looked distant and pensive. "Waiting tables
is damned hard work."

"It's tension more than anything else." She flexed
her shoulders, remembering with longing the back
rub he'd given her in Colorado.

"Coulda fooled me. You seemed perfectly relaxed."

"Just goes to show you can't read me like a book."

"As if I didn't know that." He rose.

She touched his arm lightly. "Don't go. I... haven't seen much of you lately."

His expression didn't soften as he looked down at her, but he didn't pull away. "I've been busy."

"We all have." She inhaled deeply. "I've got to admit, it was good seeing Leslie the other day. If you had anything to do with that—"

"I didn't." He said it quickly, angrily, as if he'd been waiting for an accusation.

"All right, I believe you." She released his arm. "I'm trying to be nice. What's your problem?"

Although her question had been flip, his answer was serious. "I've been sucked into something that's not really any of my business," he said at last. "Between you and your grandmother—"

"My grandmother? Are you still reporting to her?"

"Not anymore."

"She knows I'm here, though?"

"Yes."

"And has all along?"

"That's right."

"Dammit, Dev, you *promised!*"

"I didn't promise. You promised for me."

"That's not how I remember it."

"That's how it was. Look, I resigned as your keeper before we left Colorado."

"My keeper?"

Their gazes locked, hers angry and his disgusted. After a moment he shrugged and turned away.

THE PHONE RANG as Dev walked into the office next to the storage room, Sharlee's accusations still ringing in his ear. Poetic justice—it was Margaret Lyon on the line.

"Devin, dear, I just called to—"

"No dice, Tante Margaret. I told you I wouldn't be your—"

"Yes, yes," she said, "but you're my only contact with Charlotte. I must know, is her attitude changing now that she's so close to home?"

"Not that I can see, but I don't intend to—"

"Oh, God." The anguish in her voice cut off anything more he might have said. "I really must find a way to tell Paul she's back in town, even if she is still angry with us. If he found out without the proper preparation…"

Dev heard the shudder in her tone. "Then you'd better do it fast," he advised.

"I'd do it today, but he saw the doctor this morning and he's exhausted."

"Then tomorrow."

"No. The doctor scheduled tests in the morning and he's being honored by some civic group in the afternoon."

"Sounds as if that leaves tomorrow night, then."

"I'm afraid not. Charles and Alain are taking him out to dinner—I'm not sure what the occasion is. Charles was very insistent."

Little alarm bells skittered along Dev's nerve endings. "Is that a good idea?"

"They're not likely to pull anything at dinner in a public place, Devin."

"They're taking him to Chez Charles, I suppose?"

She laughed lightly. "Where else?"

"And you're going, too?"

"I can't—not that I'm invited, anyway. I promised Andy-Paul and Cory—that's Leslie's stepdaughter, an adorable child—we'd go get their school uniforms tomorrow, before the stores run out as they do every year. Then we'll have dinner out, just the three of us. I couldn't disappoint them."

"Well, Tante Margaret, it's your call, but I think you need to do it soon." He tried to separate himself from her problems.

She wouldn't let him unfortunately. "Could you come over day after tomorrow, first thing in the morning, and help me tell him?" she asked. "It would be so much easier if you're there to answer his questions."

Dev didn't want to, but he was incapable of ignoring the fear underlying her request. "If you think it'll help..." The words were dragged out of him.

"More than you know," she said with obvious relief. "I don't know what it would do to Paul if this were broken to him brutally. I've already put it off far too long. Thank you, Devin."

"You're welcome. But after that, I want out of this. I don't intend to be Sharlee's watchdog."

"Of course not."

As if the idea had never entered her head. Dev hung up the phone, fighting off a sense of impending doom.

CHAPTER EIGHT

BY EIGHT O'CLOCK the following evening, Sharlee's arms ached, her feet were killing her, and if she heard one more customer complain because the kitchen had run out of jambalaya, she'd scream.

Then she looked at DeeDee moving serenely between tables crowded with customers, laughing and joking and charming everyone, and just gritted her teeth and kept going.

Dev, who'd been helping out in the kitchen, appeared beside her.

"Everything okay?"

"God only knows. I haven't had time to—"

"Hey!" A bald guy seated in front of the window waved his arms over his head. "More hot sauce over here!"

"I'll get it," Dev offered, reaching behind the counter to retrieve a bottle of red stuff. "You take care of table six."

"Okay." Squaring her shoulders, she dug in the pocket of her apron for the check she knew they wanted.

Actually the crowd was starting to thin out a little. They'd opened at five and within half an hour, every table in the place was packed.

She placed the check down on table six and offered the family of four a smile. "Anything else I can get you?"

The mother smiled back. "Not a thing," she said with a New England accent. "Tell the cook the food was wonderful."

"I'll sure do that. Y'all come back, hear?" With a final smile for the kids, Sharlee turned to survey the situation.

For the moment things looked fairly contained. Ace was clearing dirty dishes from tables ten and eleven, which had been pushed together in front of the windows overlooking the garden out back. Momentarily without a crisis, she hurried to help him.

He gave her a grateful glance. "Man, who'da guessed we'd get this kinda turnout?"

"I'll assume that's a rhetorical question." She put a stack of plates into his pan.

"Heck, yeah. What's reterical?"

Behind them she heard the front door open and close as more customers entered. She'd have to put on that smile again, but first she'd make sure these tables were clean. She scooped up a handful of dirty silverware. "A rhetorical question is one you don't expect to be answered."

Ace frowned. "Then why ask it in the first place?"

She laughed. "I dunno, Ace. I guess I was just being a wiseass." Still grinning, she turned to greet the newcomers and stopped short.

Her grandfather stood behind a chair at the round table in the middle of the room, his lips parted in

disbelief as he stared at her. On one side of him stood
Uncle Charles and on the other, Charles's eldest son
and Dev's stepfather, Alain.

"Charlotte!" Paul gripped the chair back so hard
his knuckles turned white. "My God, is it really
you?"

DEV ROUNDED THE COUNTER with a tray of water
glasses just in time to hear Paul's shocked exclamation. He missed a step, causing the tray to slant
and several glasses slid dangerously near the edge.
By the time he caught his balance and righted the
tray, Sharlee had disappeared and Paul had collapsed
into a chair, looking as if he was about to go into
cardiac arrest.

Slamming the tray onto the counter, Dev dashed
to the old man's side and got down on one knee. He
chafed Paul's hands, which were like ice. "Mr.
Lyon, sir, are you all right?"

Paul gasped, seemed to catch his breath. Color
flowed back into his face. "Was that Charlotte or am
I in worse shape than I thought?" He pressed a hand
to his forehead.

"It was Charlotte, all right." Dev glanced up at
his stepfather. "What the hell do you mean, bringing
him here?"

Alain had long since perfected innocent outrage.
"We came to support you in your new venture, son.
How were we to know…?"

"Yeah, how?" He'd done this deliberately, Dev
thought, feeling sick to his stomach. He'd always

known Alain loathed the other side of the Lyon family, but to do something so awful...

Not that he'd done it alone. If Dev ever got his hands on his stupid little brother...

Paul clutched at Dev's hand. "Bring her to me, Devin. Please."

"Where'd she go?" Dev glanced around but saw no sign of Sharlee.

"I don't know, but you've got to bring her to me," Paul said.

"As soon as I'm sure you're all right."

"I'm all right," Paul said impatiently. "I was just...surprised, that's all. If I could have a glass of water—"

"Right here, sir."

Ace placed glasses before the two old men and Alain. Paul drank gratefully, but Dev noticed that his hand shook almost uncontrollably.

Dev rose. "I'll go get her. In the meantime..."

He saw the vacant expression on Charles's face, the avid expression on his stepfather's face, and knew he might as well save his breath.

This was no accidental meeting, but Paul had survived the shock of it. Now if Dev could just get Sharlee to come back inside and act like a grown-up.

He found Sharlee in the alley outside the storeroom, pacing back and forth in front of the loading dock. She looked half out of her mind, blond hair flying and mouth trembling. When he stepped outside, she turned on him.

"You did this! You asked him here tonight."

"I sure as hell did not."

"Then what's he doing here?" She looked at him with anguished eyes. "The shock could have killed him. Don't you care?"

He caught her by the shoulders and gave her a shake. "Yeah, I care, but apparently you don't. Why'd you run out on him that way just now? Any damage was already done by then. You left the poor guy thinking he'd seen a ghost."

"It was a shock to me, too."

"But you're not an octogenarian with a bum heart."

She caught her breath. "You're right, I'm not. I'm sorry. I was just so shocked." Her voice broke. "I'd started feeling so safe here."

She lifted her hands to hide her face. She trembled so badly beneath his light grip that he thought if he released her, she might fall.

So he pulled her against his chest and held her close. Smoothing her hair with one hand, he said, "I know you're tired but—"

"I'm not tired. I'm shocked. I had no time to prepare."

"Neither did he, *chère*." He bracketed her face with his hands and forced her to look at him. "I didn't tell him you were here. Whatever else I've done, I didn't do that."

"Then who did?"

"That doesn't matter at the moment." Dev didn't want to finger his brother until he was one hundred percent sure—as opposed to ninety-nine-point-nine percent sure. "Sharlee, you've got to go back in there and talk to him."

For a moment he thought she'd refuse. The tip of her tongue edged out to moisten her lips and her eyes remained wide and vulnerable. Then she nodded.

"Of course I do. I'm all right now." She put her hand over one of his and pressed it closer to her cheek. "Stay with me, okay? We're in this together whether we like it or not."

"GRANDPÈRE, I'M SO SORRY I ran out like that. I was just…surprised, is all." Sharlee leaned down to kiss his cheek, then dropped to her knees beside his chair.

Paul put his arms around her and buried his face in the curve of her shoulder. "Charlotte, my darling granddaughter, you can't possibly know how much it means to me to see you again."

Across their entwined figures, Dev's gaze met that of his stepfather. Alain was watching the reunion without the slightest flicker of emotion.

Eventually Paul sat up straight again, cleared his throat and with one hand dashed a tear from his cheek. "I don't understand, Charlotte. How… why…?"

"It's hard to explain, Grandpère."

Sharlee rose and Dev slid a chair behind her. With a grateful glance, she sat down and took her grandfather's hands again.

Her words sounded measured and careful. "I'm staying in the Quarter with Dev temporarily and working here while I look for another reporting job."

"If you need a job, darling—"

"Not at WDIX, Grandpère. I'm pencil press all the way. But I—" she swallowed hard "—I thank you for the thought."

His pained expression showed his continuing bewilderment. "You have a perfect right to work wherever you want to, I suppose. But why didn't you tell anyone you were back? Why didn't you come home? You know your room is waiting."

Sharlee shifted uncomfortably on her chair, and Dev could see she was trying very hard to frame her answers in a nonconfrontational way. It was clear to him that she didn't want to blame her grandmother for her predicament, not to this vulnerable old gentleman.

"I'm a grown woman," she said at last. "I should be able to handle my own problems without running to my family for help."

Paul regarded her sadly. "That's a fine commentary on modern American life," he said, his gaze rising to meet Alain's as if seeking support. Alain's expression had turned to one of unctuous concern. "What's a family for, if not to stick together during hard times and help each other out?"

Before Sharlee could reply, DeeDee sidled up. "Uh...kitchen's closing in ten minutes, so maybe you'd like to take this order." Her eyes suddenly widened. "Oh, my goodness! Aren't you the Voice of Dixie?"

Paul smiled graciously. "I'm Paul Lyon. And you are?"

"DeeDee Brown. Oh, my goodness! You're a celebrity and you're right here at Donna Buy Ya on our opening night.''

A murmur ran through the room: ''Paul Lyon! I thought that was…''

Off to one side of the table, Alain muttered a very soft, very disgusted, ''Great.''

And Charles said, ''I'm hungry! What's a man have to do to get some service around here?''

AS THE THREE MEN got up to leave, Paul took his granddaughter into his arms and held her close for a moment. How dear she was, and how like him in her refusal to be guided by good advice. ''Oh, Charlotte,'' he murmured, ''I can't tell you how much it means to me to know you're nearby.''

She clung to him, her fingers digging into his shoulders. ''It means a lot to me, too.''

''We didn't have time to truly talk tonight. May I take you to lunch tomorrow?''

She hesitated only an instant. ''I get off at two.''

''Lunch at two tomorrow, then. I'll call for you.''

She swallowed back tears; he recognized the action because he'd been doing it a lot himself this evening. With age, he'd found his own emotions lying nearer and nearer the surface.

''See you tomorrow then, Grandpère. I love you.''

''I love you, too. You hold a very special place in my heart and will until the day I die.'' He shook hands with Dev. ''I don't entirely understand your part in all this, but I thank you for taking care of her, my boy.''

Paul let Alain lead him to the limo, then settled

back into a corner of the plush seat for the short ride back to Lyoncrest. Beside him, Charles spoke in a querulous voice.

"The fish was dry and the sauce too heavy. What's wrong with Devin? He can't stay in business that way."

"Papa," said Alain, "it's just a diner, not a classy operation like Chez Charles."

Paul bestirred himself to make a quiet defense. "I found the food quite tasty and the staff outstanding."

Alain chuckled low in his throat. "Are you sure the shock wasn't too much for you, Uncle Paul? I can't believe you know so little about fine dining that you'd…"

But Paul had done his bit for fairness and let himself drift off again. He was going to have to tell Margie what had happened, and André and Gaby, too. Just the prospect of that made his heart pound painfully in his chest, but he was adept at concealing any distress he might feel and didn't think Alain noticed.

"PAUL, WHAT IS IT?" Margaret asked once Paul had sat down. He looked utterly drained. "Shall I call the doctor?"

"No, no, Margie, but you might call André and Gaby. There's something I must tell you all."

And Margaret knew.

In one horrible flash, she realized she'd been outmaneuvered by Alain yet again. He always seemed to find any chink in the armor inside which she tried so desperately to keep Paul safe.

Now Paul knew Charlotte was in town and Alain was to blame. She knew it with absolute certainty.

Before she could react, André and Gaby entered arm in arm, smiling like young lovers.

"We heard you come in," Gaby said cheerfully, "and thought..." She stopped short, exchanging an alarmed glance with her husband. "What is it? You look as if you've seen a ghost, Paul."

"I saw Charlotte tonight," Paul said.

Gaby gasped and André caught her arm, directing her into a wing chair near the fireplace.

"That's impossible, Papa," he said. "Charlotte's working in Colorado. You remember—she was home for a day in July?"

"Don't speak to me as if I were a child." Paul's voice rose. "She's living in the Vieux Carré with Devin Oliver and working as a waitress at his new café. Alain took Charles and me there for dinner this evening and I saw her with my own eyes."

"Oh, my God." Gaby pressed her hands to her cheeks. "We've got to go bring her home."

She started to stand, but André stopped her. "Not so fast, Gaby. Papa, what did she say?"

"That she's a grown woman and capable of running her own life."

Gaby groaned. "That again. She's been saying that since she was sixteen. And living with Devin? I thought *that* was over with a long time ago."

"It was." Margaret joined the fray, although she wasn't eager to have her part in all this known. Still, what choice did she have? "She's in town because I sent Devin to Colorado to bring her back."

All three stared at her in astonishment.

"She's living above the café with him and Felix Brown, his partner—nothing personal, just a place to stay. Now that she's older, though, I wouldn't object if there were more to it than that."

"I agree," Gaby said quickly, "but that's not the point. Why is she in New Orleans?"

"She…lost her newspaper job in Colorado and she's looking for another one…someplace else."

Paul was watching her with the same expression she'd seen from him so many times over the years: half astonishment and half disapproval. He'd never liked her penchant for manipulating people, but how else was she supposed to protect her loved ones from themselves and others?

André said grimly, "Why didn't you tell us she was in town, Mama?"

"Because I'm not supposed to know. Charlotte doesn't want to see anyone. Especially me."

Gaby stood, her movements jerky. "I'm going after her. Where did you say this café is?"

"No, Gabrielle." André caught her forearm in a firm grip. "That won't work."

"How do you know it won't?" she cried, her tone desperate. "She's still my baby. Why—"

"Gaby, darling, have you forgotten my own youth? Don't you remember how I reacted when *my* mother came searching for me at a low point in my life?"

He smiled at Margaret when he said that, and she sighed at the bittersweet memories his words recalled. He'd been an angry young man then, as his daughter must be an angry young woman now. They were so very much alike.

Gaby's voice trembled. "This is entirely different."

"You don't know that and neither do I. All I know for sure is that we've made many mistakes with our youngest daughter. Now we have to show a little faith in her by waiting for her to come to us."

Gaby wavered. Margaret, who knew and loved her daughter-in-law so very much, saw the battle she waged with herself. Margaret held her breath. As Devin had once said, if the family descended on Charlotte and tried to force her to come home, she'd leave.

Gaby's shoulders drooped and she looked away, on the verge of tears. "All right," she gave in. "I'll try...but I'm not sure I can do this."

"You can," André said, "because you have to. For Charlotte's sake. For all our sakes."

SHARLEE STOOD STARING down at the moon-dark garden below the balcony of the apartment, asking herself how everything had gone so wrong. The memory of her grandfather's pallor and his tears haunted her; for the first time, she'd seen his vulnerability.

"Are you okay?"

Dev's voice. He'd brought her to this point, following her to Colorado and working behind her back with Grandmère to scuttle the best chance she'd ever had to move up in her profession. Whether or not he'd had anything to do with Grandpère's unexpected appearance, Dev was not to be trusted.

"I'm fine."

"You don't sound fine." He stepped up beside her and leaned against the balcony railing. "I was as surprised as you were, Sharlee—as your grandfather was. Hell, if I'd told him you were here, it wouldn't have been near the shock to him that it was."

He was making a case for his innocence when she hadn't even asked for one. "I suppose."

"Don't close down on me, Sharlee. I like you better when you're screaming and throwing things than this...this block of ice."

She forced a laugh. "Gosh, Dev, kids scream and throw things. I've grown up, remember?"

"If I forget, you can remind me." He let out a breath. "I get the feeling you don't believe me."

"What difference does it make?"

"It makes a difference to me. I wouldn't do that to your grandfather even if he was a well man, which he's not."

She wished he hadn't confirmed her own impression. "I guess Grandmère told you the truth about that." The admission was not an easy one for her to make. She sighed. "This is all very complicated."

She turned until her back was to the railing. In the muted shadows she saw his face clearly: the hard jaw, the alert eyes. "Who knows I'm here now?" she asked. "Grandmère, Grandpère, Leslie and most of your family. That means Mama and Papa either know or will soon. Once they do, they'll want to put in their two cents' worth, no doubt."

"What if they do?"

Her jaw tightened. "That would really be the last straw. I think I'd probably just leave."

"And go where?"

"Somewhere else. It doesn't really matter, does it?" She straightened, thinking now was probably a good time to walk away from the tension she felt building between them. But she couldn't help adding bitterly, "I knew this was too good to last."

"Good?" At his incredulous exclamation, the atmosphere seemed to grow thick as a steam bath. "What are you talking about? You and me and Felix walking a tightrope twenty-four hours a day—you call that good?"

"I didn't mean good, exactly." It took some effort to realize what she *did* mean, distracted as she was by his nearness. "I meant more like...free. I've never done anything like this before, thrown reason and caution to the wind and just let things happen. I've never felt free in New Orleans before."

"That's kind of sad."

He picked up one of her hands and she, surprised by the unexpected contact, let him.

He pressed her hand against the side of his face and said thoughtfully, "I've never felt particularly free myself, now that I think of it."

"But you have your own business now. Surely..."

"I'm afraid not." The words were a mere whisper against the pads of her fingers. "Maybe you're right about this town. It could be like that old joke—a good place to be *from.*"

The strangest feeling crept over her as she stood

there with his lips brushing her fingertips. For the first time she thought perhaps he really did understand why she felt so defensive about living in the same town with all the other Lyons. She sensed the same conflicts in him, although he handled them differently.

As he had handled their inevitable breakup differently.

"Dev," she said impulsively, "now seems to be as good a time as any…" She tried to pull her hand away.

But he just threaded his fingers through hers and held her. "A time for what, Sharlee?"

She licked her lips, realizing that she was about to open a subject incredibly painful to her. "To ask you why you sent me that horrible note nine years ago. I've agonized over it ever since. I've analyzed every word and I still don't understand." She couldn't bear to look at him, so she stared down at their joined hands. "I don't know why I'm bringing it up now," she barely whispered, "when I swore I never would. I mean, it can't make much difference now, can it? Still…I need to know why."

The silence grew ominous. "It had to be done," he said at last. "We were getting deeper and deeper into a situation we couldn't handle. I thought a note would be kindest." He sounded more uncomfortable by the second. "I tried to make it as gentle as possible. You may find this hard to believe, but I took great pains over every word."

"A meat ax would have been gentler."

She had always wanted to say that to him. He groaned and she felt some slight gratification.

His breathing became heavier. "I was trying to apologize," he said.

She managed a light laugh, although her heart ached with an old pain that had never gone away. "Do you even remember what you wrote?" She closed her eyes briefly, then recited, "'Dear Sharlee, Forgive me for getting you into this mess.'"

"That's an apology."

"I didn't consider what we'd gotten into a *mess*." She forced herself to recite more. "'I'm older than you are and should have known better—did know better, but I lost my head.'"

"God knows that's true." He pressed a kiss to her palm, but there was something vaguely uneasy about the gesture.

Now that she'd started, she couldn't stop. "'I apologize for everything and wish you all the best in the future.'"

"I really meant that."

"You don't think it sounded as if we barely knew each other? That's not necessarily what a teenage girl wants to hear."

"That was kind of the point." He pressed her palm flat against his chest and held it there as if he wanted her to judge the sincerity of his heart. "You *were* a teenager, too young—"

"For a love affair?" She couldn't look at him or she'd give away the mixture of wild emotions that made her pulse soar and her breathing uneven. "I'm almost finished," she said, her voice harsh. "You wrote, 'Perhaps someday we'll both look back on this and laugh. Dev.'"

He made a sound that was not quite a groan. "Okay, maybe that was insensitive. But at the time I was stumbling around, trying to do the right thing and ease us both out of an impossible situation."

"An impossible situation… *Oh, Dev, how could you do that to me?*"

BECAUSE YOUR GRANDMOTHER convinced me if I cared for you at all, it was the decent thing to do, he wanted to shout. Your mother's tears and your father's threats didn't sway me, but then Tante Margaret got hold of me.

But he couldn't say that because he'd made a promise. With Alain urging him on and Margaret begging him to step aside because her granddaughter was too young and immature for a serious relationship, it had been no contest for a boy who knew from the beginning that he was in the wrong.

Dev was afraid of Alain, while he liked and admired Margaret. After he'd had a chance to think it over, he'd written the letter. He'd also given Margaret his promise that he'd keep her part in this just between the two of them. In his own youth and inexperience, he'd never dreamed it would affect Sharlee the way it obviously had.

He'd expected her to be angry. He hadn't expected her to be wounded. He'd never wanted to hurt her.

Now she turned still-pained eyes toward him. "Tell me, Dev." Her voice had dropped until it hardly sounded like hers. "Tell me why."

He couldn't tell her the whole truth, but he couldn't lie to her, either. "I…did what I had to do," he said. "We were too young, both of us. You know I didn't plan to get involved with you, any more than you planned to get involved with me. It just happened. Then when your mother found us together…"

In the greenhouse, kissing, their hands all over each other…

"I wasn't too young to love you," she whispered. "I did, you know."

She leaned toward him and pinpoints of light flamed in her eyes. Hell, if she slapped him, clawed his face with her nails, he'd stand and take it like a man. Because whatever retribution she felt she was owed, he figured he probably deserved to pay.

But this…how did he handle *this* without setting off a chain reaction that would make what had happened before seem like mere child's play?

GAZING INTO HIS EYES, a conviction crystallized in Sharlee's mind. She'd never even the score by yelling at him or smacking him or beating on his chest with her fists. There was only one way she could extract the appropriate revenge.

She'd sleep with him. She'd sleep with him and then leave him with a kiss-off note that *he* could agonize over for years—if indeed a man was capable of feeling anything that deeply.

She smoothed her hand across the ridge of muscle in his shoulder and up to his throat, behind his neck. Deliberately she pulled his head down until his lips touched hers. This was her first step toward that punishment he so richly deserved. She had made up her mind and was finally in control.

And then she wasn't in control at all. Wrapping his arms around her, he had her lips parted and his tongue inside her mouth before she realized that the balance of power had shifted. One hand cupped her bottom, dragging her hips so hard against him she could feel his erection.

His incendiary kiss sent sparks straight into her bloodstream. This was not at all like she remembered. Before, he'd been so careful not to frighten or hurt her. He obviously no longer considered that an issue.

He consumed her. She wrapped one leg around his, tightened her hold around his neck and let herself soar. His mouth, hot and hard and wanting, promised such wonderful things that for a moment she allowed herself to simply revel in the magic of the moment.

His hands moved smoothly over her body, touching her breasts and waist and hips. He pressed his mouth against the deep V of her T-shirt, the tip of his tongue teasing the cleft between her breasts.

"Dammit," he muttered against her breast, "I didn't mean for this to happen. I must be crazy."

"Crazy?" His hand closed over her pebbled nipple, making her gasp.

"You're nothing but trouble. Every time you come into my life, it goes to hell."

"Look—" she leaned into his busy hands "—who's talking." Then she curved her hands around his head and pulled him closer. "Besides, you're the one who came after me."

"Yeah, and now I've got you."

On that possessive note, he scooped her up into his arms and clamped her against his heaving chest. She clung to him as to an anchor, only dimly aware that her plan had gone awry and totally uncaring—

"Hey, fellow entrepreneurs! You guys up for a little celebration? Ol' Felix is here and I brought the cham—"

Dead silence. Sharlee opened her eyes and smiled vaguely at the big man framed by the light spilling through the French doors—the man with the gaping mouth and the bottle of champagne.

"Shit," Dev said softly, standing her on her feet again. He blinked and shook his head as if coming out of a fog. "What the hell are we doing?"

"I could tell you, but I think I'll let you figure it out." She summoned an unsteady smile for Felix. "I'm always ready for a celebration," she said in an unfamiliar throaty voice.

Stepping out of Dev's suddenly slack embrace, she walked unsteadily back into the apartment.

Thanks, Felix. I'll be forever in your debt.

CHAPTER NINE

THEY DRANK THE BOTTLE of champagne. Then Felix fetched another one from the refrigerator and they drank that, too. It reminded Sharlee of the all-nighters she'd pulled with pals and dorm mates in college.

Felix couldn't say enough about the opening and his plans and hopes for the future, while Dev barely spoke. Of course, he could be in some physical discomfort....

Glancing at him from the corner of her eye, Sharlee certainly hoped so. She suppressed a smile.

She could handle this. She could seduce and abandon her faithless ex-lover without suffering the slightest pang of regret. Sure, she'd gotten excited in his arms, but she wasn't as emotionally vulnerable as she'd been before. She was in charge, dammit!

It felt good.

So she smiled and flirted, turning big innocent eyes on Dev, urging Felix to expand on his vision and drinking champagne.

"This is gonna work," Felix said for the dozenth time. "I know it will. You'll make your investment back and more, Dev, guaranteed."

"Yeah, well..." Dev yawned and it looked forced

to Sharlee. "On that happy note, I think I'll go to bed."

Felix's black eyes darted from Dev to Sharlee. "Alone?"

"Dammit, Felix! You got no call to—"

"Sorry." The big man held up his hands defensively. "But considering what I walked in on earlier, the question's not that out of line."

Sharlee patted his forearm. They were sitting in a circle on the floor in front of the couch. "Of course it isn't," she agreed. "But all you saw was a 'Did we have a great opening or what?' kiss."

"That's a new one on me." He rolled his eyes.

Sharlee grinned, convinced she was the only one enjoying herself. "Don't worry, Felix," she teased. "Dev and I aren't sleeping together—" saying the last two words gave her a jolt but she pressed on "—but if we decide to jump into that fire again, you won't have to ask. You'll know."

"You having a good time?" Dev's voice was a low menacing growl. "Every once in a while, Sharlee likes to play around a little," he said to Felix. "We're not sleeping together and we're not going to. We've been there before and I'm not ready to bang my head against that cement wall again. If you'll excuse me, I'm going to bed. Alone."

"Not me." She gave him a teasing smile. "I'm going to stay and help Felix finish this bottle of champagne. See you in the morning, Dev."

Before he could reply, she turned away, as if he was already out of sight and out of mind.

SHE DIDN'T FEEL quite so confident about any of that by dawn's early light. It was one thing to let anger and adrenaline carry her along, but quite another to be in the grip of a champagne hangover and faced with a sexy half-dressed man over the breakfast table.

All the turbulence she'd sensed in Dev last night was completely absent this morning. On the other hand, she, who'd been supremely confident only hours earlier, felt diminished and confounded by memories of their brief encounter.

In fact, he treated her like a guest in his home, asking her if she'd had a good night's sleep and would she please pass the milk.

She lied and said she had slept well. As he started to leave the room, she pulled her attention away from the sagging waistband of his pajama bottoms and said, "You do remember I'm going out to lunch with Grandpère at two."

He nodded. "Have a good time."

"I will unless the entire family shows up with him," she said, referring to a scenario she'd developed over a long restless night: everyone descending on her en masse, sending her screaming out of town.

"You're up to it."

She watched him walk away, all narrow hipped and broad shouldered and obnoxious as hell. He'd be singing a different tune very soon, if she had anything to say about it.

She stationed herself by the front window of the café at five before two, determined to spare her grandfather any wait while the chauffeur came to fetch her. When the long black limo glided to the curb in the No Parking zone, she hollered a quick, "I'm leaving now!" and rushed outside.

The chauffeur held the door for her and she climbed in beside her grandfather, grateful for the blast of cool air. He greeted her with a smile.

"I was afraid I was dreaming last night."

"And I was afraid you'd bring half the family with you today."

"They wanted to come," he said. "I wouldn't let them. Told them this was my date with a very special young woman and they could find their own." He winked.

"Oh, Grandpère." She gave him a rueful little laugh. "I'm not nearly as special as I used to think. That's a dog-eat-dog world out there."

"You're too young to have learned that, Charlotte. If you'd stayed home where you belong..." He ended his lament with a sigh. "Sorry, I don't intend to belabor that point, but I won't let you think I agree with you when I don't."

"Then let's change the subject entirely. Where are you taking me for lunch? Someplace elegant and expensive, I hope. Antoine's? Brennan's?"

"How does Chez Charles sound?"

She laughed. "Doesn't anyone in the Lyon family ever eat anywhere else?"

"Yes," he said with a smile. "Last night, and look what happened. I'm not sure my poor old heart could take too many more surprises like that one." He reached out to squeeze her hand. "Of course, it was worth any risk to have you back again. Let's just relax and—'' he gave her a sly look ''—I'll save my questions for later.''

Which didn't bode well for a casual lunch.

The staff at Chez Charles greeted them effusively and immediately ushered them into one of the several dining rooms. Although she hadn't been here in years, everything was exactly as Sharlee remembered, from the glowing crystal chandelier overhead to the royal-blue tablecloths with bud vases sporting red carnations. Coiled white napkins protruded from crystal water goblets like horns.

Extra place settings disappeared as they were seated in elegant leather-inlaid chairs. When she saw Alain approaching, Sharlee nearly groaned.

He hadn't come to join them, however, but to make sure everything was properly done. He soon had waiters and busboys jumping, though they'd been doing perfectly well all by themselves.

When the flurry of activity had passed, Alain said to Sharlee, ''How long may we anticipate the pleasure of your company in New Orleans this time? It seems your infrequent visits over the past several years have been quite brief.''

She felt reasonably sure he already knew the answer, but she replied lightly, ''I've not made up my mind about that, Uncle Alain. I'm in the process of job hunting now.'' Or would be as soon as she found time to hook up to the Internet and start putting out queries to her friends in the business.

''I'd give you a tryout here, but as you can see, we rely heavily on men for our wait staff. They're much more reliable.''

"I expect the Equal Opportunity Commission would love hearing you say that," she said, softening her words with a smile. "But of course, that's a family secret and I never betray a confidence."

She had the pleasure of seeing Alain's face darken, but he didn't rise to her bait.

"Well, then, I'll leave you to enjoy your lunch." Bowing slightly, he moved away.

"Very good, darling." Paul, apparently, was under no illusions where his nephew was concerned. He flipped open his napkin and placed it on his lap. "Now, Charlotte, tell me all about yourself—and don't skip a thing. It's been such a long time since we've been able to have a real talk."

So she told him the easy parts: college, jobs, funny stories about the trials and tribulations of the working journalist. But she was thinking about the undercurrent between Alain and Paul, which, now that she thought about it, had always been there. Why had it never really registered with her before Leslie mentioned that detective's report?

When I find an opening, she thought, *I'll ask Grandpère what it means—and introduce the subject of family secrets.* She almost felt as if she'd been sleeping and had suddenly awakened to a world entirely different from the one she'd left behind.

As her recitation wound down, Paul picked up the wine list beside his plate but didn't open it. "Would you care for a glass of wine?"

She didn't, but it seemed called for in these surroundings. "Maybe a Merlot," she decided.

Paul gestured to the waiter hovering nearby. "A glass of your best Merlot for the lady."

"And for you, sir?"

"Nothing, thank you."

He wasn't drinking because of his age and health, she supposed, protective feelings sweeping over her. She had never known him as a young man, but neither had she ever thought of him as really old—until now.

When the waiter had gone, Paul turned back to Sharlee. "Please go on. I enjoy your stories immensely. Almost makes me feel like a young newsman again."

She entertained him throughout the meal: sweet-potato catfish for him—"Don't tell your grandmother!" he warned, as if they saw each other every day—and mixed-grill jambalaya for her. She'd have preferred the crab cakes and fettuccine, but Felix was bound to question her about her meal, see how it compared to the fare at the Donna Buy Ya.

She judged the food to be excellent but not extraordinary.

As the dishes were whisked away, Paul sighed and said, "This has been truly delightful, but I'm afraid now that our lunch is drawing to an end, I'm obliged to ask questions that will perhaps annoy you."

"You're entitled, Grandpère." She felt such affection for him she was willing to satisfy his curiosity if she could.

"I know about the trust fund of course."

"I supposed everyone in the family did."

"Not everyone. Some. What I'd like to know,

dear, is if you have any other reasons for continuing your estrangement from us.''

That was a hard one. She thought about it for a minute and then said carefully, ''The trust fund is a symptom, not a cause. If you want the honest truth, I suppose Mama and Papa withheld it because I didn't measure up to family expectations.''

Paul frowned. ''What exactly does that mean, dear? It veers dangerously close to psychobabble.''

She smiled. ''You must have been a great newsman in your day because you sure know how to cut through all the cr—garbage.''

''I also know how to pursue my quarry until I obtain a satisfactory answer,'' he said.

She chewed on her lower lip. ''You can't deny I was the 'baby' for a long time.''

''That's true.''

''Even after Andy-Paul came along.'' She looked away. ''I love my little brother, I really do, but I couldn't help feeling…''

''Left out?'' he suggested softly.

''Yes.'' She sighed. ''And then when mother wouldn't release my trust fund as she had Leslie's…''

''It was a joint decision made by both your parents, Charlotte. You can't lay the blame entirely at your mother's feet.''

Couldn't she? ''Whoever's feet—it was just another indication I didn't measure up to the mighty Lyon standard.''

''Measure up,'' Paul mused. ''I can't imagine where you got such an idea. You've always been a chip off the old block—just as André is." He smiled, his charisma shining through. "Would it interest you to know that there was a time when *I* didn't measure up?"

She laughed. "It would surprise me greatly. In fact, I'd never believe it."

He raised thick white brows mockingly. "I wasn't born with these gray hairs. I've sown a few wild oats in my time...." His face took on a faraway look, as if he saw into the past. "I wasn't always the model senior citizen you see before you."

Alarmed by the pallor of his face, she squeezed his cold hand, noticing for the first time an old scar that looked as if it might have resulted from a burn. He seemed so much more fragile than he'd ever seemed before, even as recently as July.

"What are you getting at, Grandpère?"

He looked at her with sad dark eyes. "Many things, but there are other people—André and Margie and..." He halted his ramblings. "Nothing's ever simple, is it? Would you like another glass of wine, my dear?"

"No, thank you." She watched him with deep concern. He seemed almost to fade before her eyes.

"In that case, I believe we should be going. You don't mind, do you?"

"Of course not." A movement through the archway across the room caught her eye, and she saw Uncle Charles peering at them. Struck by inspiration, she said, "I think I'd like to walk back to the café, Granpère. It didn't look like rain on the way over, so I may even make it without getting wet."

"If you're sure." He rose stiffly. "We must do this again soon, dear. I've enjoyed myself enormously."

She couldn't imagine how. He'd hardly touched his favorite dish and had left his bread pudding untasted.

She grinned. "It must have been the company." She kissed his cheek. "I'll walk out with you."

"Thank you," he said wearily. "I'd like that."

So she did, worrying that she'd placed undue strain on him, worrying that her efforts to be considerate were too little, too late.

As the limousine pulled away from the curb, she turned to Chez Charles again. Mentally bracing herself for the possibility of a confrontation, she walked back inside.

It almost seemed as though Alain was waiting for her, his father by his side. "Forget something?" he inquired with a slight curl of his lip.

"No," she said, "I remembered something." She gave him her most engaging smile. "Uncle Charles, do you have time for a little talk? There are a few questions I think you could clear up for me."

"Such as?" Charles demanded.

She thought fast, not wanting to reveal too much in front of Alain. "Well, for instance, do you know how my grandfather got that scar on his hand? It looks as if it might have been a burn."

Alain raised a brow. "Why didn't you ask Paul?"

"I intended to, but we were talking about something else and I forgot."

"You can hardly expect my father to remember—"

With an evil little laugh, Charles said, "I remember perfectly."

They both looked at Charles and he nodded his grizzled head. "It happened when Paul was about twelve and I was six or so."

He didn't immediately go on, so Sharlee urged gently, "What happened, Uncle Charles?"

"I hit him with a poker! Got him good, I did."

Sharlee was aghast. "But why? What on earth did he do to deserve such a thing?"

Charles frowned. "Y'know, I can't recall that part now—but I can guarantee he did deserve it. He deserved everything he got for the way he treated me, him and that woman he married. And after what she did to him, too. Margie is not the paragon of—"

"That's enough, Papa," Alain commanded brusquely. "This isn't the time to get into any of that. You said you wanted to go home *now*. I'm sure the car is waiting out back."

"But if missy here wants to talk, I can tell her tales—"

"No, you can't." Alain waved to the maître d'. "Help me take my father out back and put him in the car."

"But Alain," Charles whined, "I want—"

"To go home and get some rest. You know it's for the best."

Sharlee watched Alain hustle the old man out with the maître d's help. Her mind was whirling. *Margie 's not the paragon of*—she supplied the missing word—*virtue*. But Margaret Lyon *was* a paragon of virtue and everybody knew it. Why on earth would Charles suggest otherwise?

Alain returned and stopped short at the sight of her. "You still here?"

"I thought maybe we could...I don't know, have a drink and chat a little."

"I don't think so, Charlotte."

"Why not? You don't seem all *that* busy."

"Looks are often deceiving."

And so are words. "That's true. For example, it looked to me as if you didn't want Uncle Charles to talk to me about the family. Was that impression correct?"

"Not at all." The maître d' returned, and Alain came out from behind the counter. "You didn't believe any of that, did you?" He waved toward the door through which his father had departed. "It was nothing more than the ravings of an old man."

"He certainly seemed rational to me."

"But then, you don't have the life experience to know, do you?"

"I can tell when someone's lying to me."

"Can you, indeed? Then you should find employment as a judge, instead of waiting tables."

His insult hit its mark squarely, and Sharlee's cheeks grew warm with annoyance. Still, she was determined not to lose her temper. "Since I know I can trust *your* memory implicitly, perhaps *you* can tell me about the skeletons in our family closet, Uncle Alain."

"What makes you think there are any?"

She shrugged. "Reading the family biography Leslie wrote, for one thing. I can't imagine any family so lacking in black sheep—present company excluded."

He hauled himself up to his full height until he towered over her. "I beg your pardon?"

"Oh," she said hastily, "I meant me, not you. Sorry if you thought…" She gave him an ingenuous smile. "Surely you have some tales of your own to tell, Uncle Alain."

He shrugged and looked at her with such calculation her blood ran cold. She took a hasty step toward the door.

"Just one more thing— Was it Dev who told you I was in town? You didn't seem all that surprised to see me at the Donna Buy Ya last night."

His smile was cunning. "I have many sources of information, Charlotte."

He waved negligently. "Run along now, and give my best to my son."

"And you give my best to your father. Tell him I'll be calling on him soon for a nice long visit."

Alain's superior smirk slipped away. "I'm afraid he's not up to visitors."

"But he seemed—"

"I don't care how he seemed. I'm his son and I know what's best for him."

"Then maybe you'll talk to me yourself. It's nothing important, just a few—"

"No, Charlotte. I'm far too busy to waste time on idle gossip."

Walking slowly and thoughtfully back to the

Donna Buy Ya, Sharlee wondered why he was lying to her, well aware there was very little she could do about it at the moment.

GABY AND MARGIE were waiting for Paul when he returned from lunch. He'd expected that, but hadn't looked forward to it. He was tired, too tired to go into details. But when he saw the hope and dread in their faces, he couldn't find it in his heart to stall.

Inviting them into his study, he prepared to face up to his responsibilities as family patriarch.

Gaby couldn't even wait for him to collect himself. "How did she look? I thought she was a little thin when I saw her in July, didn't you, Margaret?"

Paul responded impatiently. "She looks fine. She's a lovely young woman, but also a troubled one."

"Troubled?" Gaby looked vulnerable. "I don't understand. Has something else happened?"

"Gaby, dear." Margaret smiled gently at her daughter-in-law. "Let Paul tell us."

"Yes, I'm sorry. It's just that I worry so much about her." Gaby bit her trembling lower lip.

Paul sighed. "It's not what anyone has said to her, it's what *no one* has said to her."

"I don't understand." Gaby glanced from one to the other.

"She feels like an outsider in her own family, Gabrielle."

"But why?"

"Rightly or wrongly, she feels excluded."

"That's ridiculous. We're trying desperately to *include* her."

"She doesn't feel as if she's lived up to our expectations."

Margaret caught her breath. "Does she really, Paul? She's so beautiful and talented that this comes as a complete shock to me."

"And me!" Gaby rose to stand behind her chair, hands convulsing on the tall seat back. "What could we possibly have done to give her that idea? If there's one thing Charlotte has always had, it's self-confidence."

"She still does, except for this one area—her family. Look at it from her point of view, if you can. We've all tried to influence her to do what we think is best, but she calls it interference." He glowered at the two women. "And if either of you say you were only thinking of her..."

Neither did so he went on, "Then she was cosseted and protected from the seamier details of the Lyon family." He licked dry lips, loathe to start a battle but knowing he had to for the good of them all. "You should tell her everything," he said, looking uncompromisingly at Gaby. "And then you should give her that damned trust fund and be done with it."

Gaby had the stunned expression of a person who'd just been slapped. "That's what this is about—the trust fund? That's why she came back?"

"No!" Paul shook his head. "You're not listening to me. I don't really know why she came back and I don't care. She's here, but if she leaves again with this situation unresolved, I'm afraid...I'm afraid..." Gasping for breath, he couldn't finish.

Margaret was at his side in an instant. "Paul, are you all right? Should I call—"

"No, no, I'm fine," he managed to choke out. He knew he should put this off, but for his granddaughter's sake, he had to press forward.

Gaby looked miserable. "I don't like to disagree with you, Paul, but I can't lay out all our dirty linen. It would be a horrible mistake. You agree with me, don't you, Margaret?"

Margaret turned a tortured face to her daughter-in-law. "I'm...not so sure anymore."

Gaby's eyes widened in surprise. Paul knew she'd learned her family protective skills at Margaret's knee and she could hardly believe her mentor might be changing her mind at this late date. Together they'd protected the family and its reputation from all comers, even from within. How often had he heard Gaby say that what Sharlee didn't know couldn't hurt her?

Until now he hadn't challenged that flawed logic, since he knew it to be born of love.

But Gaby wasn't about to go down without a fight. "No good can come of sullying our family name. As for Charlotte's trust fund—" she shook her head "—I'll never agree to give her control of all that money until I'm sure she can handle it wisely. Paul, when you two set up trusts for your grandchildren, you put control of distribution into our hands and that's my decision."

"And André's?"

"He'll go along with me on this."

Her inflexibility annoyed Paul and he shifted angrily in his seat. Although he loved and admired his daughter-in-law, he was not blind to the stubborn streak she shared with his wife—and his granddaughter.

"It's only money," he said. "It's not worth ripping the family apart over." And then from the dim and distant recesses of his memory a quote from George Bernard Shaw floated to the surface. "'If you cannot get rid of a family skeleton, you may as well make it dance.'"

Margaret rose to stand beside him. "You'll have to make your point clearer than that, Paul."

He wouldn't hurt this woman for the world, so he chose his words with care. "You and Gaby have been quite successful over the years in keeping all the Lyon skeletons under lock and key. But ladies, the times are changing. If we don't set those skeletons free, I have a feeling we're going to regret it— soon, and for the rest of our lives."

His gaze locked with that of the woman he'd loved for so long. Her eyes asked a question.

He nodded. "Yes, Margie," he said so softly only she could hear, "even *your* secret." He raised his voice. "Now I've said my piece. If you'll both excuse me, I think I'll lie down right here on the couch and rest for a minute or two."

"You're sure you're okay? I could—"

"Margie, I love you but you worry too much. Go."

CHAPTER TEN

IT HAD BEEN RELATIVELY EASY for Sharlee to talk herself into going with Dev to the Achords' *fais do do* when it was just a far-off date. But when the time came, it took everything she had to climb into Dev's pale yellow Mercedes convertible on a brilliant Sunday afternoon and drive away from the Vieux Carré.

She'd been to Bayou Sans Fin before, but only once. Of course *that* visit had changed her life. To Dev, it was probably just the place where his mother had lived.

He glanced at her as they sped northwest on Highway 10. "I haven't had a chance to ask how the lunch went with your grandfather," he said.

"Fine," she said shortly. She was too tense for idle chitchat.

"It's that way, is it?"

One thing about Dev: he could take a hint. He didn't say another word until he'd pulled into a parking space along the road near Bertie's Café where the party was already under way. Killing the engine, he looked at her, his expression inscrutable. Strains of zydeco music and yelps of approval from dancers and other revelers carried clearly on the still hot air.

"Don't be that way," he said.

"What way?"

"*That* way. This is a party. Don't spoil it."

"I've never spoiled a party in my life."

"Good, because—"

"Hey, coozin!" Beau Achord banged on Dev's car door with his fist and grinned broadly. "You gonna set there all day or you gonna come raise some hell with the rest of us?"

Dev threw open his door. "Lead the way, Beau."

Beau trotted around to help Sharlee from the car, his dark eyes appreciative. "So this is little Charlotte Lyon," he said. "Come along and meet the folks."

Sharlee followed him to the makeshift stage set up alongside the café. A wooden walkway in back led to a wooden wharf at which several bateaux—flat bottomed swamp boats—were tied up.

Beau guided them into the small café and straight to a table where an old woman of at least eighty held court. "You gotta meet my grandmother first or she'll have me for gator bait," Beau declared loud enough for the old woman to hear. "This is Charlotte," he said, drawing her forward. "Charlotte, my grandmother, Riva Bechet."

"How do you do?" Sharlee spoke politely, impressed by the woman's proud-to-the-point-of-arrogant demeanor as much as by her attire: a brilliant purple dress as all-enveloping as a tent.

"Charlotte who?" The old woman looked up with a mischievous expression. "Beau, where do you keep findin' blondes, you rascal?"

"This is Dev's blonde. You remember Dev Oliver? His mama was Yvette LeBlanc."

A smile of genuine pleasure creased Riva's lined face. "Where you been, boy? Don't think we've seen you around here since your mama died. Give me a kiss." She pointed to her cheek.

Dev did as she ordered. "I've been busy, ma'am. Forgive me?"

"Ah!" She stroked his arm archly. "And who's this pretty thing you brought to my party?"

Dev laced his fingers with Sharlee's. "This is my friend, Charlotte Lyon."

The old lady caught her breath sharply and her dark eyes widened. For a moment she stared; then a look almost of panic crossed her face.

Sharlee smiled uncertainly. "If the name's familiar, it's probably because you've heard of my grandfather, Paul."

"Your papa is…?"

"André Lyon." Confused, Sharlee glanced at Dev, but his raised brows told her he understood the woman's reaction no better than she.

Beau put one hand on Sharlee's shoulder and the other on Dev's. "My grandma used to work for Lyon Broadcasting a long time ago," he explained. "She knew all the Lyons."

"Big mouth!" Riva kicked her grandson on the shin with a foot shod in an orange sandal. "I don't know anything about the Lyons," she said to Sharlee, "but you're welcome." She touched Sharlee's hand lingeringly, almost like a caress. "You young people go along now. I'm tired of talkin'."

Mystified by the old woman, Sharlee followed Beau out onto the porch again.

They paused on the wooden ramp and Dev said, "What was all that about, Beau?"

The other man shrugged. "She's gettin' old, is all. She moved to the city when she was young 'bout a hundred years ago. She got a job at that Lyon radio station and had her a high old time, so my mama says. After a while she come home and got married."

Beau glanced toward the band, which consisted of a fiddle, an electric guitar, a hand-held triangle, an accordion and a rub-board—a corrugated metal vest played against the chest. He tapped his toe as if the music with its strong beat wouldn't let him stand still. "Hey, Dev," he said, "before I forget, someone busted into your mama's house the other day. We couldn't see anythin' missin' so we didn't report it, but you might want to check."

"Okay." Dev hauled the car keys from his pants pocket. "Maybe I'll go take a look now. It's in escrow now, but if anything's damaged, it could cause problems." He glanced at Sharlee. "This shouldn't take long. I'm sure Beau will see you get something to eat if you want to wait for me here."

"I'll go with you," she said. For some reason she didn't feel at all comfortable here. Something about the old woman had unnerved her.

Back on the road again, they drove in silence. Increasingly nervous, Sharlee looked out the window, concentrating on the rush of wind through her hair and the heat of the sun. Finally, because it was on her mind, she said, "I didn't know you'd spent that much time on the bayou, Dev. You seem completely at home here."

"My secret life." He gave her a cautious glance. "I didn't talk about it when I was a kid. It pissed Alain off too much when I visited my mother, and when Alain's pissed off..."

She shivered; she could well imagine. "But why would he care?" she wondered out loud.

"Are you kidding?" Dev turned onto an even smaller road, actually little more than a dirt trail. Trees and vines and undergrowth threatened to overwhelm it at every turn. He slowed to a crawl to protect the Mercedes.

"Why would I kid?" She searched her memory. "Actually I don't know much about your mother. I knew she was Cajun and that she was beautiful. I don't really remember her because I was only about five when she went away. After that, it was like she never existed. No one ever talked about her, including you."

"That's because Alain decreed it so." His mouth turned down scornfully.

"I thought— Dev, can I be honest?"

"Something tells me I should say no, but I'll say yes."

"I thought nobody ever talked about her because she'd done the unthinkable—given up her children."

"She didn't give them up, they were—" He stopped abruptly. "I don't want to talk about that. Just get one thing straight. Alain destroyed my mother's life, not the other way around."

"But you lived with him and not with her. Why? If you felt that way, why didn't you—"

"Shut up, Sharlee." He spoke roughly. "None of

the Lyons—no, check that. Only one Lyon ever understood.''

"Who?'' She didn't take offense—or pay the slightest attention—to his order. She snapped her fingers. "Grandmère. That's why you're so protective of her, right?''

"God, you're pushy. Is this an occupational thing with reporters?''

"The good ones, anyway. Dev, I remember asking you about your mother once before.''

He gave her an almost hostile glance. "I didn't want to talk about her then, and I don't want to talk about her now. It's ancient history, anyway.''

She made a face at him. "Okay, but I sense a few more family secrets here. Why don't you just go ahead and tell me whatever it is you're determined *not* to tell me and get it over with?''

"Then it wouldn't be a secret.'' The road they followed ended, and he pulled slowly into a clearing before a small house on the edge of the water. Painted bright blue, it had a steep roof and a long porch surrounded by iron grillwork.

She'd seen it before and the blood seemed to freeze in her veins despite the heat of the day. Why had she ever thought she could come back to this place without being overwhelmed by memories?

SHE DIDN'T GO INSIDE with him. Couldn't. While he headed for the front door, she turned toward the dock jutting out into chocolate-colored water.

Vegetation, dense and foreboding, grew right up to the water's edge. Off to the right an egret stood

at the edge of the shore; overhead a hawk soared. A
rustle in the water caught her attention. Swinging
around, she saw a small dark animal dart past. Shiv-
ering, she laid a hand on the brittle wooden rail.

She didn't belong here, then or now. She should
have known how hard this would be.

Time crawled past and Dev still hadn't come out
of the house. Wilting in the heat, she looked around,
finally noticing a tall oak tree among many others.
This one was distinguished by an old folding chaise
longue beneath its spreading branches. Leaving the
dock, she picked her way across the broken ground.

She lowered herself onto the dusty plastic webbing
carefully, fully expecting to wind up flat on her back
on the mossy earth. The longue groaned but didn't
give. Composing herself with her hands clasped at
her waist, Sharlee looked up at the lacy pattern of
light and shadow filtering through the leaves and
Spanish moss.

Too bright. She let her eyes drift closed. The hum
of insects filled her ears and she relaxed. The other
time she'd been here, she'd noticed nothing beyond
the fact that she and Dev were totally alone, finally
in a place safe enough for them to do what they'd
been burning to do....

He'd undressed her carefully, as if she wasn't
made of flesh and blood at all. But she was; she'd
ached for him, trembled with impatience. "Are you
sure?" he kept saying, until she wanted to scream at
him: *What has this all been for if not leading to this
moment? Hurry, my love, hurry!*

But he hadn't hurried. He'd gone so slowly she thought she'd die.

In her dream, she groaned with pleasure. Or was it in her dream? She felt a touch on her forearm and then his voice saying, "Sharlee? Are you all right? Wake up, chère."

It was an effort to force her eyelids open. Heat swam around her in waves and insects still buzzed, but all she saw was Dev, kneeling beside her, touching her lightly, cautiously.

"Oh." She swallowed and tried to push away the beautiful cobwebs of her dream. "I...I can't believe I fell asleep."

"No problem." He dropped to a sitting position beside the longue. "It took me longer than I expected."

The dream was hanging on, giving her trouble getting her bearings. "I don't know what's wrong with me," she mumbled, stifling a yawn. "It was just so hot—" She remembered the reason for this side trip and added, "Is everything all right inside?"

"I can't see anything wrong. My guess is someone just needed a place to sleep for a night or two."

"That's good. Are you ready to go, then?"

"There's no hurry. You're not fully awake yet." He cocked his head. "Were you dreaming? You were making funny little noises."

She groaned and raised a hand to shove damp hair away from her face. "Please don't tell me you were sitting there watching me."

"Actually I was." He smiled that beautiful seductive smile. "You looked so peaceful."

It made her feel funny to think he'd seen her looking so vulnerable. She opened her mouth to castigate him and somehow couldn't do it. Was she still asleep?

"Sharlee." He leaned closer. "It wasn't something awful that happened here, you know."

"I know."

"When we came, I really wanted you to meet my mother."

"Only she wasn't here."

"No, she was in the hospital. But I didn't know that."

"So we were alone, two kids in..." She wasn't quite willing to use the word "love."

He took her hand in his. "My memories of that day are incredible," he said, his voice silky and convincing. "I cared for you...a lot."

"I cared for you, too." The words were ripped from her throat. "Making love with you was the most wonderful thing that had ever happened to me. Even now, I can't regret it."

"Then why are you so hostile?"

She sat up and swung her legs over the edge of the longue, bumping into him with her knees. "It was what happened later," she said. "All the family upheaval, my parents' disappointment, threats, punishments..."

"I wish I could have spared you that."

"You couldn't. Nobody could. God, Dev, the sky fell and they didn't even know we'd gone beyond the heavy-petting stage. It was surreal." She looked at him, her eyes burning. "But I could handle it when

I thought we were in it together. Then I got the note.''

''That damned note.'' He reached out to rest both hands on her knees. His gaze captured hers, his eyes dark and turbulent as the water whispering against the dock.

''That damned betrayal.'' She looked down at his hands, strong and masterful, and suddenly she had an insane desire to lean forward and wrap her arms around his neck and just *go* with all the emotions and sensations she was feeling.

But this time it wouldn't be love. It would be payback.

''Sharlee,'' he said into the stillness, ''we can't start up again.''

She blinked. ''Start up again?''

''Get involved, or at least, any more involved than we are. The attraction is still there, obviously, but what's the point? You'll be leaving, I'll be staying....''

Every vestige of sleep had long since been swept away. She looked at him, at the dark hair and eyes, at the full firm mouth, at the lean bronze cheeks, and she had to slide her hands beneath her thighs to keep from touching him. Still she managed to say calmly, ''I get the feeling you're trying to tell me something, Dev.''

His nostrils flared. ''Yeah, that we've got to stop with the games. What happened after the opening...that was a serious lapse in good judgment on both our parts.''

And at last she understood perfectly; he was

dumping her again, this time even before they'd done anything. She felt her blood spike, but she forced a faint smile. "Are you afraid I'm going to jump your bones beneath an oak tree at your mother's house?"

"You know that's not what I meant." He looked embarrassed and his hands fell away from her knees.

Her smile widened. Lifting her arms, she yawned and stretched, very much aware the movement would pull the light cotton fabric of her dress tightly across her breasts. "Okay, Dev," she said cheerfully. "If that's what you want."

"It's *not* what I want, it's what—"

"Sure." She jumped up off the chaise longue and looked down at him, still sitting cross-legged on the ground. "I think we understand each other. Shall we go?"

FELIX HESITATED, holding the huge vat that had contained jambalaya in his arms. "So how was the food?" he asked, intensely interested.

Sharlee sighed and flexed her shoulders. It was Monday night and closing time at the Donna Buy Ya, and she wasn't eager to relive her adventures of the previous day.

"Okay," she said noncommittally. "I didn't actually eat much. By the time we got back from Dev's mother's house, there wasn't all that much food left."

He nodded sympathetically. "Too bad. Some of those country cooks are great. Wish I'd been there, but I had to catch up in my own kitchen."

"I wish you'd been there, too," she said with

heartfelt sincerity. "Anything else you need me to do now?"

"Nah, I think that's about it." He hiked the pot higher. "What's your hurry? You got a date?"

"No, but I'm feeling…I don't know, restless, I guess."

His broad mouth quirked up. "Yeah, I can tell."

She managed a smile. "Since you don't need me, I'll go on upstairs."

"Yeah. See you later, Sharlee."

But upstairs didn't do the trick. Wandering out onto the balcony overlooking the street, she stood there pulling deep breaths into her lungs and listening to the night sounds of the Quarter: snatches of conversation in both English and French, sultry laughter, the plaintive notes of a saxophone.

God, she'd go crazy if she didn't get out of here! Ever since the trip to Bayou Sans Fin, she'd been edgy as hell, while Dev acted as if nothing had happened.

Restless and keyed up, she stalked back inside only long enough to grab her shoulder bag and head down the stairs again. Felix hollered from the kitchen.

"Hey, where you goin' in such a hurry?"

"Bourbon Street!" she yelled back. "A little music is just what I need."

"You be careful," he warned. "There's more happenin' on that street than just sounds."

She shrugged and let herself out the front door, locking it behind her. She'd been on her own for a long time now. She certainly knew how to take care of herself.

Sharlee strolled down Bourbon Street, watching the crowds swirl around her. She'd never spent much time here—just enough to alarm her parents—but she'd always considered it tawdry and tacky.

Maybe tawdry and tacky fit her mood because even the sleaze appealed to her tonight.

Wandering past jazz clubs and neon-framed strip joints, gay dance clubs and karaoke bars, she watched the people she passed with new curiosity. On the corner of Bourbon and Orleans, a man and a woman stood locked in a fierce argument. Suddenly he grabbed her by the hair, hauled her up against him and kissed her.

A couple of drunk kids—college students by the looks of them—cheered. The man and woman walked away arm in arm, and the kids turned back to assist a fallen comrade, so drunk he couldn't sit up on the sidewalk even with the building to lean against. Grabbing him by the arms and lifting him bodily, the steadier duo dragged him into the nearest bar.

Sharlee dodged a few more tourists, then hesitated. Music poured from nearly every door: jazz, Cajun, zydeco, rock and roll and every variation thereof. But this particular sound, a straight-ahead hard-driving jazz, drew her closer. Then she saw the band on the small stage at the end of the room and knew why.

Crystal Jardin, playing saxophone, had lived at Lyoncrest for years and was probably more a part of the family by now than Sharlee was. The last Sharlee had heard Crystal, in her late twenties, held some kind of job dealing with numbers at WDIX. Her grandmother, Justine, had been the sister of Paul and Charles, so of course, Margaret had gathered Crystal into the fold—and into the house.

Sharlee hesitated while letting the music sweep over her. The small group was good, but Crystal was best of all. Eyes closed, long black braid swaying, she gave herself up to the music pouring from her instrument.

Must be nice, Sharlee thought with naked envy, to care for something so much that the rest of the world faded away.

The tune rose to a crescendo. Should she stay and say hello or move on? That was an easy one, despite the fact that she liked her second cousin. The first words out of Crystal's mouth after saying hello would be: "When are you coming back to Lyoncrest?"

Sharlee moved on. She didn't think Crystal had even seen her.

DEV HIT THE JAZZ CLUB just as the band was leaving the stage for a break. Looking around, he didn't spot Sharlee, but maybe Crystal had seen her.

Crystal saw him coming. "Where y'at, Dev? I haven't seen you on Bourbon Street in ages."

"Yeah, sorry, Crystal. I've been busy."

"So I hear. WDIX isn't the same without you." She grinned. "Good luck with your café anyway."

"Thanks. Uh...actually, I'm looking for someone. I thought you might have seen her."

"Aha! A woman!" She raised her brows.

"Aha, Charlotte Lyon. She hasn't been in here, by any chance?"

Crystal's eyes widened. "Good grief, that *was* Charlotte!"

"You've seen her?"

She nodded. "About fifteen minutes ago. She came in and stood near the door for a few minutes. I thought I was seeing things. When she didn't stay to say hello, I figured it probably wasn't her, after all. I mean, I heard she was living with you—"

"Not living with me," he objected. "There are three of us who just happen to share an apartment."

"A ménage à trois?" she said with impish delight. "Shame on you, Devin Oliver."

"Okay, okay," he said sheepishly, "I can take a joke. It's just that I don't want that kind of story going around."

"Too late," she said cheerfully.

"I don't suppose you'd have any idea which direction she was headed."

"Actually, yes. She turned left on the sidewalk— the door was open for a whole pack of people to come in so I could see." She frowned. "I hope you catch up with her. She really shouldn't be wandering around Bourbon Street this late."

"You got that right. Thanks, Crystal."

"Anytime, Dev. Tell her I'd love to see her."

"I will, but don't hold your breath. She's doing her Garbo thing these days—she wants to be alone."

"Alone with you, apparently." Crystal waved and turned away.

Dev made his way to the door through the small tables filled with music lovers, finally managing to get out the door and onto the sidewalk. When he'd returned to the Donna Buy Ya and Felix told him where Sharlee had gone, Dev had nearly had a fit. But he was hot on her trail now. And when he caught up with her...

SHARLEE SAT AT THE RAUCOUS BAR drinking a martini, tapping her foot and nodding to the beat of a zydeco group performing on a stage along the opposite wall. Young and aggressive, the musicians responded to the enthusiasm of the crowd with renewed vigor.

Someone nudged her shoulder and she glanced around. A thirtyish guy grinned at her.

"Can I buy you a drink?" he shouted into the din.

"No, thanks." She turned back to the music.

"How about a dance, then?" He moved index fingers in circles and nodded toward the postage-stamp-size dance floor.

"No, thanks."

"Then how about..." Apparently he couldn't think of anything else to offer her because his voice died away in a gurgle. Which suited her fine. She'd been fending off advances since she'd walked into this place.

The band finished the set to deafening applause. Time to move on, she decided. She'd just go on down the street until she found—

"Good band," the man on the other side of her

said. He was younger than the guy behind her, probably about her own age.

"Yes." She replaced her empty glass on the bar behind her without looking.

"Can I buy you another drink?"

"No."

"Okay, just asking. Uh...are you a college student?"

"No." The rush to the door had begun. She'd be better off letting the crowd thin out before tackling it.

"I saw the bartender check your ID."

"The light's bad in here." She slid off the tall bar stool.

Before she could walk away, he caught her wrist. "Are you sure you don't want to—"

Another hand snaked out from behind her and clamped down on the man's wrist. With a little cry of pain, he released her.

And Dev Oliver said, "She's sure."

CHAPTER ELEVEN

SHARLEE AND DEV stood face-to-face on the sidewalk in front of the club, arguing. They drew only an occasional curious glance from the crowd that eddied around them.

Apparently no one considered the altercation serious enough to merit calling the police.

"...no right to stick your nose in my business!"

"No? What were you going to do—karate chop that guy?"

"I could have handled him just fine without your interference!"

"Yeah, right. You're obviously in your element, drinking alone in a bar on one of the wildest streets in America. If I hadn't come along..."

As he continued to berate her, she felt an old familiar wildness rush over her, a wildness she thought she'd long since conquered. She'd show him! She abruptly turned away in the middle of his tirade.

"Where the hell do you think you're going?" He stepped in front of her again.

"Into the nearest bar to get a drink."

"Dammit, Sharlee, you—"

"I'm of age! Now get out of my way or I'll call the cops."

He let her go and she made good her pledge. Walking into the nearest bar, she took the first stool she saw.

"What'll it be?"

Much to her surprise, the bartender looked vaguely familiar. "A martini," she said.

He raised his brows. He was in his early thirties with fair hair and blue eyes. "Maybe I'd better take a look at some ID, in that case. Martinis are not for the uninitiated."

Opening her purse, she laid out her Colorado driver's license with the horrible picture that made her look cross-eyed. "Hey, martinis are all the rage with the younger set," she said, "at least in Colorado."

"Yes, ma'am." He gave her a curious look before turning away to mix the drink.

By the time he put it before her, she had him pegged. "WDIX-TV's fiftieth anniversary celebration—that's where I saw you."

"Yes, ma'am." He looked pleased she'd remembered him. "I saw you there, too." He stuck one big hand over the bar. "I'm Sean McKenna. Actually, my grandfather, Patrick, was chauffeur to the Lyons during the forties and fifties."

"No kidding. It really is a small world."

He watched her sip her drink. "You sure you can handle one of those things?"

"Sure. I take it slow and easy. This is only my second one tonight and it'll be my last."

He looked relieved. "Second one, huh. You must handle your liquor better than your grandfather did."

Her eyes widened. "My grandfather? What—"

"Bartender! Can I get a drink or what?"

With an apologetic glance, he moved away, leaving her staring after him.

And thinking, Grandpère couldn't hold his liquor? This was news to her.

DEV SAT DOWN beside her just as Sean returned. "I'll have what the lady's having," Dev said.

While Sean made the drink, Sharlee waited impatiently. Even Dev's presence didn't cool her burning curiosity.

When the drink was delivered, she leaned forward eagerly and asked Sean, "Where did you hear that about my grandfather? That he couldn't hold his liquor, I mean." She heard Dev's quick intake of breath but ignored him.

"Don't want to gossip about a great man." Sean swiped at the gleaming bar with a wet rag.

"I think he's a great man, too. I'm on his side, Sean." She gave him a coaxing smile. "Besides, if it's true it isn't gossip."

"Yeah, probably. Okay, it was a long time ago and doesn't matter now, anyway. What my grandfather said was, he saw Mr. Paul when he finally came home from the war, and he couldn't hold his liquor at all. That's why he decided early on to avoid alcohol entirely."

Was he kidding? Sharlee frowned, trying to remember. Her grandfather—drinking water when others drank wine. No, that couldn't be; she'd seen him make champagne toasts—but now that she thought about it, she'd never seen him drink the champagne afterward.

And when he'd turned down wine at lunch the other day, she'd thought it was because of his age and precarious health. Why hadn't she paid more attention over the years?

"What else did your grandfather say?" she urged.

"That Mr. Paul might have been born rich, but he had his problems just like the rest of us. He was a real man, Grandpa said, one of the greatest in Louisiana. Grandpa was proud of the years he worked for the Lyons." Sean saluted her with a finger tap to the forehead and turned away to check out the needs of the rest of his clientele.

Sharlee sat in surprised silence. She'd just learned one of the family secrets. Not a big one, perhaps, but hinting at others. What had Grandpère said? "Would it interest you to know there was a time *I* didn't measure up?"

She turned on Dev, saw his expression and instantly deduced, "You knew."

He looked down into his martini glass. "I...might have heard something about it."

"Why keep a thing like that secret?"

"Why not? It's no big deal, Sharlee. Whatever happened to make your grandfather give up booze obviously happened years ago. Why are you so determined to discover he has feet of clay?"

"I just want to know he's human, not some great icon to whom I never measured up." She shivered with excitement. "He and Grandmère got married not long before he went to the war as a correspondent, Dev. When he came back, he must have been...different.''

"My guess is war can do that to a person."

She made a face. "Of course, but what, exactly?" She gritted her teeth with frustration. "The problem is, I can't really imagine him as anything but old. I know he loves Grandmère, but I can't picture either of them young and hot-blooded and...and mad for each other. I wonder—"

"Why don't you just ask?"

"I have, lots of times. Not about this specifically, but I've tried 'Tell me about when you were young.' All I ever got was this rose-colored Ozzie and Harriet song and dance. Mama and Grandmère guard the family honor like dragons at the gate.''

For a moment, Dev simply looked at her. Then he shook his head wearily. "Sharlee, sometimes...most of the time, I don't understand you at all. A lot of people would be sorry to discover that a relative they loved might have once had a drinking problem. Yet you sit here looking as if you'd just learned you're related to royalty.''

"I already knew I was related to royalty," she said lightly. "What *I've* just learned is that Grandpère really was young once, that he had a life and apparently screwed it up on occasion." She grinned. "Just like me.''

"Yeah, well, I guess I'm glad if you're glad." He tossed off the last of his martini. "What say we head on back to the apartment now? I'm beat and I'd like to get some sleep without worrying about you.'' He looked at her warily, as if dreading a fight.

"You'd worry about little ol' me?" She slid off her stool and dropped a bill on the bar. "Thanks, Sean," she called to the bartender.

"Thank *you*. My best to the old gentleman."

She turned to Dev, still sitting on his stool watching her. And she thought, *Will this be the night?* She was too wound up by Bourbon Street, by Sean's scant revelations, by being here with Dev, not to wonder.

"Well?" she asked, raising her brows.

"I'm coming." He got up and stood in front of her as if waiting for some sign.

Smiling, she tucked one hand beneath his arm and leaned into him as if they were partners. He gave her a startled glance before leading her to the door and out into the craziness that was Bourbon Street twenty-four hours a day.

THE HUMIDITY FELT even higher on the walk back to the café than it had been earlier, Dev thought. It was probably just the company. Sharlee was getting him all steamed up, and he wasn't sure how much was deliberate.

Whatever—she had him so worked up that he was finding it damned hard to control his physical responses. He reminded himself that he didn't want to get any more mixed up with her than he already was. Their lives were complicated enough, and she came with a lot of baggage he'd just as soon not deal with.

Charlotte Lyon was a high-maintenance woman. If they slept together now, it would make it even harder when she left—which was going to happen soon. He sensed her impatience and restlessness growing daily. Soon she'd simply stand up and walk away, out of New Orleans and out of his life. And this time when she left, no amount of scheming by her family or anyone else would get her back.

So he would cling to his resolve, he decided bravely as they entered the café through the back door. What he'd said in the bayou still stood: no way would he start up with her again.

Quietly they crept up the stairs to the apartment. Pausing in the hallway, they looked at each other through the shadows and the tension soared off the charts. Dev felt as if he were surrounded by a cloud of steam that blurred his vision and slowed his movements and responses.

"I'm hungry." She spoke softly out of consideration for Felix, leaning forward so he could hear her. "I think I'll go see what I can find in the kitchen before I turn in. You don't have to wait for me."

"Okay." Yet he made no move to leave.

"Is something wrong?" Her voice was breathy. "I'm not mad at you anymore, if you're worried about that."

"I'm not."

"Then what?"

"I meant what I said at my mother's house."

She became very still. "I never doubted you for a moment."

"Good, because we can't get involved again." He took a step forward; they were almost but not quite touching.

"I agree absolutely. It would be insane."

She lifted her face as he lowered his. Their lips touched; that was all. Nothing else to pull them together, to hold them together, just their hungry mouths. Either one could pull away at any time.

Neither did. Her lips parted beneath his and he thrust his tongue inside, displaying a possessiveness she met without hesitation. Fire exploded in his blood and coursed wildly through his body to pool dangerously in his groin.

She moaned, a soft agonized sound, and stepped back. By moonlight shafting through the open living-room windows, he saw her breasts rise and fall with the fierceness of her breathing. He wanted to pick her up and carry her off to his room and lay her on his bed and ravish her—

"Dammit, Sharlee, we can't do this."

"Then...don't." She smoothed her hands up his torso beneath his shirt, her nails scraping lightly.

He shuddered. "You think I can't stop. Look—" he thrust both hands through his hair to keep from grabbing her "—I'm on the brink here, but I'm a man of my word." Which only an idiot would have given in the first place.

"That's very decent of you, Dev." Her tone was noncommittal, but her fingers had found his right nipple.

He gasped and started to shake. "Look, I'm going to go take a shower." From some deep reservoir of will he summoned the strength to push her hands away. "If you decide you want to join me later..." He almost strangled on the words.

The silence spun out a web of tension. "That almost sounded like an invitation. Do you want me to join you or not?''

"You know I do." Could that guttural growl be his? He licked his lips. "But don't."

"Do, don't—make up your mind, Devin."

He heard a note of laughter in her tone but also an underlying excitement. Flipping him a flirty little wave, she turned and disappeared into the deeper shadows, heading toward the kitchen.

Gritting his teeth, Dev made the lonely trek down the dark and lonely hallway to his bedroom. And with every miserable step, he assured himself that he was doing the right thing. Too bad he felt like a damn fool.

THE HEAT WAS KILLING HER—the heat of a Louisiana night but worse, the heat created by Dev. He had scorched her with that kiss. Every part of her ached for him.

Still, she thought she'd handled it pretty well. She stared at the contents of the refrigerator. There was plenty to appease her hunger: leftover *étouffée,* half a *muffaletta,* seven cheesecakes—

Seven cheesecakes? Felix must have run out of room in the refrigerators below. Unfortunately what she hungered for wasn't cheesecake. What—*who* she hungered for had gone off down the hall with his newly acquired scruples intact.

She closed the refrigerator door and leaned her forehead against the cool enamel surface. She felt as if she'd been in this town and this apartment and this job forever, treading water, marking time. She lived in a house of cards and she had to get out before it all came tumbling down around her.

She had so much to deal with and she wasn't getting on with any of it: her family, her professional future and, perhaps most unsettling, her feelings for Dev. She hadn't thought she *had* any feelings left for him, but she'd been fooling herself. Before she could go, she somehow had to bring their past to a final closure.

While she wrestled with that, she had to find a real job and brace herself to face her parents and grandparents like the mature adult she kept insisting she was. If she didn't, she'd never be able to hold her head up again.

All right, she bargained with herself; tomorrow she'd get on the Net and contact several journalist friends who worked on the West Coast. Surely one of them could give her a job lead. She'd also go to the library and check out *Editor and Publisher*. It was a start at least.

As for her family…

Her silk blouse was sticking to the damp skin between her shoulder blades. Straightening, she unbuttoned the offending garment and let it drop to the floor. Clad only in a lacy bra from the waist up, she fanned her torso with her hands. God, it was hot!

As for her family, there were apparently plenty of secrets ripe for discovery. Perhaps if she could speak to Uncle Charles privately…

Not that she intended to use anything she discovered to hurt or even to alarm anyone at Lyoncrest. She just wanted to know—no, she *needed* to know or else she doubted she'd ever really figure out what her own place was in the scheme of things.

Moving carefully through the darkness, she walked to the door leading to the balcony. The room was open with all doors and windows flung wide to catch any slight breeze. A burglar could probably get away with everything they owned, assuming there was anything in this apartment actually worth stealing.

Even moonlight couldn't penetrate to the garden below, shrouded as it was in shadows cast by the buildings surrounding it. Just as the truth she sought was shrouded in shadows. Just as her feelings for Dev lay so deep that no light could penetrate to illuminate them for her.

She had loved him—past tense. Now she only wanted to make him suffer a tiny little bit. It was called revenge, not a pretty word but one that resonated through her.

Her linen pants felt like wool leggings and she hesitated with her hand on the waistband button. Why not? she decided. The house was dark and everyone was asleep. No one would know she'd stripped down in the kitchen.

The pants hit the linoleum. Sucking in her breath, she raised her arms and arched her rib cage. This was the coolest she'd been without air-conditioning since she'd returned. She could actually feel the lazy swirl of air moved by the ceiling fan.

Her breasts felt heavy beneath the light confines of lace. Maybe she should go all the way....

Amused, she laughed out loud. Maybe she should

look for a job as a stripper on Bourbon Street. Then
she could write an exposé—"I was a stripper with a
penchant for words"—and really shock her family.

Damn. She glared at the door leading to the hall
down which he'd disappeared. He'd invited her to
his bed—sort of—and she wanted to go, but maybe
she shouldn't. Not yet, anyway. She should probably
wait, make him want her as much as she wanted him.

"Damn you, Devin Oliver," she whispered in a
tight little voice. "You're not going to get off so
easily this time."

DEV WASN'T ASLEEP but he was trying like hell. On
his back in bed, he stared up at the ceiling with steely
determination.

He would *not* chase her, dammit. She would come
to him or not.

The kiss had told him everything: she wanted him.
Had his rambling rationalizations put her off entirely? Maybe she was waiting for him to make a
move so that she could...what? Slap him down? Pile
on the guilt?

Pick up where they'd left off?

He groaned and lifted an arm to cover his eyes.
Talk about the best of times and the worst of times.

But he would *not* go looking for her, even if it
meant spending the rest of the night fighting that and
other, more compelling, urges. He wasn't some kid...

He slid one leg off the side of the bed, bending
his knee until his foot hit the floor. Maybe what he
needed was a drink of water.

The door to his room opened and he tensed—not

that he was expecting a burglar. Soft running feet sped across the floor and stopped at the side of the bed.

"Dev, Dev, are you awake?" Sharlee whispered urgently. Leaning over, she touched his arm hesitantly.

"Wha—" He strove to sound sleepy when he was anything but. "What is it? What's wrong?" It was only natural that he'd turn toward her and pull her onto the bed with him and— Jeez, was she naked? But no, he felt the bra strap across her back and the edge of elastic around her hips. Bra and panties. He stifled a groan. "Is anything the matter?"

"Does something have to be the matter? I thought I was invited. If I'm not—" She caught her breath and he felt her hand on his hip. "Are you naked?"

"I'm in bed," he countered. "What did you expect?"

Her body trembled with nervous laughter. "I know you don't want to start anything again, but I was hoping—" deftly she insinuated a knee between his thighs "—you'd have your manly way with me at least once."

"Bingo!" He slipped a hand inside the elastic of her panties and grabbed the sweet curve of her bottom. "Is this something along the lines you had in mind?"

She caught her breath. "It's a beginning, anyway." She pressed her lips to the runaway pulse at the base of his throat.

"I couldn't have said it better myself." With one

quick motion he rolled her on top of him. Let her feel his arousal, since she was the cause of it.

She let out a long luxurious groan. "I guess you meant what you said at Bayou Sans Fin," she whispered, reaching for him with both hands. "We sure can't start up again...."

WHEN HE PULLED HER on top of him, she almost lost it. He wasn't wearing a stitch, not that she wanted him to be, but it was still a thrill to feel that expanse of warm muscular male body beneath her.

It was an even bigger shock to feel sixteen again, as young and inexperienced as a virgin. As he kissed her mouth, he deftly stripped away the panties. The bra followed, leaving her completely exposed to the wonderful things he was doing to her.

When all along, she'd intended to do things to him, to show him that in the years since they'd been together she hadn't been sitting by the fire knitting mittens. With his face buried between her breasts, intentions both good and not so good flew out the window.

She was here because she couldn't not be here. Maybe tomorrow she'd remember other, truer, motives.

SHE OPENED HER LEGS and he moved inside her in one strong stroke that drew a blissful "Ahhh!" from her.

It was like coming home, like finding paradise, like...

He began to move and she quivered beneath him

just as she had in the past. Her harsh breathing caught on a sob. Just like that, she convulsed and he knew she'd already reached an orgasm.

The first one, anyway. He drove into her, his own breathing coming in harsh grunts. Shoving his hands beneath her buttocks, he slanted her hips to accept his thrusts more deeply. She felt like putty in his hands, still trembling with aftershocks. Then in an instant she began to come alive again, to respond.

She moved with him once more in perfect rhythm, as if they'd been doing this forever without that awful gap of years between them. He withdrew, plunged deeper, repeating the sequence over and over until he couldn't withstand the building pressure for another instant.

When he hit the peak he didn't leap off alone, for her breathy little cry told him she was with him all the way.

HE AWOKE WITH SUNSHINE lying across his face and Sharlee's right arm and leg lying across his body. A feeling of infinite peace and contentment possessed him.

If only he hadn't found her crying in the arbor at Lyoncrest that day so very long ago. If they'd waited to discover this connection between them, how different their lives might have been. Instead, they'd both been bruised by the consequences of that premature loving.

This time it would be different, he vowed without the slightest notion how that might be accomplished. Careful not to wake her, he covered her shoulder with his hand and stroked down to her wrist, across skin as soft as the proverbial baby's behind. He'd been fighting it, she'd been fighting it, and suddenly last night they'd both seemed to run out of excuses at the same time.

He didn't know when she awoke, only that the hazel eyes suddenly opened. She looked at him searchingly, as if she could see inside him to where he guarded his most private thoughts and feelings.

He smiled. "Good morning."

"Mmm." She snuggled closer with a great sigh. "It was a good night, anyway."

"I certainly thought so. Real nice of you to drop in."

"How could I have turned down such a charming invitation?"

"I guess you couldn't," he said, "for which I'm grateful."

She smoothed a palm across his chest. "I hope I don't regret it."

He reveled in the stroking of her hand. "I hurt you once. I didn't mean to, but I did. I don't want to hurt you again."

"You won't." She lifted herself away just enough to look squarely into his face. "You don't need to worry. I'm not sixteen anymore."

"I can see that."

"The truth is," she said, settling her head on his shoulder, "I was getting really tired of being constantly distracted by you. I have other things to think about."

He wasn't quite sure how to take that. Was he an

itch that once scratched would fade away? "Such as?"

"Leaving."

He tried not to let her see his reaction. "You've made plans to do that already?"

"I'm in the process. There are certain things I have to do before I can, though."

"Such as?"

"Well—" she kissed his chest, using her tongue "—there was *this,* but now I can check it off my list." She made an imaginary tick mark in the air. "Go to bed with Dev and see if it's anything like I remember."

He couldn't believe what he was hearing—and he couldn't resist rising to the bait. "Is it?"

"That's for me to know and you to find out." She gave him a teasing grin. "Anyway, that's one down and two to go. Now I've got to find out what Grandpère and Uncle Charles meant by something I overheard at the anniversary party."

He levered himself up on a bent elbow, supporting his head with his hand. "This is the first I've heard about that."

Her lashes lowered provocatively. "I guess I'm just feeling expansive this morning. What Charles said was, 'There are more secrets in this family than candles on that cake.' And as you know, there were fifty candles."

Dev felt faint stirrings of unease. "He was probably just making conversation."

"Oh, no, he was dead serious, and that's the way Grandpère took it. When I told Uncle Alain that I

wanted to talk to his father, he turned me down flat.''
She chewed on that delicious lower lip. ''Leslie told
me a little the day I saw her at JAX, and then I ran
into the bartender last night and he told me some
more.''

She sat up, curling her legs beneath her. Her
breasts rose full and inviting, the dark-rose nipples
already tightening beneath the intensity of his gaze.

She leaned over him. ''I've only seen the tip of
the iceberg,'' she said. ''I know just enough to realize there's much more to be discovered. I don't
honestly expect that anything horrendous has been
hidden from me. But even if it's only small
things…''

''Sharlee…'' he began in a warning tone.

''No, this is important to me.'' Her lower lip thrust
out stubbornly. ''I hate secrets. I've always hated secrets, which is probably a good part of the reason I
became a reporter, I suppose.''

He covered those beautiful breasts with his hands
and she leaned toward him. ''Don't you have any
secrets yourself?'' he asked.

''No!'' She caught her breath. ''Do you?''

''Maybe one or two.'' He kneaded the soft flesh,
then lightly pinched the nipples.

She smiled and her eyes half closed. ''What do I
have to do to get those secrets out of you? I'll do
anything at all. Just tell me…show me.''

''*Chère*,'' he murmured, ''I can't show you a
thing, especially now. We're out of condoms.''

''Then I guess we really *can't* start up again.''

''Well…maybe just a little.'' And his hungry lips
closed over one tempting nipple.…

CHAPTER TWELVE

SHARLEE WAS IN THE SHOWER when the telephone call came. Dev spoke briefly, slammed down the receiver and stumbled into the kitchen, intent on locating that badly needed first cup of coffee. Instead, he found Felix standing at the window with his own cup in his hands, a brooding expression on his face.

Dev hitched up the pajama bottoms he'd donned for propriety's sake. "You look like hell, Felix," he announced.

"And you've got canary feathers sticking outta your mouth."

"Passing moral judgment, are we?" Dev took a cup from the rack on the counter and reached for the coffeepot.

Felix seemed to consider Dev's comment. "Yeah," he said at last. "I guess I am. I just don't want to see either of you guys mess up. You're my partner and she's a decent gal—hard worker, too."

"Okay, I'll watch out for our mutual roommate."

"Ain't nothin' mutual about her at this point." Felix's gaze swung to a piece of fabric on the floor near the refrigerator.

Sharlee's blouse. Dev fought a smile.

"Yeah, grin." Felix's mouth turned down at the

corners. "I've been expectin' this to happen, but I kept hopin'—ah, to hell with it." He finished his coffee and slammed the mug down on the counter. "You're both old enough to take your lumps."

"Felix, you don't understand how it is with us."

Hell, Dev thought, *I don't understand how it is with us.*

"I understand no good is gonna come of it. Now I'm buttin' out."

Felix left the room just as Sharlee walked in. She looked fresh and pretty, wet hair clinging to her neck and not a speck of makeup to hide her glowing skin. "Felix looked like he got up on the wrong side of the bed," she said. "I, on the other hand, got up on the right side." She grinned. "Although it wasn't my bed."

"It is as long as you want it to be."

A flash of vulnerability crossed her face, followed by a teasing tilt to her lips. "Careful," she warned. "I might take you up on that—and then again, maybe I won't." She paused on her way to the coffeepot to grab her blouse and pants off the floor and toss them over a chair as casually as if she stripped in the kitchen every night.

She poured coffee and faced him with a faintly challenging smile.

He set his empty cup in the sink. "Listen, I've got several errands to take care of this morning. When you go downstairs, will you tell Felix I'll be back in time to help open for lunch?"

She stopped smiling. "All right."

He waited for her to ask him where he was going,

what he was doing, maybe even ask if she could go along. But apparently she still had her pride, for she simply turned away, to his vast relief.

But not before he'd seen a flash of something he didn't like in her face.

Something very like disappointment.

THE MAID SHOWED Dev into the living room at Lyon-crest. Margaret joined him almost immediately.

"Thank you for coming so promptly," she said, sitting on the elegant gold-brocade couch and smoothing her navy blue skirt over her knees. "Would you care for anything to drink? Coffee, iced tea?"

"No, thanks. I just had breakfast."

She nodded, folding her hands in her lap. "What was Charlotte doing wandering Bourbon Street alone last night?"

"Ah." Dev looked past her, at the magnificent fireplace with the oil portrait of Alexandre Lyon above it, old Alexandre who had started it all. "You've been talking to Crystal, I see."

"Of course." Margaret pinned him with her glance. "Charlotte's all right, isn't she? Crystal said I was making too much out of this, that you were only a few minutes behind her, but it still worried me."

"She's fine," he said impatiently.

"That's a relief." Margaret's shoulders sagged slightly. "Why did she go to Bourbon Street by herself? Did the two of you quarrel?"

Had they? He wasn't even sure himself, so he said,

"No. She went there because she was restless." He hesitated. "There is one other thing, though."

"Yes?" She leaned forward attentively.

"She's asking a lot of questions about this family."

"Oh, dear." Margaret's lips thinned. "That's an ongoing bone of contention around here. Paul wants to tell Sharlee everything, Gaby and André want to tell her nothing, and I...I'm somewhere in the middle. Until we reach some consensus, I must ask you to head off Charlotte's inquiries."

"No way. I told you I was out of this and I meant it." He picked up a glass figurine of some kind of bird—hawk, eagle, he didn't know one from the other—and turned it over in his hands. Lights gleamed from its depths, reminding him of Sharlee's eyes.

He put the bird down abruptly. "She intends to talk to Charles."

"Charles!" Alarm flared on Margaret's face. "Anyone but Charles. He and Alain would put everything in the worst-possible context." She chewed her lip for a moment. "Under no circumstances is my granddaughter to speak to Charles. I'm surprised Alain would allow it, actually."

"Alain's against it, but you know how determined Sharlee can be." Dev felt words he hadn't intended to say pressing on the back of his throat.

"Devin, you must—"

"Don't even go there. I did what you asked me to do. You can't expect any more of me."

For a moment she stared at him as if she really

couldn't believe he was serious. Then she sighed. "All right, but if you had a child, you'd understand." She beseeched him with her glance. "She really mustn't speak to Charles."

"I'm not entirely sure I agree with that."

"Then perhaps it's best you *have* bowed out," Margaret said gently.

Later on the drive back to the Quarter, Dev breathed a sigh of relief. He really was in the clear. If he was smart, he'd keep it that way.

SHARLEE DIDN'T GO to his bed that night, nor invite him to hers. After the café closed and her work was done, she made a great pretense of yawning and stretching and declaring herself exhausted.

She saw the look that passed between Felix and Dev but ignored it. She was determined to make Dev want her more than anything else in the world, so that when she left he'd feel it at least half as deeply as she'd felt his defection nine years ago. The only way to do it was to withhold what she longed to give.

It wasn't easy. When he caught up with her on the stairs, she didn't even want to talk to him for fear she'd weaken.

"Wait a minute, Sharlee. I have to tell you something."

Her stomach felt as if she'd just gone over a rise on a roller coaster and was headed down. This did not bode well. She turned toward him, her stomach still doing flip-flops, and said a cool, "Yes?"

"Your grandmother called this morning and asked me to drop by Lyoncrest."

"Grandmère?" She frowned. "What did she want?"

"Crystal saw you last night on Bourbon Street and Tante Margaret was concerned."

"You gave her a full report, I suppose."

"No, I told her you were fine and reminded her that I'm not your keeper."

"You obviously weren't very convincing."

He looked disgusted. "What am I supposed to do? Tell her to buzz off?"

Her temper soared. "Yes—in a nicer way, of course."

"Ah, be reasonable." He shook his head help-lessly. "Do you think I like being in the middle this way?"

"You should like it. You do it so well."

"Dammit, Sharlee!" His anger matched hers. "I'm trying to be honest and you're not making it easy. I didn't want to bring it up at all but…ah, forget it." He turned to go back down stairs, then hesitated. "Just one more thing. I want you to promise you won't leave town without talking to your family first."

"I'll promise no such thing. Why should I?"

"Because you don't want me to think you're a sniveling coward. How's that for a reason?"

They glared at each other, eye to eye because he was on a lower step. The truth was, everything was up in the air and she didn't *know* what she intended to do.

"We'll just have to wait and see," she said at last.

"As you said, you've resigned as my keeper, so what difference can it possibly make to you?"

His dark eyes flashed. "When you put it that way, *chère,* I can't think of any difference at all."

That night she undressed in her room, not in the kitchen. She could hear Dev moving around next door and it almost killed her to have him so near and yet so far. She was still too angry to go to him, though. If only those sounds would stop...

And then they did, with the opening and closing of his door. He was going out.

He was going out without her.

To hell with that!

SHE BOOTED UP her laptop and got on the Internet that very night. Filled with fresh resolve by his disloyalty, she set to work with a vengeance, sending an e-mail to every journalist for whom she had, or could scrounge up, an address; then she cruised the web pages of every California newspaper she could find—and she found plenty. Checking out bylines, she discovered that several belonged to reporters she'd worked with or at least met. At the San Franciso *Globe,* she even found the byline of an investigative reporter she'd met at a conference last year in Denver.

Well, nothing ventured, nothing gained. She e-mailed him along with all the others.

The next day she received a dozen responses in her mailbox. It was fun catching up with old friends, but what she was really seeking didn't seem to be there—until she opened the last message.

She could hardly believe it: a reply from Jere Bryce, prize-winning investigative reporter for the San Francisco *Globe*. She scanned in frantic haste:

Hey, Sharlee, I remember you! You asked good questions. About what's happening around here: The *Globe* will shortly be opening up a couple of new bureaus in the hinterlands. I'll nose around and see if anyone knows the timetable. Of course, this doesn't mean you'd have an in; you'd still have to bump shoulders with a million other unemployed journalists. But if you've got good clips and you're a workaholic, who knows? All best with your job-hunting efforts. Say hello to the Big Easy for me.

> Jere.

Jere. A Pulitzer prize winner signed his e-mail to a little ol' nobody like her "Jere." She was in heaven.

"Dear Jere," she e-mailed back, "Competition doesn't scare me. Just get me those dates and I'll be forever in your debt...."

THREE DAYS LATER she received his reply. "I like your spunk, kid. Applications for GAs are being accepted right now. Include clips and tell 'em you took my workshop. Send your stuff to..."

GAs—general-assignment reporters. Right up her alley.

SHE WENT DOWN for the dinner shift that night with only half a mind on her work. Her life seemed to be moving at warp speed all of a sudden. It was dawning on her that this time when she left New Orleans, it probably *would* be for good.

But there were still certain things she had to know. Experience as a professional snoop had taught her that the best way to find out what you needed to know was to ask the right question of the right person. During her break, she called Alain at Chez Charles.

"I was just wondering how Uncle Charles is doing," she said. "I thought maybe I could drop by and see him in the next day or two."

"Sorry." Alain's voice was curt but didn't sound sorry in the least. "His asthma is acting up, so he's not seeing anyone."

"That's too bad. I'm not just anyone, though. I'm family. I wouldn't upset him."

"Yes, you would. Maybe in a month or so he'll be up to it."

"I can't wait a month."

"Oh? Are you leaving town?"

"I didn't say that. I just happen to be a very impatient person."

He laughed. "You and your entire family. I wish I could accommodate you, but it's impossible. I'll tell the old man you called."

"Do that," Sharlee muttered, hanging up just as Dev came out of the kitchen where he'd been chopping what Felix called "the Trinity"—celery, onions and peppers.

He raised his brows. "Any problems?"

"I wanted to drop by to see Uncle Charles tomorrow, and Uncle Alain says he's not up to having company."

"Really? I saw Charles yesterday and he seemed fine."

"You saw him?"

Dev shrugged. "Sure. He's my step-grandpa."

"Can you get *me* in to see him?"

Dev glanced at the full café just beyond the storeroom where they stood. "I think we'd better talk about this later. DeeDee's running herself ragged out there."

"Okay, but don't forget. I won't."

"Sharlee," he drawled, "I don't think you ever forget anything. That's probably your most annoying trait."

She followed him into the café and got right to work, but she was thinking about something entirely different.

Like the fact that many people knew many things, and one who knew more than most was Devin Oliver.

HE KNEW THAT LOOK. Sharlee was going to pin him to the wall in her quest for the same "secrets" her grandmother was trying like hell to keep from her. What a nightmare.

At closing time, he dallied in the kitchen, doing odd jobs for Felix until Sharlee gave up and went upstairs to the apartment. The talented chef watched her depart and said, "Avoiding her won't get you off the hook."

"Who are you—Dear Abby?" Dev snatched off the heavy apron he'd donned for scrubbing pans.

Felix laughed. "It don't take a Dear Abby to see what's going on here. Playin' hard to get just ain't your style."

"It is when I'm trying to avoid all those questions."

"She is a nosy little thing," Felix agreed. "My advice is, tell her the truth and then run."

"I think I'll do the running first and skip the truth."

"Meaning?"

"I'm gonna hop over to Chez Charles and have a little talk with my stepfather. If anyone asks…"

"Yeah, okay. I don't know what's going on, but what the hell. I only work here."

Dev wished he could say the same.

ALAIN OPENED A FRESH BOTTLE of Perrier and poured it into a crystal goblet. Leaving the empty bottle on his office wet bar, he walked back to his huge steel-and-glass desk and sat down in the sculpted jet-age chair.

The open books on the transparent surface stared back at him with the same message as before: Chez Charles was in financial trouble.

Again.

Somebody was going to have to go to Paul and André, hat in hand, and finagle another of the many "loans" that had kept the restaurant afloat over the years. But not recently, dammit. For the past eight years, Alain had managed to avoid that little ego-buster.

He'd be damned if he'd subject himself to it again. He'd send his father to beg. If Paul and André wanted to play hardball, Alain would be more than glad to oblige. But he'd spin it to look like a couple of bullies picking on a sick old man.

He took another sip of water. This humiliation would be a thing of the past once he figured out the details of his plan to take back what was rightfully his. When André was revealed as the impostor he was, Alain would assume the mantle of authority at WDIX-TV. It would be the ultimate payback, but it had to be done carefully.

He had his troops in place at WDIX-TV: his brother Raymond worked in accounting, brother Jason was in sales, and brother Scott was a cameraman though sometimes his loyalty was in doubt. Son Alex was a part-timer in news and would go for an on-air position if he ever got his friggin' degree. The kid seemed to be majoring in wild women and song, instead of communication. Still, he occasionally proved useful, as he had when he'd reported the return of Charlotte Lyon.

Then there was Dev.

Alain's stepson had been in the most important slot of all, as assistant to André. Alain had not had a single doubt that Dev would do what he was told—as long as his mother was alive. Once she died, all bets, unfortunately, were off.

Still, it was blatantly disloyal of Dev to turn his back on his own family. Alain had raised the little bastard like a son, and look how he'd repaid the favor.

Hell, the only thing Alain had asked for was a little industrial espionage. What was wrong with that? Happened all the time.

The office door opened and Benedict Arnold himself walked in. Alain smiled at his stepson.

Dev sat in a curved crystal chair and slumped down on his spine. "Glad to see you're so happy," he said.

"Life is good," Alain replied.

Dev's brows shot up. "Care to tell me why?"

Alain laughed. As if he'd tell this little traitor anything about anything. "Sure. Business is great, the weather's great, and my turncoat son has come to visit me."

Dev didn't smile. "I'm sorry you feel that way about me. I haven't turned on you, Alain, any more than I can turn on the other side of my family."

"Ah, but it's not your family. You've simply been granted visitor privileges—unless of course you decide to marry your way in as you nearly did once before." He peered at Dev through narrowed eyes. "And how is the headstrong Ms. Lyon?"

"I won't talk to you about Sharlee, Alain."

The older man assumed an injured expression. "You used to call me Dad like the rest of my children. What have I done to deserve such an ungrateful son?"

Their gazes met and locked. Dev wasn't the first to look away, which surprised and displeased Alain.

He had to quit thinking of Dev as a boy when obviously he no longer was.

Dev straightened in his chair. "I'm not your son and I don't owe you a damned thing," he said quietly. "You had a lot of ways to keep me in line, but not anymore."

They both knew what he meant. Alain shrugged. "So to what do I owe this unexpected and unpleasant visit?"

"Sharlee said you told her Charles isn't doing well. Is that true?"

"Why would I lie about a thing like that?"

"I can think of a hundred reasons."

"I bet you can." Alain leaned forward, placing his arms on the cold glass surface. Suddenly he felt an overpowering urge to tell Dev everything. Surely if he knew what was to come, he'd return to the bosom of his true family.

For the truth was, Alain had cared about this boy a great deal. He still found it hard to believe Devin would betray him out of a desire for justice. Perhaps if he explained…

Alain sucked in a deep breath and controlled that impulse in the nick of time. Dev was out of it now, and common sense dictated he stay out.

So Alain said, "It's Papa's asthma. He can't see anyone, even you. Tell your girlfriend to leave him alone, Dev. That's an order."

Dev rose. "I've taken my last order from you, Alain. Please let Charles know I hope he feels better soon."

"I'll do that."

Frustrated because there was so much he longed to say and so little that wouldn't foul up long-range plans, Alain let Dev walk out of his office.

Then he angrily dumped the rest of his Perrier and filled his glass with vodka.

"WHERE HAVE YOU BEEN?" Sharlee stood at the top of the stairs glaring at Dev. "I thought we were supposed to talk after closing."

"It *is* after closing. What's your problem?"

"I've been waiting for more than an hour. I repeat, where have you been?"

"That's none of your business."

Sharlee followed him into the living room, then watched him walk on into the kitchen. What in the world had made him so testy?

Not to be put off, she went into the kitchen, too. He'd be sorry he'd kept her waiting, because it had given her time to get her thoughts in order. And what she'd thought about was not necessarily going to make him happy.

He stood in front of the open refrigerator, drinking out of a half-gallon milk carton. She wouldn't even dignify such behavior with a rebuke.

He kicked the door closed and sat at the dinette table. "You just gonna stand there and glare at me all night?" he asked.

"I would, but I've got other things on my mind."

"Such as?"

"Such as..." She took the seat across from him and leaned forward, betraying her eagerness. "Dev, I've been thinking—"

"Always a dangerous thing."

She ignored the crack. "You know how much I want to fill in the blanks about the family."

"Yes. I'm just not sure why."

"At this point, neither am I. I just have to know."

"Lots of luck." He rose to toss the empty milk carton into the trash. "If you don't mind, I think I'll head off to—"

"Dammit, I do mind!" She jumped up and grabbed his arm. When he looked down pointedly, she released him and stepped back. "I want you to help me get in to see Uncle Charles."

"Can't be done. Alain's got him locked up tight."

"Do you really believe he's sick? Or is Alain just keeping him away from me?"

"It doesn't matter what I think."

"It does to me."

Their gazes locked. He broke away with a frustrated exclamation.

"Sharlee, I don't *know* what Charles knows. Whatever it is, Alain doesn't want him spilling it."

"You know what *you* know, though."

He shook his head slowly. "I can't tell other people's secrets."

"But you can tell your own secrets." Impulsively she took his hand in hers and looked earnestly into his eyes. "There's something I've always wanted to know about your family, but every time I mention it, you clam up."

He looked as if he knew better than to say what he said. "And that would be...?"

"What I mentioned at Bayou Sans Fin. Why did

your mother leave you and your brother and sister behind with Alain when she moved back there? No one on my side of the family ever understood why you didn't hate her for that.''

CHAPTER THIRTEEN

DEV LOOKED as if he'd been blindsided.

"I'm sorry," she said, immediately contrite. "I've always wondered but you've never given me much of an opportunity to ask."

He caught his breath and his balance. "It's okay," he said in a strangled voice. "I've kept the secret so damned long…" He gave her a crooked smile. "Secrets again. You're right, Sharlee, there are a lot in this family, but I don't need to keep this one anymore. It's just…hard to say out loud what's only been whispered."

His voice grew stronger, more determined. "Nobody knew about this except me and Alain and my mother. Now that she's gone, who am I protecting?" He looked around the brightly lit kitchen. "But not here. Let's get a glass of wine and take it into the living room. Then I'll tell you all about the time my mother shot my stepfather."

SHARLEE SAT ON THE COUCH with Dev on the floor by her feet, her hand on his shoulder. He talked and she listened, although she had to swallow back the tide of sympathy she knew he didn't want.

"The only father I ever knew was Alain Lyon,"

he began. "He married my mother when I was about two." Dev gave her a crooked smile. "She had rotten taste in men. My real father was a fast-talking charmer who knocked her up without benefit of clergy, then split. She was working at WDIX and somehow she and Alain…" He sighed. "I'm pretty sure she married him because she thought she'd be moving up in the world. He married her because she was beautiful. They were both disappointed.

"Alain's a complicated man. In many ways he was a good father, but he was a terrible husband—and a worse enemy. He was good enough to me when I was growing up, though, treating me just as he did his own two children. Teresa's a nun—did you know that?"

"I'd heard."

"And you know Alex, who's the spitting image of his father unfortunately." Dev looked pained. "Anyway, Grandfather Charles and Grandmother Catherine never liked my mother, although they seemed to have no trouble accepting me.

"Alain and my mother were married in 1972 and divorced in 1980. Sounds simple but it wasn't. Alain was playing around on her and she knew it. Hell, I knew it and I was only ten. When she couldn't stand it any longer, she took her kids and went back to her family home in Bayou Sans Fin."

Dev sat silently for several moments, staring into the ruby-red wine in the jelly jar that doubled as a wineglass. Then he said, "Alain came after us of course. He said he wanted all of us back, including her.

"He held all the cards. She defied him as long as she could, but he had money and resources on his side. When she finally broke down and said she'd return, he told her—" Dev shivered "—he didn't want her back, after all. He just wanted the kids, including me, and I wasn't even his. I was in the room when he told her this, and his voice was like ice."

Dev shook his head. "But he didn't do anything right away. He let her live with that uncertainty for weeks. Then he showed up unannounced on her birthday to take us away."

"Oh, God, Dev." She touched his shoulder, wanting some physical connection with him. "That must have been awful."

"Yeah, well, I wasn't going," he said flatly. "Someone had to stay and take care of my mother. I had it all planned—how I'd hide in the bayou until Alain got tired of looking for me and left. But on the day he came, as I was sneaking off the porch, I heard them screaming at each other—and then a gunshot."

Sharlee's heart stopped beating and her grip on his shoulder tightened. He didn't seem to notice.

"I dropped my pack and rushed into the house, sure my mother was dead. Instead, I found Alain with blood dripping from his fingertips."

"She shot him?"

He nodded. "In the arm. He was very calm about it. She was hysterical. He took my hand then and said we were leaving. The other two kids were already waiting in the car."

Rage at Alain warred with sympathy for the little

boy Dev had been. Almost unconsciously, she began to knead the tight muscles beneath her hand.

"I said I wasn't going. He said fine, stay if I wanted, but if I did, my mother would go to jail forever for shooting him. He wouldn't report what happened if she gave up all claim to her children. Otherwise…"

Sharlee had never heard anything so shameful in her life. "So she let him have his way."

"She didn't see any other choice." He set the now-empty jelly jar on the low coffee table. "That guilty secret pretty much paralyzed any rebelliousness I felt under Alain's iron rule. Until my mother's death, I always knew he'd make her pay somehow for any misdeeds of mine."

Sharlee sighed. "No wonder everyone thought you were perfect. That's what you were trying to be."

"Yeah. And I was the only one of her children who kept in contact with her. The others were too young when they lost her. Teresa was five and Alex was only two. They forgot, but I never did. And I never stopped loving her and worrying about her and trying to take care of her even at a distance."

"So at the age of ten, you began keeping family secrets. I don't think even my parents or grandparents know about this."

He looked at her, his face bleak. "I saw secrets everywhere I looked. People…talk to me, Sharlee. I don't really know why. Maybe it's because I don't talk about myself much—except to you, apparently. Whatever it is, I learned to keep my own counsel.

I've got a reputation as a person who can keep a secret.''

''And you don't like that?''

''It's a hell of a responsibility.''

''Poor Dev.'' She stroked his temple. ''I had no idea you'd gone through anything so awful. All I remember about your mother were whispers about 'the kind of woman who'd abandon her children.' That was so unfair.''

''Life's unfair, Sharlee. That doesn't mean we quit trying.''

''Yes.'' Bending forward, she pressed her lips to his cheek. Slipping her arms around his neck, she rested her forehead against his and pressed tiny kisses on his jaw, on his mouth.

And she felt her heart swell with a brand-new kind of emotion. She had never felt so connected to him—and it all tumbled out in a plea.

''Take me to bed and make love to me, Devin Oliver,'' she whispered. ''Let's forget our problems and just think about each other for at least a little while....''

They undressed each other slowly by the light of the moon streaming through the balcony doors, then, still standing, ran caressing hands smoothly over each other's bare skin, molding curves and angles, coaxing and teasing.

Nothing could go wrong now. There was no need to rush, because the outcome was no longer in doubt. They were together in a way they'd never been before, anticipating without words, reacting without thought, everything perfect...so perfect....

"Oh, Dev," she murmured against his mouth, "I never knew it could be so good."

"Oh, ye of little faith."

She felt his smile against her flesh as he kissed her throat. His tongue flicked out to touch the indentation at the juncture of her collarbones and she shivered with reaction. Using both hands, he explored the curves of her hips, then lifted her into the rigid length of his arousal.

She clung to him, trembling like aspen leaves in a Colorado high-country wind. And then she raised her feet off the floor to twine her legs around him, completely vulnerable, totally open. With a sudden arching movement, she felt him enter her.

Gasping, he took a few staggering steps forward until the wall was against her back, offering some support. Holding her by the waist, he thrust again and again.

He didn't apologize or make excuses for taking her so hard and fast, and she didn't want any. His mouth seized hers in a kiss that mingled their harsh uneven breaths.

And then she splintered. For the first time in her life, she cried out in the throes of passion. Her nails bit into his shoulders and she soared, her pleasure drawn out and intensified.

He was with her, convulsing into her, uttering a guttural sound of satisfaction that ripped into her heart.

And this was just the beginning of a very long, very sweet night of love....

LAST NIGHT HAD BEEN a good thing for a woman about to leave town and determined to avoid heartbreak at any cost. Waking in Dev's arms, Sharlee realized she'd been dreaming about that very thing. With a little moan of self-pity, she snuggled closer to his chest and refused to open her eyes.

He'd shared his secrets with her, but she couldn't share hers with him, at least not the most important one: that she'd fallen in love with him all over again. Or maybe she'd never fallen out of love with him in the first place. There was something she *could* share, though.

"C'mon, you're awake, sleepyhead." He slid one hand sensuously over her bare behind. "I've been lying here for almost an hour waiting for you to stop snoring."

She dug the pads of her fingers into his ribs. "I don't snore."

"Actually you don't. But you do have a lovely little moan when I touch you right—"

"Stop!" She rolled onto her back, opened her eyes and grinned at him, thinking that a girl could only take so much. "I'm awake."

He covered her left breast with his hand and began kneading the soft flesh. "Not as awake as you could be."

"That's...true." His touch took her breath away and pressure began to build anew in the pit of her stomach. "Dev—" she caught his hand, stilling it, pressing it tightly against her breast "—you told me about your mother last night. Now I want to tell you about mine."

"I know about yours." Leaning over her, he replaced his hand with his mouth. Scraping her nipple lightly between his teeth, he flicked it with his tongue, then sucked strongly.

She gasped.

"That's the sound, all right." He spoke around her breast, cold air rushing over her heated flesh. And for the next fifteen minutes, neither of them uttered a coherent word.

Eventually, though, Dev raised his head mere inches from the pillow and said, "I apologize. You wanted to tell me something about Gaby?"

Sharlee pulled her fragmented thoughts together. "The main reason I've stayed away so long is because she wouldn't give me my trust fund," she said as simply and as honestly as she could. "Grandpère set up trusts for all of us—Leslie and me and now, I'm sure, Andy-Paul. Les got hers at twenty-one, but me?" Despite her best efforts, the old bitterness crept back. "I still don't have it."

"You're on the outs with your entire family over *money?*"

"No!" She glared at him, her warm glow dissipating. "It's what the money represents, don't you see?"

"Maybe you need to spell it out."

"It's about trust, and acceptance. It's about letting me take my place as an adult member of the family."

"*Chère,* how could they know you've grown up when you've been gone for so long?" He cupped her chin with his hand and looked into her eyes, drop-

ping a soft kiss on her lips. "Right or wrong, your
parents did what they did for your own good."

The old familiar outrage surged through her and
she opened her mouth to sting him with angry words.
But there was something in his expression, some unfamiliar tenderness that said he wasn't trying to hurt
her, only suggest that she *might* be wrong.

Her anger melted away and she began to laugh,
and soon he was laughing with her. When she could
speak again, she said, "For my own good! That's
what parents always say when they break your heart,
you know?"

"What if it's true?"

"Even if it's true, it stinks!" And she began to
laugh again, helplessly. He held her until laughter
gave way to tears and he held her through that, too.
Finally, sniffling, she pulled away and said in a
hoarse voice, "Mama and I had an awful fight the
day she and Papa told me they'd be holding the
money until they were sure I was 'mature enough to
use it wisely.' I stormed out of the house and she
followed me. We stood on the steps of Lyoncrest
screaming at each other."

"Poor Sharlee."

She gave him a grateful glance. "My birthday's
in January and I was graduating only a few months
later. Mama wanted me to move back to Lyoncrest
then, so they could assure themselves I was ready for
the responsibility of that damned trust fund. I could
work at WDIX...."

Turning, Sharlee slammed her fist into the pillow.
"I told her to keep the damn money, that I'd never

set foot inside Lyoncrest again as long as I lived, and hell would freeze over before I went to work at WDIX.'' She met his gaze, feeling horribly vulnerable. ''It's not the money, Dev. It isn't. It's control.''

He stroked her naked back. ''I believe you.''

She believed *him,* too, which astonished her. ''I really do feel better telling you,'' she confessed. ''I've never mentioned it to anyone, except Leslie that day at JAX, because...well, you know, they'd just think I was mercenary, which I'm not. I have a lot of faults, but that's not one of them.'' She drew her nails lightly over his chest, enjoying the way he shivered. She swallowed hard. ''That's one more family secret out in the open. Too bad I won't have time to dig up all the others.''

He covered her hand with his. ''You're really getting ready to leave, aren't you.''

She nodded. ''I've got to. If I don't, one of these days I'll wake up and discover I'm forty years old and still waitressing at the Donna Buy Ya.''

''It's not that bad.'' But his tone sounded remote.

''Yeah, it is,'' she said. ''But if I go before I know...'' She took a deep breath. ''Dev, you're the only one who can help me.'' Scrambling around to her knees, she bent over him earnestly. ''I've got to know the truth about this family and then maybe I can get on with my life. Will you help me? Please? Pretty please with butter and sugar on it?''

DAMMIT, SHE'D MADE a reasonable request. She had a right to know at least as much about her own family as he did. But he couldn't be the one to tell her—

for a lot of reasons, not the least of which was Margaret.

Looking up into Sharlee's serious face, he realized that with or without the truth, with or without the money in that trust fund, her family wasn't going to force her to do anything she didn't want to do. If she ever spoke to them again, it would be her choice, not theirs. Why couldn't they see that?

"Well?" Sharlee bent closer. "I'm tired for being saved from myself. Help me."

"All right." He didn't know when he'd made up his mind, but the answer was there. "I will."

"Yippee!" She leaned over and kissed him on the mouth. "When?"

"Today. We'll leave early. Felix has a cousin who's been begging to work here, so I'm sure he can bring her in for a tryout. Alain will be at a board meeting at WDIX and Charles will be home alone. I'll get you in to see him then."

"Yes!"

She jumped out of bed, completely unself-conscious in her naked glory. Grabbing a towel from the rack behind his door, she wrapped it around her body. "You won't regret this," she said happily. "I swear you won't."

God, he hoped neither of them would.

AFTER DEV WENT DOWNSTAIRS to help with the lunch setup, Sharlee jumped on the Net to pick up her messages. There was one from Jere Bryce and she clicked it open with fingers that trembled.

Sorry, kid, you didn't make first cut—not enough hard-news experience. But Lisa Bing, the lifestyles editor, needs a feature writer and I mentioned you. I know it's not your dream but it'd be a nice place to start. Hope you don't mind my presumption. You'll be hearing from Lisa soon—she's a damn good editor and you could do worse.

"Oh, God," Sharlee said softly, her heart beating so hard and fast she could barely breathe. He was right; this wasn't her dream job, but she'd take it in a heartbeat if she got the chance.

San Francisco was a long way from New Orleans.

She looked around the living room of her communal apartment. She'd known something would break and that her days here were numbered. She'd thought she could leave without a qualm. Now she knew she'd have qualms aplenty.

The biggest qualm of all was Devin. She loved him—she knew that now—but there were too many years and too many tears between them. He belonged here and she didn't. It was as simple—and as complicated—as that. She hadn't been after revenge. She'd been after love. What she'd gotten was great sex.

Shaking with reaction, she clicked out of her e-mail program and closed down the computer. The possibility of a job added fresh impetus to her determination to uncover all she could about her family, and fast.

SHARLEE COULDN'T REMEMBER ever being inside the beautiful and spacious home of the other branch of the Lyon family. Although Alain's home was also in the Garden District, it was on the opposite end from her own family home. Since neither Charles nor Alain was particularly sociable, family occasions were automatically held at Lyoncrest.

Dev parked at the curb in front and they entered through an arched wrought-iron entryway laden down with mandevilla vines so dense they created a dark passage all the way to the front door. Pulling a key from his pocket, he inserted it into the lock. In an instant they were inside an elegant foyer dark with marble and rich woods.

A middle-aged woman in a black uniform was coming down broad curving stairs, and she paused with one foot in the air. Obviously startled to see them, she still gave Dev a tentative smile as she continued down.

"How's it goin', Lorraine?" he greeted her.

"Very well, thank you. Uh...your father is out I'm afraid."

Dev's hand tightened on Sharlee's elbow. "We didn't come to see Alain. Is my grandfather home?"

She fidgeted, looking very uneasy. "I'm afraid...Mr. Charles isn't well enough to see anyone."

"So he's in?"

"No," she said in a rush, "he's—Mr. Alain took him to see the doctor."

"Funny, I thought Alain would be at the WDIX board meeting this afternoon."

Lorraine's cheeks reddened. "Normally he would be, but not today. He—"

From another room, the strident notes of a piano shattered the tension. Lorraine jumped and cast an apprehensive glance over her shoulder.

Dev smiled. "I think Charles has returned without letting you know, Lorraine. We'll go on in and say hello."

"Please don't." She held up a hand. "Mr. Alain said no one was to bother his father."

"Seeing me won't be a bother to him."

"But you're the one Mr. Alain doesn't want in here," Lorraine blurted. "He left specific instructions that you are not to enter."

Sharlee's entire body tensed in anticipation of being shown the door. If Dev couldn't get her in, there was no way she'd be able to corner Charles on her own.

Dev seemed unperturbed. He dangled his house key in front of Lorraine and said, "What if you never saw us here today? What if you weren't coming down the stairs just now and what if I snuck in while you weren't looking?"

"But I *was* looking."

"No, you weren't." Putting his hands on her shoulders, Dev turned her around and gave her a small but encouraging push back up the stairs. "I just want to talk to my grandfather. There's nothing wrong with that."

For a minute it looked as if Lorraine would turn around and argue. Then she squared her shoulders and walked up the stairs without a backward glace.

Sharlee breathed a sigh of relief. "That was close."

"It's *still* close. I'm not sure I really convinced her, so we'd better hurry. She could decide to call Alain the minute she's out of sight."

Sharlee shivered. "I'm ready. Let's do it."

THE BEAUTIFUL NOTES of Beethoven's *Für Elise* drew them forward. At the door to the living room, they stopped to let the music flow around them like a curtain of sound.

Charles sat at the baby grand, his hands moving over the keys, a little more slowly than a younger man might have done but with great confidence and feeling. Dev, who'd grown up hearing the man play, was not surprised; Sharlee obviously was. She looked up at him with astonishment on her face.

Her beautiful wonderful face. A feeling deeper than anything he'd ever imagined washed over Dev, shocking him with its intensity. He wanted to put his arms around her and hold her always and keep her from any possibility of hurt or harm.

Which was, of course, impossible. She didn't want anyone looking after her. She wanted to do it herself—in another state.

She stepped into the room and Charles glanced up, confusion on his face. He stopped playing.

"It's me, Granddad—Dev." He moved forward, steering Sharlee before him.

"Dev?" For a moment it didn't look as if Charles even recognized the name. Then he frowned. "Oh, yes. Dev, Alain's boy."

"This is Charlotte Lyon. You remember her—André's daughter?"

Sharlee approached him with her hand outstretched. "I saw you recently at Chez Charles," she reminded him. "Remember? I said then that I'd drop by to visit you."

"André's girl—Alex said you were back, living with Devin. No morals, just like that father of yours." Charles banged his hands down on the piano keys, flinching at the cacophony he created. "Alain says..." He looked as if he suddenly couldn't remember what Alain said.

Dev glanced at Sharlee and saw her astonishment when she realized Alex had betrayed her. Kneeling beside the piano bench, he spoke to his grandfather. "Charlotte's interested in hearing family stories, and you know more about the Lyons than anybody else. I hope you'll answer a few questions for her."

"Why? So she can tell me I'm crazy?"

"Nobody thinks you're crazy, Granddad, least of all me. I think you've had a tough life, and not all the things that have happened to you were your fault."

"Paul does. Margie does. They hate me."

"They don't!" It was Sharlee, shock strong in her voice. "I know there are a few bad feelings between your branch of the family and mine, but believe me, nobody hates you."

"Who *are* you, girl?" Charles stared at her suspiciously.

"André's girl, Charlotte," Dev repeated patiently. "Will you answer her questions? The truth, that's all she wants. You won't hurt her feelings and she won't get upset.'' Would she? He gave her a quick glance.

She nodded. ''Come sit over here on the sofa where you can be comfortable. Anytime you want to stop, I promise I won't push you.''

Charles peered at her through watery blue eyes. ''You're a pretty little thing,'' he said. ''Not as pretty as Margie, though. Margie was the most beautiful woman I ever saw.''

Sharlee and Dev exchanged startled glances. He'd never heard Charles speak of his sister-in-law with anything but scorn or anger.

''I've seen pictures of Grandmère as a young woman,'' Sharlee said, helping Charles stand. Slowly she maneuvered him toward the couch. ''Did you know her before she married Paul?''

''Before, after and in between.''

Charles sank onto the sofa but didn't relax into the cushions. He clasped his hands between his knees and rocked forward. ''In between,'' he said softly, ''before Paul came back from the dead...she almost married me.''

CHAPTER FOURTEEN

SHARLEE SAT DOWN HARD on the coffee table in front of the old man, so astonished she couldn't speak. A quick glance at Dev told her he was just as surprised by this revelation as she was.

Charles and Margaret...before Paul came back from the dead?

"Everybody loved Paul," Charles rambled on, his tone dripping venom. "It must have been his voice, because he never cared about anyone but himself and that radio station. He loved it as much as I despised it, but *I* wasn't important. Nobody asked *me* what I wanted."

"I'll ask, Uncle Charles. What *did* you want?"

"A career as a concert pianist," he responded instantly. "I could have had it, too, only my father..." He trailed off with great sadness in his voice.

Sharlee knew her great grandfather Alexandre had had definite ideas about who should do what in his family—and his word had been law. She felt an unexpected sympathy for Charles. Perhaps he wasn't entirely to blame for the way he felt.

"I couldn't do anything right," Charles went on mournfully. "But then Margie came home from college with her bastard son and Paul left her. After that, I didn't look so bad.''

"What are you talking about?" Sharlee leaned forward, frowning. "Margaret had another child besides André?''

"I'm talking *about* André." Charles was visibly annoyed by her inability to understand. "He's not Paul's, you know. He's not a Lyon at all.''

The poor old man had lost it. "Why would you say such a thing?''

"Because it's true. I could count months. So could Paul. Check their wedding date and André's birthday and you'll see, too.''

Although this could only be the rantings of a failing mind, Charles spoke with such conviction that Sharlee shivered. It wasn't something that should alarm her, was it? She glanced at Dev, but his face was a blank.

A careful blank?

"Anyway," Charles said, his voice growing stronger, "after that, Paul went off to war as a correspondent, but we all knew he just wanted to get away from his unfaithful bride. Everybody was going to war except me. Was it my fault this asthma got me classified 4-F? It's a good thing I *was* here, though, because someone had to keep a rein on Margie. But did I get any credit for keeping the business going?" His face twisted. "Why did *I* always get the raw deals?" His glance grew sly. "At least Margie was here. We worked together every day. I was like a father to André and I know she noticed that. When the war ended and Paul didn't come home when the GIs did, I thought I saw a chance…''

This was not what Sharlee had expected to hear. What *had* she expected? Little things, long ago resolved—maybe the occasional shady business deal, hurt feelings, misunderstandings. Suddenly she wondered if she'd opened a Pandora's box.

''Margaret was the one who pushed us into television,'' Charles confided. ''I only went along with her because I wanted to stay on her good side. Then she found Paul drunk in some gutter and dragged him back to Lyoncrest. That's when it all blew up in my face.''

''I really can't believe—''

A light touch on her arm stopped Sharlee's outburst, and Dev shook his head in silent warning. ''When was that, Granddad? Nineteen forty-six, -seven?''

''Later. Maybe forty-eight or -nine. Margie hadn't heard a word from him for years. Everyone thought he was dead. Everyone except her. She always said he'd be back.''

Obviously Paul's return had not been a happy occasion for his brother.

''Then what happened, Uncle Charles?''

''I saw the handwriting on the wall and left Margie and Paul to their folly.'' He gave a harsh laugh. ''She brainwashed him into believing in that television stuff, so we made a deal. They'd get the TV station and I'd take the real family business—WDIX Radio. Papa wasn't too enthusiastic about splitting the management that way, but we finally convinced him.

They got to him, though. When he died, they got sixty percent of Lyon Broadcasting and I only got forty. That was my thanks for years of hard work and dedication while Paul was out drinking and whoring, avoiding his responsibilities. That's why André is in charge today, instead of Alain, the right-ful Lyon heir.''

Sharlee finally saw rhyme and reason. ''You hate my father because of what *your* father did in his will?''

Charles affront was obvious. ''I don't hate André. I told you, I was a father to the boy when Paul re-fused to even acknowledge his existence.''

''That's surprising,'' Sharlee said slowly, ''when they're so close today.''

''I was there,'' Charles said sharply. ''Paul knew André was Margaret's brat. In the end he wanted her enough to overlook her indiscretion. But one of these days, Alain will prove that André is not a true Lyon. When that happens—'' He snapped his mouth closed and glared at his two visitors.

''He can't prove it because it isn't true,'' Sharlee argued, although she knew she'd never change the old man's mind. She was hearing only one side to this story, anyway, and it was obviously slanted. ''Why are you pursuing this vendetta? What did my father ever do to you?''

''He disgraced the Lyon name and it isn't even his,'' Charles said bitterly. ''He was a good boy, but he grew up to be like Paul—a playboy and carouser. He was well on the road to ruin when Margie and Gabrielle got hold of him again. If they hadn't straightened him out, we'd have been shed of him early on. Then Alain would already have his birth-right.''

Sharlee's heart beat painfully in her chest. "You obviously don't like my mother, either.''

"She's a meddler and a slut. Her first husband, assuming they ever actually married, was scum who—''

"That's enough." Dev gripped the old man's hand to stop him.

Sharlee gave him a grateful glance. No matter how angry she was with her mother, she didn't want to hear Gaby trashed by anyone.

"You can't change the truth," Charles said. "Gabrielle married your father—if he is your father—for power. Then she did her best to turn André against Alain. That day Paul had his second heart attack…'' His voice trailed off.

"Go on, Granddad," Dev urged him gently.

"It wasn't Alain's fault," Charles said queru-lously. "He couldn't help it if Paul got upset.''

"What did Alain say?''

"The truth. That the birth certificate wasn't…that Gabrielle…and André had just married a bitch who'd leave him when…parish records didn't…'' Charles stopped floundering and said plaintively. "Paul had a right to know, didn't he? But they all blamed Alain when Paul had that heart attack—kill the messen-ger!'' He puffed out his chest. "They hate me and mine and the feeling's mutual.''

"Not true." Dev released his grandfather's hand.

"Tante Margaret has always hoped for a reconciliation."

Charles snorted. "When pigs fly."

"Think about it, Granddad. You and your brother are both getting on. Why cling to a family quarrel that stretches back fifty years?"

Charles looked confused. "So long? Sometimes it seems like…yesterday. We were all young then, and life was so much simpler—"

"What's going on?"

At Alain's shout, Sharlee started in surprise. He strode into the room so angry he looked apoplectic.

Which set off a round of coughing in Charles.

Dev rose. "I thought you'd be at the board meeting, Alain."

"I was until Paul had a fainting spell and called the whole thing off." He glared at the unwelcome visitors. "Why are you two harassing my father this way? Have you no heart?"

Charles gave a final hacking cough before straightening, eyes streaming. He looked at Dev and Sharlee as if they really *had* forced him to talk to them.

"I'm sorry, Uncle Alain," she said. "We didn't intend to upset him. We were just…talking."

"Talking, my ass. You were trying to weasel personal information out of a poor old man. You should be ashamed of yourself, Charlotte."

"Hold it right there." Dev stood nose to nose with his stepfather. "Charles was fine until you came barreling in here."

"Really? How would you know, you ungrateful young pup?" Alain turned on Sharlee. "Looking for those family skeletons you asked me about? Trying to get dirt on us for your father? *I'll* tell you a secret if that's what you want to hear.''

She didn't trust him, but she nodded, anyway.

Alain poked hard at his own chest with a stiff forefinger. "I was the only Lyon who supported your romance with my stepson, did you know that? Everybody else thought he wasn't good enough for you, but I, in my blind loyalty—"

Dev let out a sharp bark of laughter. "Careful, Alain, or I'll tell her the real reason for your support.''

"That's right, twist everything around. The truth is, once you found out her side of the family wouldn't stand still for it, you couldn't bail out fast enough." He turned his ire back on Sharlee. "He was only after you to further his own ambitions, not because he found a spoiled little sixteen-year-old so irresistible.''

"Damn you." Dev's face was filled with fury and he hauled back a fist.

Sharlee grabbed his arm. "Let's go," she said. "There's nothing more to be gained here.''

Dev flexed his biceps as if itching to take a poke at Alain. "I don't know if I'm finished yet or—"

"I do." Still clinging to his arm, she turned to Charles. "Thank you for talking to us. We didn't mean to upset you.''

"The whole truth and nothing but the truth," he said defensively.

"Goodbye, Alain." She wouldn't address him by the honorific title of uncle ever again.

"Don't come back here, Charlotte."

"I don't expect I'll need to."

The short walk to the front door felt like one of the longest treks of her life.

Heading back to the Donna Buy Ya, Sharlee said, "We have to talk about this."

"I know."

"How much of what Alain and Charles said was true?"

Dev didn't take his attention off the busy street ahead. "Quite a lot of it actually. Not all. And Charles put his own spin on it of course."

"But not about my father. Why would they say those things?"

"Because they believe them, Sharlee. They've never believed Paul was André's father. Charles raised his children to think that way and so did Alain."

"What about you?" Such a possibility dismayed her. Dev had always seemed so levelheaded it would lend Charles's incredible story considerable weight if he believed it.

"Once I grew up enough to know who was who and what was what, I knew it wasn't true," he said. "André is a Lyon through and through."

She felt vastly relieved. "Do they have any evidence?"

"If they did, Alain would be general manager of WDIX today—trust me on that. André is the only person standing between them and what they believe should be theirs—control of every facet of the family businesses."

She thought for a moment. "Okay, I can see that. But what about you? You seem as certain of your point of view as they do of theirs."

He gave her a quick grin. "Margaret Lyon is the most faithful of women," he said. "There is nothing she won't do for her family, which sometimes leads her to make mistakes, but they are based on love and family loyalty."

"Did she really say she wanted Charles and Paul to make up their differences?"

He nodded. "She's worried about Paul. She wants all the loose ends tied up while there's still time."

"Loose ends like me."

"Yes." They crossed Canal Street and entered the Quarter where the going was considerably slower. "So...what do *you* think?"

"I'm not sure. I have to digest this. What Alain said about you and me..."

"That I was just preying on a sweet young thing for what it could get me?"

"Yes, that."

He pulled up to the garage where he kept the Mercedes and stopped. Turning toward her, he said, "Sharlee, you don't believe that."

"No...but on the other hand, I never understood why you changed so suddenly. One minute you were standing by me and the next I was getting that god-awful note in the mail."

"I told you I was sorry about that." He punched a button and the garage door slowly rose.

"Why did you even write it? Why didn't you just

come to me and explain what was going on? We could have faced it together.''

He drove into the cooler darkness and turned off the engine. ''Did it ever occur to you that I didn't trust myself to say those things to you? That if I had, I wouldn't have been able to make them stick?''

She thought about that for a moment. ''No,'' she said, ''that didn't occur to me. Are you saying that's what happened? That you had no other reason for breaking my heart?''

''Who counts the reasons?'' He said it lightly but with a curious undertone that warned her he didn't want to go on with this. ''Listen, you wanted to know the family secrets, and I think now you pretty much do. So are you sorry you started that boulder rolling downhill?''

''I... No.'' She lifted her chin. ''No, I'm not sorry.''

But that could have been bravado.

THE CALL SHE'D BEEN waiting for was on the answering machine when she checked: the lifestyles editor of the San Francisco *Globe* wanted to interview her. Was she available later this week?

She telephoned and gave Lisa Bing a resounding yes, then checked flights at the airport before she got cold feet. There was a plane leaving at two tomorrow afternoon.

The one-way ticket cost everything she had, but she would be on that plane.

Then the doubts started.

Should she sneak away without a word? Should

she tell Dev she was going or just do it? Tell her grandfather? Her parents?

She didn't need anything from any of them, she reminded herself. She had the money to buy her plane ticket and survive—barely—until she got on a payroll. She didn't think that was going to take long.

It *couldn't* take long.

She was going to get this job and it would lead to what she really wanted to do. She'd finally be on her way professionally, and she'd do it without any of them. Let them keep their damned trust fund. Let them keep their damned secrets. She no longer cared.

And that went double for Devin Oliver.

Waiting tables that evening, she tried not to watch him, tried not to think about him, but when he was in the room, it was impossible. She could smile and kid around with the customers, take orders and deliver food, but it was done with only half a mind.

If she let him, Dev could become her universe again.

Well, she didn't want her universe to be firmly tethered to New Orleans. This wasn't home anymore. She didn't know where home was, but she'd keep looking until she found the place that spoke to her heart. When she did, she'd settle down, but not before.

Dev paused on his way past with a tray of water glasses. As usual he was filling in where needed: bussing tables, manning the cash register, cutting and chopping in the kitchen.

"You okay?" he inquired.

"Of course. Why do you ask?"

"You seem distracted."

She shrugged. "I have a lot on my mind."

"Don't let that stuff Charles said get to you," he advised. "There's another side to the story."

"I suppose."

"Don't you want to know what it is?"

"I'm not sure. Maybe it would be better if I just quit while I'm ahead."

"Are you ahead, Sharlee? I don't think so." He looked at her with a world of disappointment in his expression. "But it's your life," he added. "Do what you want. You always do."

SHE SLEPT WITH HIM that night because she couldn't help herself.

When he held out his hand, there was nothing for her to do but take it and follow him down the hall to his room. Not a word was spoken because none was needed. They came together for lovemaking all the more powerful because it would be the last time.

Satisfied, exhausted, she lay in his arms unaware that tears were falling until he roused and said a surprised, "Hey, what's this? Why are you crying?"

She scrubbed at her eyes with a corner of the sheet. "I didn't know I was," she said.

"Ah, *chère*." He pulled her closer. "I did make a mistake taking you to see Charles today."

"Oh, no. I'm grateful you did."

"But you got more than you bargained for."

A *lot* more, on many different levels. "Maybe," she hedged. "But I'm all right with that…mostly."

"What still bothers you? Maybe I can help you understand…"

"You can't, Devin," she said firmly. "I'm not a little girl looking for someone to kiss my booboo and make it all better. I can handle my own problems." Rolling away from him, she sat up on the side of the bed.

From the darkness came his voice, a little hurt and a little puzzled. "Don't go away mad. I was just—"

"I know what you were just." Leaning down, she snatched her T-shirt off the floor and hauled it over her head. "I'm not mad. I'm tired. I've been working hard, in case you haven't noticed."

"I have noticed. Everybody has. I guess I should have mentioned it to you."

"As long as you sign my paycheck, you don't have to say a word." She scooped up her shorts and pulled them up her legs, then stood to settle them around her hips. "I need some rest, Dev. If I stay here tonight, neither one of us will get any sleep."

"True, but I still wish you'd stay. I've got some things I want to say to you and—"

"Some other time, okay?" She didn't think she could stand any more emotional turmoil. "I'll see you tomorrow."

"Okay, but it'll be later than usual. I've got to go over to the wholesalers first thing and get our standing order straightened out. They keep sending over the wrong napkins."

"Okay, no problem. Later."

Later. Maybe years later. Because her plane was leaving and she had no intention of missing it.

SHARLEE SPENT a restless night, awaking exhausted the next morning. What had troubled her sleep? Secrets. Family secrets.

And family loyalty and family obligations.

She'd had a hard time rationalizing a decision that had been solidifying ever since she'd arrived in New Orleans: she would return to Lyoncrest one last time. She owed her family that, even though it meant breaking the angry vow she'd made years ago.

She was pouring cereal into a bowl when Felix came in to grab a folder stuffed with papers off the table.

"How's it goin'?" he asked absently.

"Fine. Uh...Felix..."

He looked up sharply. "Yeah?"

She laughed a little self-consciously. "I, uh, just wanted to tell you I'm leaving."

"Sure, I know that." He did a double take. "You mean now?"

She nodded. "I hate to leave you in the lurch, but I've got a job interview coming up."

"Oh. Then you'll stay until you see how it turns out, won't you?"

"The job's in California and my plane leaves at two. This just happened or I'd have given you more notice."

"Getting a new waitress won't be a problem. I've got relatives standing in line." He took a sip of coffee. "I'm sorry to see you go, Sharlee. When Dev brought you here, I thought he'd screwed up big time. But you turned out to be all right."

She gave him a watery smile. "Th-thanks. I'll miss you, too."

"How did Dev take it?"

"I haven't had a chance to tell him," she said.

"Are you kiddin'? You slept with the dude last night and the subject never came up?"

She felt her cheeks redden. "I didn't want to spoil things."

"I can guarantee you'll spoil things if you go sneaking out of here like a damned—" He bit off his words, glaring at her. "Tell the man."

Speechless, she watched him stalk out of the room. She'd never expected such an outburst from good old easygoing Felix. Suddenly the cereal didn't look too appetizing.

She went back into her bedroom, dragged her suitcases out of the closet and spread the first one on the bed. She filled the first case quickly and opened the second. Staring at it, panic grabbed her by the throat.

She had to get out of here and fast. She knew what she was going to do, and she didn't need everyone else putting in their two cents.

"What the hell are you doing?"

She whirled around, her heart beating erratically. Dev stood just outside the open door, anger radiating from him.

"Felix sent you, I suppose."

"Felix? I haven't even seen Felix this morning." Dev stalked into the room and looked pointedly at the suitcase. "Does this mean what I think it does?"

"What do you think it means?" She dumped an armload of underwear into the open case.

''That you're running away.''

She faced him, hands planted on hips. ''I am not running away. I'm *going* away. There's a world of difference.''

''Not from where I stand.'' His lip curled. ''Did you at least tell your family?''

''That's none of your business.''

''Sharlee!'' He looked as if he wanted to grab her and shake some sense into her. ''You owe them that. For weeks they've been sitting in that big house waiting for you to make the first move. Now you say you're leaving town without so much as the courtesy of a telephone call?''

''I didn't say that. I said it was none of your business.'' She wedged her laptop computer into the middle of the suitcase, burrowing into clothing to provide it a cushioned resting place. ''Don't forget, none of this was my doing. You and Grandmère got me here under false pretenses.''

''No, we didn't. We got you here because we care about you. There's nothing false about *that* pretense.''

''You *care*, do you?'' She stared at him, thinking that ''caring'' didn't begin to cover what she wanted from him—and would never get.

''Yeah. Makes me feel kinda dumb, since you were leaving without telling *me*, either.''

A pulse hammered in her throat. ''Maybe I wanted you to remember me the way I remembered you— the last time. Maybe I wanted you to feel half as bad as I felt then.''

''Revenge, huh?'' He shook his head wearily.

"Okay, you got it. I feel like hell. Now at least go tell your grandfather goodbye. It'll probably be the last time you ever see him."

She gasped. "That's an awful thing to say. For your information, I'd already decided to go by Lyoncrest on my way to the airport." She slammed the suitcase, swung it off the bed, grabbed the other one and started for the door.

He stepped into her path, his dark eyes blazing. "Just like that?"

She faced him, knowing it wasn't "just like that" at all. "Look," she said desperately, "I'm doing the right thing. What more do you want of me?"

"Nothing, I guess." The angry light went out of his eyes. "Nothing at all."

"Then—" she licked dry lips "—goodbye, Devin."

He was still standing there motionless when she rushed out the door.

SO THE PRODIGAL DAUGHTER would return home, at least for a little while.

Dev stood in her bedroom long after her footsteps had faded away, trying not to take her defection personally. She had never suggested she might stay.

He had never suggested he wanted her to.

He sighed. At least she was going home first. Now all that would be missing from a Lyoncrest reunion was the prodigal brother.

CHAPTER FIFTEEN

HOW STRANGE IT FELT to enter the grounds of Lyoncrest after all this time. Sharlee stood for a moment just inside the wrought-iron gate, trying to calm herself for the ordeal to come.

She'd seen the various members of her family on a few occasions since her twenty-first birthday, but never at Lyoncrest. The memory of storming away without her trust fund had never left her, and she had never expected to return.

Yet here she was, walking up to the front door of the house where she'd grown up. She felt like a total stranger. Pausing with her foot on the lowest step, she took a deep breath. The heady aroma of gardenias and jasmine and sweet olive filled her senses.

Sheltered by live oaks and surrounded by carefully manicured lawns and gardens, Lyoncrest rose a majestic three stories. Looking up at the second-floor gallery, she thought she caught movement behind the gauzy curtains and clenched her teeth.

Whomever she found inside, *whatever* she found inside, she'd just have to deal with it. Mounting the steps, she reached for the polished brass knocker. Almost before the first clap of sound, the door opened.

Grandmère stood on the threshold, her pleasant expression quickly becoming anxious.

"Charlotte." Stepping forward, she wrapped her arms around her granddaughter. "Oh, Charlotte, you're home."

Sharlee neither resisted nor returned the embrace. Even so, tears gathered behind her eyelids and she blinked them back. She would not cry; she would not. She was an adult now, no matter what the people in this house believed. She would act like one.

Margaret drew back, her own eyes bright with moisture. "Oh, this is wonderful! We've just finished a late breakfast and everyone except the children is having coffee in the garden room. Will you join us?"

Sharlee nodded, not yet willing to trust her voice. Numb, she followed her grandmother across the ancient oriental runner in the foyer and through the French doors opening onto the glass-enclosed sunroom. Everyone *was* there: grandparents, parents, sister and brother-in-law.

When they saw her, all conversation ceased and an electric awareness expanded to fill the room. Leslie gasped and started to rise, then sank back into her chair. Gaby seemed too stunned to move.

Sharlee paused uncertainly just inside the doorway, trembling with apprehension. She felt as awkward as the child they took her for.

Paul, seated on one of several couches in the room, smiled. "We're so glad to see you, my dear. Please, come sit beside me."

"Yes, do." Margaret frowned. "Didn't Dev come with you?"

"No, Grandmère. I came on my own to say good-bye. I'm catching a plane to San Francisco in just a few hours."

"Charlotte, no!" Gaby half rose, held back only by André's firm grip on her arm. "Now that you're finally here, there's so much to talk about. If you love us enough to come—"

"Don't do this to me," Sharlee said sharply. "I won't be manipulated that way ever again."

André leaned forward. "That's not what she meant," he said. "Your mother loves you and wants what's best for—"

"Oh, Papa!" Sharlee's shoulders slumped. "I believe you. That's never been the issue. I love you, too—" her glance swept over all of them "—but I can't live with you, not ever again."

"Not at Lyoncrest, perhaps." André slid an arm around Gaby's waist to anchor her. "But New Orleans is a big town. Haven't we proved that we can give you space? There's no need to go all the way to California."

"That's where the job is, Papa."

"There are plenty of jobs here."

Sharlee smiled grimly. "And many of them are at WDIX-TV, no doubt. Forget it. I won't let you force me into a mold where I'd be miserable." Not for all the money in the world, she thought. She doubted she'd take the trust fund now even if it were offered. "Before I go, though…" She licked her lips, her anxiety skyrocketing. "I spoke to Uncle Charles yesterday. He told me a lot of things about the family that I'd never heard before."

Margaret's sharp intake of breath brought Sharlee swinging around. Grandmère put out a hand to brace herself against the back of a chair. "I wish you hadn't gone to Charles, Charlotte." She glanced at André and Gaby, her expression disconsolate. "We should have been the ones to answer her questions."

"Oh, Lord." Gaby shook her head wearily. "You're right, Margaret, but better late than never." She looked straight at Paul. "You warned us it was time to set our family skeletons dancing."

He nodded. "I did."

"The unvarnished truth, then, Charlotte. I don't know what good can possibly come of it, but if you want to know our secrets, so be it. Where shall I start?"

The pain in Sharlee's aching heart deepened. Slipping into a chair facing both parents and grandparents, she struggled to find words.

Before she could begin, Leslie spoke up. "Mama...Papa, should Michael and I stay or—"

"Please stay," Gaby said quickly. "This concerns you, too. Everything out in the open once and for all." She looked at her husband, then at his parents sitting close together on the couch. "Agreed?"

Margaret spoke for everyone: "Agreed."

The digression had given Sharlee time to collect herself. When they all turned to her again, she said, "Please understand that I'm not trying to hurt anyone. I just want to know the truth."

Heads nodded. She took a quick breath and plunged on. "Grandpère, Uncle Charles seems to think you and Grandmère hate him and his entire family. I know there's been bad blood between the two branches of the family over the years, but we've still always managed to come together as we did for the fiftieth anniversary celebration. Yet I'm absolutely sure Uncle Charles believed what he was saying.''

"Charlotte, I..." Paul looked almost befuddled.

Before he could find words, Margaret intervened. "Let me, Paul. If I go astray, you can pull me back." Her smile was beautiful and just for him. "As you've done for so many years."

"Thank you, Margie." He lifted her hand to his mouth for a kiss.

Tears leaped to Sharlee's eyes and she blinked them away. Her grandparents' love had always filled her with awe. And yet, Charles claimed it had once been entirely different between them.

Margaret said calmly, "We don't hate Charles or his side of the family. We've tried very hard to get along with them, but they've been so fixated..." She stopped, biting her lower lip.

Sharlee finished her sentence. "Fixated on Papa. They don't believe Grandpère is his father and thus don't consider him a true Lyon." She looked quickly at her father. "I'm sorry, Papa, but that's what Uncle Charles said."

"It's all right, dear." André didn't seem in the least perturbed by Charles's accusation. "Charles and Alain have made that claim for years." He cocked his head and regarded her quizzically. "You didn't believe him, did you?"

"No. But then Uncle Charles said Grandpère got

angry when you were born, because he knew you weren't his. That's why he went away and didn't come back until years after the war was over. Uncle Charles said Grandpère spent those years, and I quote, drinking and whoring.''

Margaret's face had grown pale. ''Such language for a lady,'' she said faintly. ''Charlotte, we…your grandfather and I did have a misunderstanding shortly after André's birth. Our reasons were personal and I don't feel I can share them even now. It was a matter between husband and wife, but I swear to you, there has never been infidelity in this marriage.''

A glance at Paul, who nodded, and she continued, ''Paul was away for seven years, seven long horrible lonely years. When he came back to us…'' She steeled herself with a trembling breath. ''When I found him living in the swamps and brought him home, it wasn't easy for any of us at first, André included. Paul had been through hell.''

''I'm sorry to bring up such painful memories,'' Sharlee said. ''Now I have to ask Grandpère—when did you realize you couldn't handle alcohol?''

Paul's smile was grim. ''Long before I acted on the knowledge,'' he said. ''Once Margie found me passed out in the bayou and dragged me home—''

''Oh, Paul, it wasn't like that! You'll make the children think that you were a drunk, and you weren't. You simply have an intolerance to alcohol, that's all.''

''No one thinks worse of you for it, Paul,'' Gaby said.

He sighed. "I thought worse of myself," he said. "You see, Charlotte? I'm not such a perfect old gentleman, after all. What Margie isn't saying is that I deserted my family by not coming home after the war."

"Not deserted, Paul." Margaret looked distraught.

"Yes, deserted. Didn't we agree not to garnish the truth? By the time Margie found me and dragged me home, I was pretty used up. I wanted nothing to do with her or my son or Lyon Broadcasting, and I sure as hell didn't want anything to do with television." He smiled at his wife. "She changed all that," he said, "and I bless her for it every day of my life."

Margaret reached for his hand. She seemed finally reconciled to having the truth come out. "You see, dear Charlotte, there's more than one Lyon who has been hauled, kicking and screaming, to do his duty to his family."

Paul smiled. "You're right as always."

Someone was sniffling, probably Leslie. Sharlee cleared her throat. "Grandmère, Charles said that if Grandpère hadn't come back, *he* would have married you."

"Of course not! Charles and I spent a lot of time together because of the radio station, but..." She groaned. "Charles got more and more...difficult."

"You could say that," André agreed with a chuckle. "Actually, Uncle Charles was very good to me before Papa came home." He gave his mother a curious glance. "I guess now I know why. He was probably using me to get to you, Mama."

Margaret's sigh sounded long-suffering. "He was

also trying to turn you against your father, should he ever come back. For a while I feared he'd succeeded.'' She leaned closer to Paul as if to reassure herself he was all right with her explanation. ''Eventually we worked everything out.''

Paul looked straight at Sharlee. ''André *is* my son,'' he said, his voice rising. ''All my brother's accusations won't change a thing.''

''Charles says Alain will eventually replace Papa as head of Lyon Broadcasting.''

''Did he say how?''

''No.''

''Because it will never happen.'' Margaret took up the story again. ''On top of everything else, Charles is bitter because he failed to see a future in television. After Paul came back, we made a deal with Charles and Alexandre. Paul and I took control of the TV station and Charles WDIX radio. Then when Alexandre died, Paul and I received sixty percent of the stock and Charles got the remaining forty. He never forgave us for that, conveniently overlooking the fact that my father and Alexandre started the original station together.''

Sharlee turned to Gaby. ''Why does Uncle Charles hate *you* so much, Mama? You weren't even around in those early days.''

Gaby started to reply, but André spoke first. ''Let me, Gaby. He hates her because without her I'd probably never have amounted to much.''

''André!'' Gaby's laughter diffused some of the tension. She added impishly, ''That's only part of it. I was always a threat to them, at first because I was close to Margaret and then because I was moving up through the ranks at WDIX. Once André came back to the station—''

''Came back from where?''

''The Merchant Marine,'' André said. ''You knew about that. What you may not know is that I also spent several years running swamp tours. I was shiftless enough to give ne'er-do-wells a bad name, for a while.'' His grin made him look a decade younger than his fifty-eight years. ''Mama was after me constantly during those last years to join Lyon Broadcasting—sound familiar?''

Sharlee had to smile. ''A little.''

''It runs in the family, Charlotte. We all think we know best.''

''But you did come back to WDIX in the end.''

''Yes. Mama said it was inevitable, which is probably a good part of what kept me on the run for so long. Right after Papa's first heart attack, I saw the handwriting on the wall.''

''All I ever wanted,'' Margaret said, ''was to see WDIX-TV in the hands of my children and their children.''

''You wanted it so much that you nearly drove me away from it for good,'' André said, but without heat, for that was an issue long resolved. His eyes widened suddenly. ''My God, it's the same way Gaby and I have driven Leslie and Charlotte away.''

''Papa!'' Leslie shook her head. ''You didn't drive me away. I'm just totally unsuited for such a highpowered business.'' She clutched her husband's arm.

"Instead," she said with a smile, "you got Michael."

"Whom we greatly appreciate," André said with a smile for his son-in-law. "But to return to the point, the ill feelings toward Gaby came to a head when Papa had his second heart attack. Alain was with him seconds before it happened. We've always felt he was responsible."

"Let that go," Paul said. "It would have happened regardless."

"Papa's never told us what Alain said, but we can guess," André continued, eyes narrowed. "While Papa was lying in his study perhaps dying, Alain lit into Gaby. He accused her of marrying me for power, called her a name or two and said she wouldn't be so smug when he proved I wasn't a true Lyon."

"So now," Gaby said with a grimace, "we've gone full circle. Charles and Alain still insist they will eventually wrest control of Lyon Broadcasting from André. In the meantime they do all they can to cause problems in the family and at the station."

"Such as?" Sharlee asked curiously.

When Gaby hesitated, André squeezed her hand. "It's too late to hold anything back now, Gaby."

"You're right." She looked almost frightened when she said it. "There have been a number of incidents over the years, but the scariest was a bomb threat at WDIX. André and I were working late one night when we got a phone call saying there was a bomb in the building. At the time we thought it was part of an attempt to take over Lyon Broadcasting by killing both of us. The bomb turned out to be an elaborate dud, but it was one of the most terrifying things I've ever lived through. The authorities never figured out who was behind it, but we knew.''

She smiled suddenly. ''One very good thing came of it, though. It took the fear of dying to make your father and me realize how much we loved each other. We were married that very night—or rather, that morning, because it was after midnight.''

Her mother's straightforward recitation had provided the final shock to chip away the icy core Sharlee had cultivated for so long. Undone by all she'd heard, she was struck for the first time by the undeniable fact that life and love had not come easily to any of these people. Why should *she* have it any easier than they had?

Leslie clung to Michael's hand, her face registering shock but also compassion. Leslie was too nice to even suspect such a lurid family past, but that very niceness made it easier for her to be accepting.

Sharlee's approach, as always, was different. She respected, even admired, Margaret and Gaby for what it had cost them to reveal what they'd hidden for so long. Dev was right when he said that nothing was all black or all white, she realized. *Mama is human and made human mistakes. She's suffered for them—all of us have. God knows I haven't always been perfect, either.*

Her father seemed at ease now, actually relieved. Her grandparents looked exhausted, Paul watching the proceedings with a brooding expression, while Margaret seemed more and more uneasy. A soft word from her husband and she settled back with her hands in her lap, but her granddaughter recognized a Herculean effort when she saw one.

Gaby looked at her two daughters anxiously. "I'm sorry now that I kept all this from you girls. At the time I thought I was doing the right thing."

"You didn't do it alone," Margaret said. "We both did what we thought was best. What could possibly be gained by laying out this sorry tale?"

"Nothing," Sharlee said, "in *public*. Les and I should have been told, though. This is family history and it's important. Until today, I never understood what always seemed to be a fanatical insistence on family loyalty. Now I can see that we all have to hang together, or Charles and Alain will surely hang us separately."

Margaret nodded. "Is that all you've gained here today, Charlotte?"

Sharlee chewed her lip, feeling the pressure. "I think...I've also learned that dragging Lyons into the family business, kicking and screaming, as Grandmère said, is a matter of tradition and not always such a bad thing."

"Bravo!" Paul said softly.

Gaby's laughter was shaky. "And now that you know, are you...?"

"I'm glad I know, Mama. You've finally treated me like a grown-up member of this family. That means more to me than anything." They faced each other, hope a tentative thing drawing them together for the first time in too long.

But it was Leslie who stood, and Gaby rose to meet her. Tears streaming down their faces, they embraced. Then Leslie stepped aside and looked at her sister, her expression pleading.

Nearly blinded by tears she'd vowed not to shed, Sharlee almost hurled herself into her mother's embrace. As her arms closed tightly around Gaby, Sharlee admitted at last how very much she'd missed her mother. Her father, too, who stood waiting for his own hug.

Brushing damp eyes, she gave her parents a wobbly smile and said words she'd vowed she'd never say to them: "I'm sorry. I'm sorry about all the time we've wasted." Her heart was in those words.

Turning, she knelt to kiss her grandfather's cheek, then her grandmother's. "I love you both," she whispered. "That's never changed. I'm sorry I've caused you pain."

"We regret we kept so much from you, dear," Margaret said. "Having you reconciled with us is my fondest dream. But I want it all, and there's still something more—"

"You've always wanted it all, Margie," Paul interrupted fondly. "Be grateful for what we have."

Margaret's laughter carried an edge. "If I had been satisfied with what we had, we'd all be in radio today. What I was about to say is, I want it all, and that includes a reconciliation with Charles and Alain. This constant friction in the family—"

Movement at the French doors shattered her concentration and she glanced around. Her eyes widened and she gasped as if she'd seen a ghost.

Puzzled, Sharlee turned to find Dev standing in the

open doorway, Charles beside him. His questioning gaze was on her his expression looked anxious.

So did Margaret's. One thin hand flew to her throat. "Charles! What are you doing here?"

Charles blinked. "Don't you want me here, Margie? Once I thought you might, but then…" The old man sighed. "Devin said I should come, but perhaps I've made a mistake."

Margaret caught her breath sharply. "It's no mistake, my dear." Crossing to her brother-in-law, the other man who had loved her, she put her arms around him. For a moment the old man stood there helplessly. Then he smiled and returned the embrace, saying her name in the softest possible voice.

After a long moment she pulled back to look at him. "Lots of water under that particular bridge," she said. Her gaze turned to Dev, who'd taken a step back. "Thank you."

Taking Charles's arm, she led him to the empty chair next to Paul's end of the couch. Paul offered his hand; after the tiniest of hesitations, Charles took it.

Sharlee let out the breath she'd been holding. Perhaps everything in the Lyon family would be all right now. Perhaps Margaret's fondest dream of family reconciliation was about to come true.

Gaby leaned forward urgently. "Charlotte, there's one more thing we need to talk about."

"What, Mama? Hasn't it all been said?" Sharlee found herself hoping to avoid any more revelations. She'd learned quite enough for one day.

"There's the little matter of your trust fund."

"I don't care about that," Sharlee said quickly—
and it was true. She was beyond all that now.

"But it's yours. Your father and I want you to
have it. I'm sure you can use the money."

*Because I'm living off what I make and not on the
family dole?* but Sharlee wasn't about to say that. "I
never cared about the money," she said, "just what
it represented. I told you that before, but I know you
didn't believe me."

Which didn't speak all that ill of them, since she
hadn't entirely believed it herself. Until this moment,
she hadn't been absolutely sure, in her heart of
hearts, that she'd be able to turn down that kind of
money if it was ever offered. A new sense of freedom
followed the realization that she could.

Gaby didn't look too certain, either. "Your father
and I..." She glanced at André, who nodded.
"We've realized we probably *were* trying to use that
money to control you."

Sharlee stared at her parents, fighting a giddy
smile. "Probably?"

"Okay, we were," Gaby said sheepishly.

André grinned. "I don't suppose you'll like hearing this, but we—"

"Did it for my own good!" Sharlee finished the
platitude and followed it with a groan and a grin.

"Anyway—" Gaby clung to her point, tenacious
as always "—the money is yours to do with as you
choose."

Sharlee raised her brows. "Don't say anything
you'll regret," she warned. "Not all that much has

changed. I'm as determined as ever to live my own life.''

"We know," her father said. "That's part of your charm."

Sharlee laughed. "Thanks, Papa, but I really am moving to California, money be damned."

Dev, who'd been standing beside her chair, put a possessive hand on her shoulder. "And I'm moving with her," he said in a steady voice. "If anyone has a problem with that, say so now—and that includes you, Charlotte Lyon."

"Oh, God." She stared at him, afraid to believe her ears. Without thinking, she pressed her hand over his, still curved around her shoulder. "Do you mean it?"

"If you want me." He looked vulnerable when he said it.

"I want you but—"

"That's all I need to know." He gave her a crooked little smile. "We'll iron out the details later. I just wanted everyone to know right up front."

"Which means that if you walk out on me the way you did before with one of your detestable little notes, my menfolk can go after you with a clear conscience."

"Dev sent you a note?" Gaby frowned. "What are you talking about?"

"It was a long time ago," Sharlee said, but the knot in her stomach didn't feel as if it had loosened much in the intervening years. "Dev dumped me and—"

"That's why you were so determined to go to

boarding school? Devin, how could you do such a thing? We didn't want you two getting serious—you were far too young—but there was no need to be cruel."

Everyone in the room looked at him as if he'd just fallen off his pedestal. Sharlee felt guilty for putting him on such a spot. Before she could say anything, her grandmother intervened.

"It wasn't Dev's fault."

Now everyone looked at Margaret, at her proud yet somehow defensive expression.

Sharlee said, "Excuse me?"

"I begged him to write that note. I now publicly beg his pardon for the grief it's caused both him and Charlotte."

"Margaret!" Gaby recoiled. "We begged you to stay out of it. You promised."

"And I would have honored that promise if you and André had been capable of resolving the situation," Margaret said. "Don't you remember how difficult things were? Charlotte was inconsolable and everyone was taking sides. It seemed wiser not to let the situation drag on interminably."

"Mama," André exclaimed, "I can't believe you went behind our backs that way."

"My darling, I've gone behind your backs innumerable times." Margaret sounded tired and old but not sorry. "Why do you think your daughter suddenly returned to New Orleans?"

"I assumed...hoped she was homesick."

"Wrong." Margaret's lips compressed into a thin line. "It was time for her to return, so I sent Devin to get her. I will always owe him for being able to accomplish that impossible task. He—''

''Hold on a minute.'' Dev's authoritative voice stopped the old woman's words. ''I think I need to clear up a couple of points before this goes any further. First, Margaret asked me to write that note to Sharlee, but I'd never have done it if I hadn't realized she was one hundred percent right. Second—'' he scowled down at Sharlee, who was holding her breath ''—Margaret asked me to go to Colorado and bring Sharlee home, but I did it for myself, because I wanted to know what kind of woman she'd grown into.''

Sharlee squeezed his hand. ''And what kind am I?''

''My kind, obviously.''

''Wait a minute!'' André looked from one to the other with shock on his face, finally zeroing in on his mother. ''Mama, I can't believe you've been so manipulative.''

''I would do that and more,'' Margaret said, ''for those I love.''

''Including,'' Sharlee said, ''getting me fired from my newspaper job in Colorado. You shouldn't have done that, Grandmère.'' *Get it all out now,* she decided. *Leave nothing to fester and divide.*

Margaret did not flinch. ''That was wrong of me,'' she admitted, ''but look how well everything's turned out.''

Sharlee started to utter a tart reply, but the words died on her tongue. Her grandmother had indeed done her a favor. If she'd torn Sharlee and Dev apart before, she'd surely brought them back together now.

"Grandmère," she said, "I may not always agree with you, but I always love you." Her fingers tightened on Dev's hand, sending him a silent message that she'd make verbal just as soon as she could: *And I love you, too.*

The excitement of multiple reunions finally proved to be too much for Paul. Rising stiffly, he smiled fondly at his assembled family.

"This is the way we should always be," he said in that famous voice, which always resonated with authority. "Thank you for this day, Sharlee."

She walked to him and put her arms around him, shocked by how fragile he felt. She'd always thought her grandfather to be strong and utterly invincible.

"Grandmère was right—it was time," she said. "Besides, I had just a *little* help deciding to do the right thing." She smiled at the man she loved.

Paul kissed her cheek. "I love you. Don't ever forget that. In years to come, when I'm no longer here to remind you—"

"You'll always be here, Grandpère." She caught her breath before succumbing to the onslaught of emotion. "As long as there's a single Lyon left, you'll be here."

He touched the dampness beneath her eyes with a gentle knuckle. "That makes it all worthwhile, you know."

Margaret, hovering in the background, took his arm. "I'll go up with you, dear," she announced.

"Charles? Would you care to join us upstairs? We can have a tray sent up and enjoy a good long talk."

"I don't like climbing stairs," Charles said. "My knees—"

"We've installed an elevator. Please come."

Sharlee watched the three old people move slowly out of the garden room, Margaret in the center with an arm linked with an arm of each brother. So much history! And to think they'd once been young and vibrant and looking forward, instead of back.

Gaby stood, all smiles. "Charlotte, you and Dev will stay for lunch of course."

Sharlee stiffened. Her plane left at two o'clock. Had she already missed it? She'd been so swept up she wasn't even sure.

"We'll stay," Dev said, adding softly for Sharlee's ears alone, "Forget the plane. I have a plan. Trust me."

She did. Implicitly.

JOINED BY ANDY-PAUL and Cory, everyone gathered for lunch in the dining room, which soon rang with laughter and excited conversation. Seated next to her mother, Sharlee found herself answering the most inane questions about her former job, her work schedule, her friends, her social activities, her dreams and ambitions.

Questions with answers only a mother could hear with such rapt interest. Sharlee was seeing her mother in a whole new light, no longer as simply the tyrant who made her life miserable with lectures and rules. Instead, she saw a woman with hopes and dreams not just for herself but for her children.

Sharlee glanced at Dev. She still didn't know what he had in mind, but she was more than ready to risk everything for him.

Lunch passed in a happy glow. She had no idea what she was eating and didn't care, safe once more in the family circle. After the meal the children scampered away to play while the adults retired to the library where André walked behind the leather-tooled bar.

"Drink, anyone? I think we have a great deal to celebrate today. I'm having a brandy and Gaby enjoys cream sherry after a meal."

"Perrier for me," Leslie said. "I'm not drinking for two."

Dev and Michael opted for brandy.

"Charlotte?"

"What?" She'd been admiring Dev's profile, instead of paying attention.

"Would you like a drink?" André asked.

"You mean alcohol?"

Gaby laughed. "Honey, you're of age."

"Yes, but this is the first time you've ever offered me a drink." She felt peculiar saying, "I'll have what Mama's having."

When all drinks were in hand, André lifted his goblet in a salute. Conversation quickly died away as everyone turned to him expectantly.

"To the Lyons," André said, his voice so full of satisfaction it overflowed. "May we always be as happy as we are today."

"Hear, hear!"

They drank.

Michael lifted his glass again. "To all of us. May we be in heaven thirty minutes before the devil knows we're dead."

"A good Irish toast," André said approvingly.

"Well, my grandfather was Irish," Michael said with a grin.

Dev lifted his goblet. "Okay, how about this? Here's to Charlotte and—"

He stopped short and everyone turned toward the door to see the cause. Margaret stood there, as still and pale as a marble statue, her face totally devoid of expression.

"Grandmère?"

Margaret said, "He's gone," her voice faint.

"Charles?" Dev frowned. "He came with me. How could he—"

"Not Charles." She drew a quivering breath. The room was intensely silent.

André set down his glass carefully. "Papa's gone? I don't underst—" And then he did and his face contorted with pain. "My God," he said, "has anyone called an ambulance? Tell us what—"

"André." Margaret lifted one hand, palm forward.

"We have to do something. Why are you just standing there as if we have all the time in the world?"

"Because," Margaret said, "it's too late."

André barely reached his mother before she crumbled in a faint. He caught her before she hit the floor,

and it was then they all heard the wail of an ambulance siren in the driveway.

But Margaret was correct; it was too late for Paul
Lyon.

EPILOGUE

SHARLEE LAY IN DEV'S ARMS that night and cried for the loss of her grandfather, but she felt a sense of gratitude, too. If she hadn't been there, if she hadn't had that final chance to tell him she loved him, she didn't think she'd be able to live with herself.

Dev stroked damp hair away from her face. "He died happy, Sharlee, and that's worth a lot," he murmured through the darkness—no moon tonight. "His family was whole again, at least for those few minutes. That meant more to him than anything."

"Oh," she choked, "I hope so."

"Did you hear what your grandmother said about that?"

"No. When?"

"Just before we left. She said your grandfather was just hanging on in hopes that some miracle would bring his family together. She said his time was running out and they both knew it. Only an iron will was keeping him alive."

Sharlee sniffled against his bare shoulder. "And they say *Grandmère* is made of iron."

"He was just as strong in his own way. He went as he wanted to go, surrounded by family."

"Even Uncle Charles was there. It was a miracle, Dev. And you did it."

"Yeah, well, it meant a lot to your grandparents to have Charles there, but don't count on too much family togetherness." He stroked her hip possessively. "The family feud has lasted too long and goes too deep. I think you know that as well as anyone now."

She nodded, beginning to tear up again. "At least Grandpère died believing there was a chance."

He kissed her cheek. "There's always a chance."

"Grandmère and Grandpère were together for so long that it…it just seems completely unfair to separate them now."

"Shh. Fifty-plus years of happiness isn't unfair. Nothing lasts forever, Sharlee—except love. Tante Margaret will love him until her last breath, and so will your parents and so will you and the rest of the family. He's dead, but he isn't gone—not really. Not as long as you remember him."

"I never forget anything, even the things I wish I could." She shifted until her head was lying on his chest. "Like…you and Grandmère conspiring over that note." She drew small circles on his skin with a nail. "Why didn't you tell me about her part in that before?"

"I promised her I wouldn't."

"Do you always keep promises so faithfully?"

"I try to, Sharlee."

"And you always do what you say you'll do?"

"Same answer—I try to."

"You said you were going to California with me.

Did you mean that? Your life is here. Your business is here.'' She broke off in fear and dread. She'd thought about this ever since he'd made his announcement, afraid he'd been carried away by the moment.

When he didn't immediately answer, she looked up at him in a panic, but the darkness defeated her. She couldn't see a thing. He touched her cheek lightly and she sighed with relief.

''My life is with you,'' he said, his voice husky.

''What does that mean, Dev? You've got to spell it out for me.''

She could hear his quiet breathing, feel the rise and fall of his chest beneath her cheek.

''It means I love you,'' he said. ''I've always loved you. But until you'd grown up enough, we couldn't put the past behind us and go forward.''

''But what about my family and yours? What about San Francisco? What about the Donna Buy Ya? What about—''

''Hush,'' he said, touching her mouth with his fingertips. ''We love each other—you do love me, don't you?''

''You know I do.''

''You wanted me to say it, and now I want *you* to say it.''

''I love you.'' The words seemed to rise from the very depths of her soul. ''You make me a better person. You make me *want* to be a better person. I want to do the same for you.''

''Then,'' he said with satisfaction, ''all else is details.''

PAUL LYON, the Voice of Dixie, was interred in the family tomb three days later.

Afterward Sharlee and Dev stood on the front steps of Lyoncrest, saying goodbye to her parents. Leslie stood nearby with her hand in Michael's and her eyes red from weeping. Everyone else, even Charles, was inside—with one exception.

"Grandmère isn't back from the cemetery yet?" Sharlee looked around for the slender black-clad figure who had carried herself with such dignity through what must surely have been the most trying moments of her life.

Gaby swallowed back a sob. She'd taken Paul's passing as hard as his wife and son had. "Margaret wanted to spend a few minutes alone with him," she said. "I hope we did the right thing by letting her stay there by herself."

"We had to, Gaby." André squeezed her hand. His mouth, usually set in an inflexible line, trembled. "It's what she wanted. Besides, the chauffeur is there when she's ready to come home."

Sharlee touched her mother's shoulder. "Will you tell her again how sorry we are and how much we love her?"

"You can't wait and tell her yourself?" Gaby was clearly disappointed.

Sharlee glanced at Dev. "I wish we could, but we've already delayed as long as we can. We're driving straight to San Francisco and we'll get married there just as soon as we can arrange it. I rescheduled that job interview, but we don't have much leeway."

"Oh, Charlotte, can't you stay and let me give you a proper wedding?"

Where once Sharlee might have snapped a defensive rebuff, now she kissed her mother's cheek. "Thanks. We really don't have time and, besides, we want to do this our own way."

"Oh, dear—" Gaby sighed "—did I do it again?"

"Yes, but that's okay. And Mama—" Sharlee took a deep breath "—I want to thank you and Papa for letting me find my way back this time. You didn't track me down and pounce on me, which I constantly expected and would surely have resisted."

"It was hard not to," Gaby admitted. "You don't know how hard."

"I think perhaps I finally do. Maybe someday...maybe someday..."

"What are you trying to say, Charlotte?" André looked as if he knew.

"Maybe someday Dev and I will decide to follow in the family footsteps, after all. Who knows? Anything seems possible now."

"Oh, Charlotte!" Gaby was clearly overjoyed.

"Don't get carried away! I just said maybe."

"We understand," André assured her, "don't we, Gaby?"

"Oh, yes." Gaby closed her eyes. "That would make us all so happy, but I swear, I won't push."

Dev squeezed Sharlee's hand. "Time to get going, *chère*."

"There's still one other thing we have to discuss before you go," Gaby said quickly. "About your trust fund, Charlotte..."

"I don't want it, at least not now." She glanced at the man she loved. "We don't need it."

"Then what should we do about it?"

"Ask Crystal to manage it. That's right up her alley—accountant and all that sort of thing, plus she's family."

"But if you need it, you'll say so?"

Sharlee smiled at Dev. "Are we going to need it, darling?"

He grinned back. "I doubt it. Not anytime soon, anyway. Escrow finally closed on my mother's house, so we won't be paupers. We'll also be silent partners at the Donna Buy Ya, which is starting to pick up—another year and it might actually show a profit. Felix says it'll be a gold mine someday."

Sharlee laughed at his droll recitation of Felix's excited prediction. "There you have it, Mama. Please don't worry."

"I'll try not to, but that's hard for a mother. I just want you to be happy—and close, but I'm willing to wait for that." Gaby embraced her youngest daughter. "No more family secrets," she whispered into Sharlee's ear. "That's one lesson we've all learned the hard way."

ALL EXCEPT MARGARET Hollander Lyon, at any rate.

In a limousine traveling north, barely able to keep her eyes open as some unknown drug flowed relentlessly through her veins, she wondered vaguely if she'd waited too long to reveal the biggest secret of them all.

"The Lyon family skeleton still has one more dance left, Paul," she murmured as her head sagged against the soft leather upholstery. "Pray God there's still time to set things right."

*Turn the page for an excerpt from
the next book in*

the LYON LEGACY trilogy—

FAMILY FORTUNE

by

Roz Denny Fox

Watch for it next month!

CHAPTER ONE

Mid-September 1999

ANOTHER THREE thousand dollars withdrawn from Margaret Lyon's private bank account! Crystal Jardin scowled at her computer screen. In the past two weeks, identical withdrawals had been logged against Margaret's bank account via an ATM. An unknown automatic teller. Crystal found that the most worrisome. She wouldn't be as concerned if she hadn't just seen a WDIX-TV segment on a computer hackers' convention. She'd learned that bank officials haunted the convention, hiring the brainy kids who hacked into bank systems and putting them to work writing codes to plug these very types of leaks.

The segment stuck in her brain because in addition to her duties as business manager for the family-owned, New Orleans-based Lyon Broadcasting Company, she served as personal financial advisor to Margaret, the principal stockholder, and to a few other family members, as well.

The amount of the withdrawals wasn't particularly alarming. Margaret was an extremely wealthy woman, and one prone to shopping sprees. Crystal hadn't been too concerned when Margaret disap-

peared without informing the family of her where-
abouts. Until today. She recalled that the last time
they sat down to go over finances, which they did
regularly, Margaret hadn't been herself. Who'd expected her to be? It was shortly after her beloved
husband, Paul's death.

Crystal understood that Margie needed time alone.
The woman had loved Paul Lyon for nearly sixty
years. Losing him suddenly to a heart attack—after
doctors had twice snatched him from the brink of
death—had shaken the entire family, and no one
more than Margaret. The funeral had been over-
whelming, with half of New Orleans turning out.
Heartfelt eulogies given by colleagues in the broadcasting business for the man known as the Voice of
Dixie must have added to the weight of Margaret's
sorrow.

At the time Margie went missing, everyone in the
family assumed she'd gone off alone to grieve. But
when she didn't call or show up at one of the ocean
resorts she and Paul had always favored, her son,
André, and his wife, Gaby, began to panic. And now,
this complete elimination of a paper trail in Margie's
bank transactions panicked Crystal, too.

At seventy-seven, the family matriarch excelled in
anything relating to the TV station she'd brought to
life fifty years ago. But the lady Crystal loved like a
surrogate grandmother didn't have the skill to hack
into a bank computer system.

So she'd enlisted someone's help. Whose? And
why go to such extremes? Crystal racked her brain
for other possibilities. She avoided terms like *kid-*

napped. André, Paul and Margaret's only child and general manager of the business, had tiptoed around the term at breakfast, too. Though Crystal knew it was on his mind today when he debated whether or not to file a missing persons report with the police.

André was torn between allowing his mother the independence she'd always demanded and being horribly remiss if anything was wrong. Crystal felt the same pressure now. She wanted to show him the account—except that Margaret insisted on keeping her financial dealings private. And if she'd run afoul of criminals, wouldn't they clean out her account and be done with it? Crystal thought it more likely that Margaret, always a headstrong woman, had bullied a banker friend into freeing her from a cloying family for a few weeks. The days after Paul's death and before the funeral, they'd closed ranks hoping to ease her pain. "Smothered" was how she'd described it to Crystal the morning of the service. So after a lengthy internal deliberation, Crystal decided to respect her client's wishes for now.

HARLEQUIN®
SUPERROMANCE®

Join us in celebrating Harlequin's 50th Anniversary!

The LYON LEGACY is a very special book containing *three* brand-new stories by three popular Superromance® authors, Peg Sutherland, Roz Denny Fox and Ruth Jean Dale—all in one volume!

In July 1999, follow the fortunes of the powerful Lyon family of New Orleans. Share the lives, loves, feuds and triumphs of three generations... culminating in a 50th anniversary celebration of the family business!

The Lyon Legacy continues with three more brand-new, full-length books:

August 1999—**FAMILY SECRETS** by Ruth Jean Dale
September 1999—**FAMILY FORTUNE** by Roz Denny Fox
October 1999—**FAMILY REUNION** by Peg Sutherland

Available wherever Harlequin books are sold.

HARLEQUIN®
Makes any time special ™

"Fascinating—you'll want to take
this home!"
—**Marie Ferrarella**

"Each page is filled with a brand-new
surprise."
—**Suzanne Brockmann**

"Makes reading a new and joyous
experience all over again."
—**Tara Taylor Quinn**

See what all your favorite authors
are talking about.

Coming October 1999 to a retail store near you.

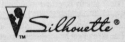

HARLEQUIN®
SUPERROMANCE

COMING
NEXT
MONTH